CUPIDITY

LUCINDA LAMONT

CHAPTER ONE

'Come on, Willy, do your coat up. This is going to be the start of a new adventure for us. You'll get to live with Charlie. I wish I could have lived with a friend when I was your age.'

Martha pulled his zip up as far as his big woolly scarf would allow and pulled his little hat over his ears to make sure as much of his young, delicate skin was covered as could be. She stood up and looked around her. Taking it all in one last time. One last breath in this house. One last smell. The last time she would smell the scent that they had created as a family. The faint scent of John's boot polish. A whiff of Willy's talcum powder, and whilst everyone else might not smell it, the sweat and tears of Martha with a slight pang of her royal jelly moisturiser. She could hardly bear to leave this house. Once she shuts the front door for the last time, she shuts out the life she had with John. She shuts out the memories. The plans. Willy's first few years. The happy times. The struggles.

Martha had accepted Johnny's death. She had no other choice. All she had now were the memories.

Every day he was serving in the army she would worry. So many people had lost their lives. So much heartbreak and families torn apart, but he would always come back. Most times with no warning. He would bound in through the front door, dump his bags on the floor, and call out to his family. Firstly, he would pick up Willy in his arms and give him a tight squeeze and plant a big kiss on his little rosy cheek. Willy's eyes would light up, and he would giggle with pure delight. His little laugh would fill the room with happiness, changing the normally nervous atmosphere instantly. Then Johnny would put Willy down next to his toys and look up at Martha who was watching them. Martha looked beautiful as always. She would be wearing her apron most of the times he came back, with her immaculate victory rolls set in her deep brown, bouncy hair. She had winter-like clear blue eyes and always had her signature slick of red lipstick on.

No matter what the occasion, she always looked glamorous and beautiful, and what made her most beautiful was that she had no idea quite how captivating she was. Johnny would forever be in awe. Everything that had happened, everything he had seen, all the trauma he had experienced, it would disappear when he saw her. She was his everything. She was what drove him when he felt weak. When he was scared, he would be brave for her and his son too. He would do everything in his power for those two. The apples of his eye, and boy, was it good to be home. He would take a step closer to Martha, and she would look at him.

Her stomach flipped every time she saw him. Twelve years together and he still made her weak at the knees; but every time he left, she felt sick to the stomach and would stay that way until he got back. She would finish drying her hands with the tea towel, a household item which had almost become like a comforter for her.

Like clockwork, the emotion would rise in her. She would try to fight it back; but the more she did, the stronger it would get. Her big blue eyes would start to fill quickly with salty tears, and then the first big tear would leak from her perfectly lined, doe-like eye and roll down her cheek; and then another and then another until she was crying uncontrollably. She would fling her arms around him and sob. He would pull her in, one arm around the top of her back and shoulders and the other at the bottom of her back, and gently rub his hand up and down her slight frame, soothe her and tell her it was ok. He was back now.

She hated doing this, and every time promised herself she wouldn't the next time, but she knew that was a promise she couldn't keep. She didn't want him thinking she couldn't cope, she didn't want to make his job any harder for him than it was, but the relief to have him home every time was a feeling that would never grow old.

Those memories, for Martha, were to be just that. On April 22nd, 1943 life changed. It was one of those life events whereby people say you will never forget it, but it hadn't been that way for her, she was already beginning to forget. It was one big blur, and that blur lasted for months.

On April 22nd, she had been playing with Willy. She had not long bathed him. He was on his baby towel on the living room floor, and she was drying him off. Although he did bear a slight resemblance to Martha, he was his father's son, and she loved that. For every day that she missed John, she could look at Willy and know that he was with her. His eyes, although only baby eyes, would bore through her and reach right into her heart and soul. Mostly that soothed her, but sometimes the darkness of his pupils staring into her used to make her nervous and unsettled and wishing that John could be there immediately. She wondered if the baby was an indicator of John's safety, and that's why she would have those feelings sometimes. Maybe she could pick up a sixth sense from Willy when John was in danger; after all, he was made by both, he shared both of their genes. She would never know.

When she did see John, he would tell her nothing. He would say that everything was fine and that she shouldn't worry so much. He was a man, a typical man, but also a gentleman and very loving. She hoped Willy would be just like him. How could he not? A beautiful baby boy. She leaned down and tickled him, and he began to laugh and coo. She then blew a big raspberry on his belly, and he laughed and giggled in sheer delight. His skin so soft and delicate – scrumptious. They played this game for a good few minutes. His laugh was so infectious, how could she stop?

There was a knock at the door. She called out that she would be just a minute. She wrapped little Willy up in his soft baby towel and stroked his face with her index finger.

'Now you wait there like a good boy, Willy. Mummy will be just a second.'

She got up and wandered just out of sight to the door. The door was a solid wooden one with no window. She patted down her skirt, checked her hair, and, with what would become slow motion in memory, turned the golden latch on the door. The gloomy, poorly lit hallway came to life with beams of the outside world flooding it with colour. On the opposite side of the door to Martha was a boy of about fourteen. He had a plain envelope with a cross on it. Of that moment, that was all Martha could remember.

The boy had delivered a telegram. Martha had known what it was as soon as she saw the envelope. She had heard it before from people she knew quite well and others she barely knew. The news was always delivered by a teenage boy and the envelope would be plain with a cross on it. It was the fastest way of delivering the message. When she opened the door, she didn't even see his face. She saw the envelope instantly and passed out.

The months passed by in a haze. Martha tried to be as strong as she could for Willy. Heavens, if it wasn't for Willy, she might not have coped at all.

Martha kept thinking back to how they had met. She wished that she could go back to then. Go back to when they were all so young and happy and carefree. John, or Johnny as she affectionately called him, was her world. She came from a normal working family and was one of three sisters. She was the middle one. Their mother had died giving birth to Susannah, the youngest of the sisters. After that, their father had never been the same, choosing to drown his sorrows and slowly lose sense of reality. He became quite a cruel man. Whether it was him that was cruel or the alcohol that made him that way no one would know, but life was certainly not rosy for the girls back then. Jane was the eldest sister and the most beautiful. She was married off at seventeen. She married into a wealthy family and had hardly looked back since. These days they only heard from her on birthdays and Christmases and that was it.

Martha didn't blame her. Although Jane wasn't as compassionate as Martha, she accepted her for who she was.

Martha just wanted to have a family of her own. A family that would always be together and never abandon each other. Susannah was to be the career woman. She went to college as soon as she was old enough to begin a career in nursing. She was a very sweet girl but possibly quite damaged. She lived in the wake of her mother's death, and although their father had never blamed her, he might as well have said it at times. Martha was extremely proud of her younger sister and slightly disappointed in her older sister. Maybe disappointed wasn't the word, just a bit sad that she married off and never got in touch. They had been so close when they were younger. Life hadn't been easy for the Henderson girls, but you could say they had all achieved a life of their own.

Jane was married and living with a wealthy family. Martha was married to an army boy and had a baby, and Susannah had the brains and a bright career ahead of her. Yet, despite all of that, they had grown quite distant. Martha often felt lonely and left out, and so she was delighted when John asked her to marry him. They had been teenage sweethearts. He had chased her for some time, but she was rather reserved whereas he was not. He had that boyish charm, played the clown, and was 'one of the lads' as it were, but it was all camaraderie. He had loved Martha from the minute he set eyes on her.

It was June 1930 when Johnny and Martha had been introduced. He was playing rugby in the local league. He had played since little school. His Dad had always pushed him to be competitive but he didn't mind; in fact, he thrived on it. He loved showing off, and he could because he was naturally very good at most sports. Martha had been invited to watch the match by her friend Mae. Mae's brother played in the team, that's how she got the tickets but that's not why they were going. Mae had a big crush on several of the boys, and she would be happy to win the attention of any one of them or all of them. Although the two girls were best friends, they were different in appearance and morals to a degree. Mae was much more voluptuous than Martha but quite beautiful. She was confident, buxom, sexy, and much more outgoing than Martha. She always gave the impression nothing phased her. She was always on at Martha to show a bit more cleavage or even just a bit of skin. 'It drives the boys wild,' she would tell Martha.

Martha just wasn't like that. She was nervous around boys, around a lot of people, in fact, and didn't like to attract attention. Sometimes she wished she had an ounce of Mae's confidence, but sometimes Mae's confidence would make her cringe. Like the time when there had been a regatta on in town. All the men were competing in strength competitions such as tug of war and who could punch the punchbag the hardest. The women would all be helping each other out on the various cake stalls and mingling together, but not Mae.

She had to have a go at the tug of war. She had to punch the punchbag. She wasn't any good at the challenges, but it would evoke a roar of applause and attention amongst the men, and she craved it, enjoyed it, and soaked it up. That day, the day of the Regatta, after they had cleared up from all the activities, they ended up at the local public house drinking until the early hours. Martha didn't drink much and didn't behave too differently from how she normally did, but Mae was dancing on the tables by the end of the night, singing at the top of her lungs, downing drinks and just being one of the boys. Sometimes it was fun to watch and sometimes it was rather quite unsettling for Martha. But that was Mae. The girls weren't normally allowed in the pubs which is why Mae told Martha she should make the most of it.

Martha and Mae were quite different, but they were the best of friends. Deep down they both admired the other for being totally different to them; and they were girls, they both wanted the same thing, to be swept off their feet and be loved and be cared for and to play the wife. That's what all the girls wanted. So, when Mae invited Martha to watch the rugby that day in June, Martha gladly accepted. She was a nervous girl, but she wasn't one to miss out either. They arrived at the pitch together, and on the way there, Mae had already given Martha the low down on the whole team. She knew everything about everyone. Sometimes Martha wondered if Mae was talking to her specifically or just talking in general, but she didn't mind. She liked the noise Mae made. It distracted her from her usually nervous and anxious mind. Mae had given Martha her top five players from the rugby team whom she would be happy to court, but with her looks, and her breasts, Martha was sure Mae could probably have any one of them.

The girls walked over to the drink stand and got a ginger beer each. Martha hated the taste of it, but Mae had told her it was a must because one of the girls at the Women's Institute had told her it flattens the stomach. So, it was decided, that's what they would be drinking until Mae got her hands on a new fad.

All the girls that were there at the rugby match knew Mae. When she walked over, there was a loud chorus of appreciation for her being there. They were the local glamour girls, if you like, all dressed up as if they were meeting royalty with as much makeup on as their faces could take and enough hairspray to piece together a broken vase. Martha was never going to be like them, not because she disapproved but because she didn't know how to look or dress like them. Anyway, one thing she did know was that as much as they all seemed the best of friends, they weren't really. Those girls would steal each other's boyfriends, lie and backstab about each other, but then they would put on the airs and graces all the time when they were together. She found it most bizarre. Mae was a loyal friend to Martha. They had been neighbours since they were babies, so you could say that they were like sisters. Martha knew she was safe with Mae, and Mae knew with certainty that she was safe with a friend like Martha.

Once Mae had finished saying her hellos, she

walked back over to Martha and linked arms with her.

'Come on, let's go and show these boys what they could have. Today we arrive as mysterious women, and we leave as wanted women.'

Martha's stomach flipped with dreaded fear, but she knew there was no getting out of it. They walked over to the side of the pitch and found a spot at the front, of course, with some chairs to put their belongings on. Mae took off her coat to reveal her modern and somewhat tight dress. Those boys were in for an eyeful today. She looked at Martha and observed her fully covered body and began undoing her coat for her to reveal her neckline.

'Come on, if you want to be noticed, you need to put in some of the effort.'

She meant it in the nicest conceivable way, but that was Mae. She wasn't good at quotes, anecdotes, advice or compliments, but the difference was she meant to be. She tugged Martha's coat off her, tidied her hair up, and looked at her like a picture had been unveiled.

'Lovely. What man isn't going to want us.'

The men were up the other end of the pitch warming up and preparing for the game. Mae was trying to find George, her brother. Well, she said she was trying to spot him, but what Martha mostly heard was, 'I think he's at the back next to Philip. Now, Philip I wouldn't mind getting to know better. Sarah Gregson wouldn't like it but that was ages ago so I'm sure he is fair game. Or is that him next to Andrew? Andrew is sooo divine. Louise from number 63 said he was big, if you know what I mean, but then he dumped her for Anna, Philip's sister, and since then she said he's nothing but a little boy, but I don't think he is with Anna anymore anyway because Philip went mad about it...'

Mae went on, and Martha pretended to listen with the odd raised eyebrow or turned down mouth.

'GEORGE. GEORGE. Over here.'

Martha wished she could put her head in her hands or that the ground would swallow her up. Mae was pretending to beckon her brother, but she was waving in such an animated way that her big bouncy breasts would sway and jiggle about. She knew exactly what she was doing, but to give her credit, she always got the result she wanted. David clocked the girls and headed over...with one of the other boys. Martha started feeling panicky.

'Mae. Marths. Good to see you. Thanks for coming girls. Marths, this is my good friend Johnny.'

David had affectionately called Martha 'Marths' since they were children. He was the only one who did, but she didn't mind. What she did mind was being set up but knew there was no getting out of it. Her face burned, and she felt like it must be a dark shade of crimson, but in fact, it was still her pretty English rose complexion, just a little bit rosier. Johnny took Martha's hand and kissed it whilst performing a curtsy in her honour and introduced himself.

'Hello, Martha, what a pleasure to meet you. I'm um, I'm uh, my name is...sorry, please excuse me, but I am taken aback by your beauty and those eyes. I'm Johnny, forgive me.'

Oh, he was good. Very good, she thought but she wouldn't fall for it. Not that easily. You see, because the Henderson girls had lost their Mum, they had had to make up their own minds about the world of romance, love, and fairy tales. Their mother was a totally devoted wife and she loved their father, but then she died and their father became a broken man. The girls had no one to guide them, and so Jane became the hopeless romantic, Martha became guarded, and Susannah showed no interest in men at all, perhaps because their father showed no interest in her. Deep down, Martha was pleased Johnny had showed her some attention. It made her feel nervous (again), but in a good way, which was an unusual feeling for her. She told him he was being silly and that she was a plain thing really, but that she was grateful for the compliment. The boys got called over to begin the match. Mae watched Johnny run back to the centre of the field; she was now half-interested in the match which was half more than when they had arrived. She was enjoying her quiet daydream about what had just happened when she was interrupted by Mae's squeal of pure delight.

'You like him, don't you? You really like him. I've tried so many times to find someone for you but never got it right, but I didn't give up hope, I knew I would crack it. You're like a little walnut, Martha. A tough nut but you can be cracked. Yes. This is so exciting.'

More wise words from our darling Mae there, thought Martha.

Martha didn't consider herself to be anything like a nut, but she was happy to stay and watch the game. In fact, she was glad she came.

CHAPTER TWO

Martha boarded the train with Willy. She was panicking. Did she have everything? She was sure that she must've forgotten something. She had never moved to a new house before. Well, she had moved in with Johnny, but she only had a few bags of belongings then. Now she had packed up a house. A house of memories and a truck loaded with a family's worth of possessions. Sometimes she would think she wasn't old enough for this.

She was, but sometimes it was hard to believe it had come around so quickly. It didn't seem like long ago that she and Jane would be playing with their dolls, dreaming of the day they would be mothers, wives, all the while Susannah would be in the corner reading. Three sisters, different hopes, different dreams. Jane would always have the grandest of the dreams. She wanted the big house, the beautiful wardrobe. She fantasised about not having to do much. She wanted a cleaner. She would be happy to cook because she enjoyed cooking and, as such, was very good at it. Being the eldest, she learnt from their mother, and when mother passed, she took over, so cooking had never been an issue. Running the house, however, that was down to Martha. She kept everyone organised, kept the house tidy, made sure all their clothes were clean and laundered. If anything, Jane had the easier job, but Martha wouldn't dare ever tell her that. As far as Jane was concerned, she was the one that kept it all together.

Martha reminisced and wished that she had enjoyed the easier times more. She never dreamt of being a widow. She never dreamt of running the house, raising the baby alone, and she never dreamt of the void that she would be left with. She didn't mind doing everything when Johnny was away, because all she dreamt about then was him coming home. Even when he did, she made sure he didn't lift a finger. She loved being his wife. She loved showing him her gratitude for everything they had, not materialistically because they didn't have much in terms of possessions, but just how much they had by being together. The love, the bond, their companionship, a friendship that never faded. Would she ever feel content again now that he was gone? She doubted it. How could anyone ever get close to her like she had been with Johnny.

Her thoughts were interrupted with a sharp squeal and then cries from Willy. A drunkard had pushed by on the train and hit Willy in the face with his case. Martha cradled him quickly and patted his hair. She then sat him on her knee and looked at his face. He had a mark just under his left eye that would bruise nicely. She looked up at the man who had hurt her son. A rage brewed inside her, but when she met the stranger's eyes, she could see he was inebriated. She held his stare for a moment, and then he broke the silence.

'What?'

He slurred and snarled aggressively. She held his stare for a moment longer and then looked down at Willy. She pulled him in and stroked his soft blonde hair and comforted him.

She turned them both away so they wouldn't have to see the angry drunk. She felt so pathetic. The old Martha would've been angry enough to punch that brute in the face, but she had lost a lot of confidence since Johnny died. She had always been a nervous character, but that would normally be pushed aside when it came to the protection and wellbeing of her baby. She felt so alone and each day she was just trying her best to get on with her life. She wished she had said something, she wished she had defended her son, but what then? He would've retorted probably and then she would've been even more scared. She knew that, as Willy got older, she would need to toughen up. She didn't want him thinking she was a pushover, and she wanted him to stand up for himself if he needed to. She continued to stroke Willy's hair and hummed him a tune; he started to drift off. He began to suck his thumb, which normally she would forbid, but on this occasion, she let him.

As Willy slept, Martha wondered what Johnny would've done if he had witnessed that drunk. She knew what he would've done. She didn't need to wonder but she liked to; God she missed him. In that moment, Martha decided that this move was to be a big part in their lives. She knew it was anyway, but if she moved and carried on with her depression, anxiety, and thoughts as she had been, then nothing would change. She had to make a conscientious effort to make this a fresh start, a new beginning. She had to make Johnny and Willy proud.

Eventually, the train pulled in at their station. Martha wondered how long she had been daydreaming whilst Willy snoozed against her. Everyone was in such a rush to get off. She sat there with Willy and waited for the mad rush to calm down. She gently woke Willy up and pointed out of the window.

'Look, Willy, look. We're here. This is our stop. Look how many trains there are.'

Willy gently stirred whilst being nonplussed about the whole situation, but she was glad he was awake. Although he was only three, she didn't feel quite as lonely when he was awake. Almost everyone had departed the train, so Martha took Willy's little hand and stood up to leave. As she tried to manage their coats and a couple of bags, she saw the old drunk ahead continue to be rude and aggressive to the other passengers. In that moment, she was glad she hadn't become as bitter as him. Whatever had happened to her, she had always managed to remain a decent person, and she felt good about that. She got to the exit of the carriage to join the platform. The drunk was a couple of people in front. She was fixated on him and still very annoyed that he had hurt her darling boy, and then, right in front of her, she watched him shove an elderly lady out of his way, giving her quite a fright.

The blood in her began to boil. The Martha that had been emotionally asleep for the last two years began to come to life. The noise around her began to fade, and the commuters around her became a blur. She found herself marching forward without any control. Her heart started beating faster, her top lip began to bead with sweat, and then, before she could even think what she was doing, she was right up behind him and just placed one foot slightly in front and across of his. She watched as he began to tumble, almost in slow motion. She stepped back still holding Willy on her hip. The drunk fell over and his drink left his hand, rolling across the platform. He was so drunk that it didn't seem to cause any injury. The worst thing for him was that he had lost his drink. A few people began to gather around him to offer help to get him up, but he just shouted abuse at them all.

Martha stepped back, and the hustle and bustle became alive. Instantly, the station had become noisy again She was shocked at what she had done and began to feel guilty. She turned on her heels and was making her way to the exit when someone grabbed her by the elbow.

'My dear, I saw what you did just there...'

Martha was horrified but turned to see her accuser.

'You did? You saw what?'

The old lady smiled at a very worried looking Martha and placed her hand on her arm.

'Don't worry, petal. I am glad you did. I saw what that old fool did to your boy. He got off lightly if you ask me. Now, you look exhausted. Will you let me buy you a cup of tea?'

And with that, she took Martha's arm and guided her towards a café just a short distance away. At first, Martha's eyes pricked with tears, but then she let out a soft giggle, and before they knew it, they were both laughing. It was then that Martha knew the old lady had been sent to her. She was a messenger. A shining light to tell her she was ok, she was doing an excellent job, she would laugh again, and that perhaps this move wasn't such a bad idea after all.

Evelyn, the elderly lady, was just what Martha needed that day. Once they sat down for a cup of tea, Martha's fears and concerns had gone to the back of her head. She was genuinely enjoying herself. This impromptu meeting had become a welcome breath of fresh air for her. Evelyn was so sweet. She insisted on buying them a pot of tea, and she bought a little cake for Willy. Martha had wanted to pay, but Evelyn was having none of it. Evelyn was fantastic with Willy as well. She sat him down and told him to enjoy his cake and not worry about making a mess.

Evelyn had two grandsons of her own. She was immensely proud of them and clearly loved being a grandmother. Even when Martha wanted to go to the ladies' room, Evelyn told her to go. Normally she wouldn't dream of letting Willy out of her sight, but she knew without hesitation that he was safe with her. She went to the ladies, and for the first time in about four years, she felt carefree, light on her feet as she made her way to the back of the cafe. When she reached the ladies room, she felt a sense of release, as if something had lifted, the grey cloud that had been hovering over her had moved on. She hadn't had a moment alone for such a long time. She was only gone for two minutes but she felt rejuvenated.

Then it dawned on her. What the hell had

she done? She didn't know Evelyn. This seemingly nice elderly lady had taken charge of the situation from the moment they met. She was the one who grabbed me, she realised. She was the one who insisted they went to a café. She was the seemingly natural one with Willy. Oh, my God, what if it was a setup? What if she was a child snatcher?

Martha's heart started to pound in her chest. What the hell had she been thinking? Willy was all she had. All she had and now she had left him with a stranger. Her head became hot. She was almost too scared to walk out in case she found him gone.

Her heart now sounded like a steam train in her ears. She began to control her breathing and walked out into the cafe. She heard Willy's laugh before she saw him. He was in fits of giggles. Evelyn had him on his back and was pretending to be a doctor whilst tickling him furiously. He was lapping up the attention, and more importantly, he was perfectly alright. Martha leaned back against the wall, and the relief that poured over her body acted like anaesthetic. She made her way back over to the table.

'You two look like you're having fun.' She smiled and picked up her teacup and saucer.

Willy was laughing whilst shouting, 'Again. Again.'

Evelyn sat him up and placed him next to her. 'My boy, you are tiresome. I can't keep up. I'm too old for a young sprog like you.'

Willy's bottom lip started to go; he had loved the attention of someone new so much and he didn't want the fun to end, so he started playing on it, but what he hadn't noticed was that Evelyn was playing with him, her hand had formed pinchers and was going straight for his chubby little knee. She gave it a good squeeze, and he howled with laughter and wriggled and wriggled. It was then that Martha realised how good it was to have someone around, how good that bit of support would be, and then suddenly she felt relaxed that they were moving in with Mae, Peter, and Charlie.

Mae and Peter had Charlie in the same year as Martha and Johnny had Willy. The children had met a few times over various holidays. Mostly they got on fine despite the odd spat. Peter was friends with Johnny. They all met around the same time. Peter didn't play in the rugby team like Johnny and Mae's brother David, but he was a friend of David's.

Peter was far too proud and flamboyant for rugby. He liked sharp suits and was always immaculately presented. He would always make quips that rugby was for men who had something to prove, perhaps he felt he had something to prove because he was always analysing other men. He was a good man nonetheless and very well suited to Mae. They loved to talk about other people and assume they were better than everyone else, but Martha always felt that they would talk this way because they were very insecure in themselves. They might have been, but they didn't act insecure when they were together. They were always surrounded by people. Always hosting parties, they always wanted to be in the thick of it yet seemed so interested in everyone else and not in a healthy way.

After Johnny died, Martha received a small sum of money from the army – the remainder of his wages and a small amount of pension. He was only in his early thirties, so the proportion wasn't huge. When he died, she didn't care about anything. For someone who worried so much about everything, the wind had well and truly been taken out of her sails, and so she gave little thought as to how they would survive.

Luckily for her, her older and now wealthy sister Jane had offered to help them out and give them financial support. She visited once to break the news but didn't stay long. Martha was still living in a haze at this point; the army pay-out had lasted about three months. It should have only lasted two, but she was very frugal and had to be like many other families at the time. She hadn't asked Jane for anything. No one in the family had any money apart from Jane, but Martha didn't consider herself to be Jane's problem. All the family knew what had happened, of course. Jane sent her condolences, Susannah stayed with Martha for a week, and her Dad called her but she couldn't make out much of what he was saying. He was drunk again, she guessed. She never heard from him again.

But, to her surprise, Jane arrived one day. She remembered it well because she was having a good day. Spring was coming, and it was about four months after Johnny's death. She had woken up, played with Willy, and cleaned the house; there wasn't much to be cleaned but she did a lot of cleaning that morning and caught herself humming a tune whilst doing so. For whatever reason, something lifted her that day, and she managed to feel slightly upbeat for the first time in a long time.

There was a knock at the door, and Martha

was delighted to see it was Jane. Jane looked glamorous and incredibly striking, with long, golden blonde hair and green eyes. She had long eyelashes and full lips. She was beautiful. No one could deny her that. Martha ushered her in and offered to take her coat which Jane accepted; in fact, she was more than comfortable with it. She had let the wealth get to her. She stood there, tall and slender, whilst Martha walked around her and removed her heavy, double-breasted, military-style coat with a fur neck collar. A couple of years ago, Martha thought Jane would've taken her own coat off, but she had clearly become accustomed to her own lifestyle. Martha didn't care really. She was overjoyed with the surprise visit. Jane walked through to the living room and looked at Willy. She kneeled and took his hand and looked at her nephew.

'Look who is a big boy now? My, don't you look like your father.'

She stayed silent for a minute; they both did. Willy stared at her with his big eyes and then looked at Martha and asked for a biscuit.

'No biscuits today, Willy. We don't have any left, and Mummy doesn't have any money.' She went through to the kitchen and sliced him up an apple. 'Jane, how lovely to see you and so unexpected. I shall put the kettle on and make us some tea.'

Jane didn't say anything; she just looked around at Martha's tired house. It was tidy and neat but it was looking a bit drab. Martha put the kettle on the hob and shouted out from the kitchen.

'So, what brings you here, Jane? I'm delighted, just delighted to have you here.'

She wanted to go over and have a big cuddle and for them to squeeze each other tight, but she could see that was not the right thing to do. Jane sat there on a dining chair looking like a movie star. Her hair, her makeup, the clothes... she looked incredible. Jane didn't seem to relax. It was like she didn't want to be there, but she eventually spoke.

'Martha, I am not staying long. I have come to do one thing only and then I am on my way.'

Martha brought the cups over to the dining table and sat down. 'What's the matter, Jane? This seems serious? Has something happened?'

Jane snapped at her. 'Of course, something's happened, Martha. Your husband died, and now you can barely keep a home going for you and Willy. I'm sorry. I just feel so helpless. Here I am with no worries like that but with nothing to spend it on and here you are with a world of responsibility and no income or help to lighten the load. I've come to help. I am going to give you some money. To help you both get by.'

Martha didn't know whether to laugh or cry. 'I don't... I don't need your money,' she stumbled.

'Yes, you do, Martha. You need it much more than I do, and so I am going to help you. I don't want a song and dance made about it, just let me help, will you?'

With that, Jane and Martha agreed an arrangement where Jane would send her the money she needed to survive every month. Partly she was relieved. She had been struggling for months. Her Dad wasn't nearby to help, not that he would be much help these days. Susannah was working seventy-odd miles away, and Jane just wasn't around. Even today, although she visited, she didn't seem like she was there. It was as if her mind was on other things. She had arrived and left in what seemed like a flash, but once the day's events had sunk in, Martha couldn't help but feel Jane had her own battles going on.

Martha slowly came to and realised that she was still in the café and that Evelyn had been chatting away, but she hadn't heard any of it. She hoped Evelyn hadn't noticed as she hadn't intended to be rude.

'Well, I must be off,' said Evelyn. 'I am visiting my son and I don't want to be late.'

Martha thanked Evelyn for what had been a lovely hour or so. She wanted to ask Evelyn if she was local. She quite fancied them being friends. She almost saw Evelyn as a mother figure in that split second and thought how nice it would be to have a friend that could take pity on her and lend her an empathetic shoulder from time to time. The hour they had just shared was mainly passing the time of day, talking about Willy and such.

Martha wished she had asked Evelyn more questions and regretted being selfish with the opportunity that she had been given. Evelyn stood and put her small silk scarf on around her neck and picked up her coat. It was quite cold outside but not as chilly as it had been, so she didn't have the need for it really. She picked up her bag and patted Willy on the head and said her goodbyes. Martha told her how lovely it was to have met and instantly felt empty as she walked away. Martha stared into space. She had been pleasantly distracted by Evelyn and now she was left with her thoughts again. Suddenly she regained focus and turned to the table where Willy was happily entertaining himself. Martha noticed that Evelyn had left money on the table for the tea and biscuits. She felt terrible that she hadn't noticed and looked out of the window, but Evelyn was gone. Nowhere to be seen. Martha felt even worse now. She hoped Evelyn didn't think ill of her. She liked Evelyn and had enjoyed sitting with her.

CHAPTER THREE

'Good evening and welcome to your news bulletin on this day May 7th, 1944. With me, Roger Stephens. Tonight's main story is that a body has been found on the outskirts of Henley. Formal identification is yet to take place, but police have confirmed that the death was indeed murder. Currently they do not know who they are looking for but have asked the public to remain vigilant after what they have described as an act of brutality. Should you have any concerns or think you may have any information regarding this incident, please contact your local police station immediately.'

The radio was on whilst the two friends, Martha and Mae, set up the table for breakfast.

It was a good-sized breakfast room although quite dimly lit. Mae and Peter could afford the finer things in life due to his wealthy background. They put out a pot of tea and some wholemeal toast. Although Peter and Mae experienced less hardship than most of the families locally, they had to make do with rationing the best they could. The boys were running around the house together playing as if they were aeroplanes and crashing down on to the floor. The two women called the boys through and sat them at the table.

'Now, boys, a piece of toast each with marmalade on and no fussing. That's all there is until lunchtime, so eat it up, and I don't want to see a single crumb left over.'

Willy looked terrified of Mae's dominance, but he picked up his toast without a sound. Charlie wolfed his down like it was going out of fashion. The two ladies took themselves to the back door with their cups of tea and went for a cigarette.

'I tell you what, Martha, I don't know about you but having Willy here to play with Charlie is working out to be a bit of a godsend. I haven't had a cigarette in peace for ages.'

'It's only been one night and this morning, Mae, I wouldn't get too ahead of yourself just yet. You'll regret asking us to move in soon enough, I'm sure.'

Mae put her hand on Martha's arm. 'Don't be silly, Martha, what are you like? This is going to be great. You can't manage on your own, we have the room, and I could do with the company. We'll be fine, you'll see. Plus, you'll be snapped up again one day, living with a man again and wishing you were still living with me, so best to make the most of it, eh.'

The two women laughed and knew Mae could well be right, right about both points.

That afternoon, Martha and Mae went out for a stroll with the boys.

'Isn't it funny, Martha, how much we have changed? Remember back in the day where we would go out looking for boys, and here we are with a boy each of our own. I guess I've still got my Peter, and you don't have Johnny anymore, but he'd be proud of you. He'd be glad you moved in with Peter and me.'

Martha wasn't quite so sure about that, but what Martha was sure of was that Mae *hadn't* changed. She was still thoughtless with what came out of her mouth, but nevertheless, she was always there for Martha when she needed her. Mae said she needed to pop into the car garage to say hello to her friend, and as normal, Martha just went with the flow and allowed Mae to take the lead as she had done for the last twenty-something years of their lives. Martha was always in Mae's shadow.

'Hello, David, how are you?'

A man not too dissimilar in age to them looked up from a greasy engine.

'Hello, ladies, Mae, how are you?'

'Very well, thank you, David. David, this is Martha; Martha, this is David.'

Martha smiled but blushed furiously. Maybe she blushed so furiously because she was furious. How could Mae do this? It was her first day staying with them and already she was trying to pair her off with someone. Johnny had been gone a couple of years but she was not interested in anyone else. She began regretting moving in with her straight away and wondered if she had made a terrible mistake. Mae could be so insensitive sometimes, insensitive and so bloody interfering. She felt a wave of emotion rise inside her, her temperature got hotter, and she felt like she was going to burst into tears. With that, she told Mae that she was going to show the two boys something outside, and she took their hands and they walked off. There wasn't anything outside to show the boys, so she instantly felt that was a stupid move, but who cared? Maybe she should just tell Mae to her face that she knew it looked stupid walking off but she was not up for sale. They weren't teenagers anymore. She couldn't pair her off again. She managed it successfully once, but now he was dead, she was heartbroken, and no one would ever replace Johnny. Mae came out looking defiant as always.

'What was that about, Martha? You made yourself look quite silly, I think.'

A rage grew inside of Martha.

'Quite silly? Quite silly? Is it silly to not want to be forced to go on a date? Is it silly for me to make my own move when the time suits me, and that's if I ever want to again? This is not your choice. This is my life. Stop trying to get me to be like you.'

Martha turned away and stroked her head. That was two people she had had a go at in as many days, and although both occasions left her shaking, both of those occasions felt quite liberating and empowering. She didn't want to be pushed around anymore.

'I'm sorry, Martha, that you don't have Johnny anymore. I am sorry you have had to be on your own, but you are barking up the wrong tree, lady. David has a girlfriend. It just so happened he was the first person I have seen this morning that I know, so I thought I would introduce you. I was only trying to help you fit in. I will ignore your insults on this occasion, but I can't promise I will if you do it again, so take that as your warning and stop feeling so bloody sorry for yourself. This is a new chance for you. A fresh start. I was only trying to help.'

Mae stopped talking. She was breathing so heavily that her breasts looked as though they were going to burst out of her over tight, ill-fitting dress. Martha struggled to take her seriously because she was so distracted by her ridiculous cleavage.

On the way back she thought about what Mae had said. Martha felt terrible. Was she really, that self-centred? Has she always been self-centred? Have people thought that of her for a long time, and it's taken Mae, of all people, to point it out?

'I'm sorry, Mae. I...I...I just thought you were trying to...'

'I know what you thought I was trying to do; you have made that quite clear and I accept your apology. Now come on, let's go and have some tea and get these boys some lunch.'

With that, Mae rounded up the boys and they all walked home with Martha feeling downcast and compunctious.

The ladies arrived back with the boys, and

Peter was home. He was high up in the army now, Martha wasn't sure how high up probably because Mae didn't seem to know and Martha didn't like to pry. Due to his position, he was home a bit more than he used to be which Mae had said was a blessing and a curse. Charlie saw his Daddy and shrieked with excitement.

'DADDY. DADDY. DADDY.'

Mae continued to go about what she was doing and eventually stopping for a millisecond to kiss him on the lips and then carried on as she was. Peter acknowledged Martha and leaned forward to kiss on her on the cheek whilst holding Charlie on his hip. She noticed he was wearing aftershave. She hadn't been close enough to a man to smell it in years. He was always very groomed, and Martha liked that in a man.

'How are you settling in, Martha. Have you got everything you need?'

'Yes, thank you, Peter. It's different but we are both very grateful and happy to be here, aren't we, Willy?' She spoke while looking down at her son. Peter had such captivating eyes which she had forgotten about until now. She never did like to look into them for too long. Willy was looking up at Peter whilst holding on to his mother's skirt, almost burying his face in it, and sucking his thumb.

'And how are you, young Willy? My, don't you look big and strong just like your dad? He would be so proud of you, looking after your Mummy the way you do. I hope Charlie is being good and sharing his toys with you?'

'Yes, I am, Daddy.'

Charlie didn't miss a trick and was desperate for his father's approval. He was giggling and looking at his father adoringly.

'I'm a good boy just like you told me to be.'

'And that's exactly what Daddy wants to hear, Charlie, and seeing as I am home for a few days, if you continue to be a good boy, I might take you both fishing down by the stream. How does that sound?'

Peter lowered Charlie down and revealed that he didn't have the strength to hold a stocky three-year-old for a prolonged period of time. They both rejoiced and made it clear that they would both like that very much.

'Ok, well, off you go and play, and we will maybe go down there tomorrow.'

'Yay, tomorrow. Fishing. Fishing.'

They both seemed to speak almost in unison. Of all the things Martha felt since moving in with

Mae and Peter, the best thing was seeing her boy happy. He was always a good boy with such a sweet and gentle nature. He had coped very well when it was just the two of them, but now seeing him so happy with a companion of his own, she knew it would do him so much good, and if she was honest, it was good for her to live with a friend too.

Although Mae hadn't given Peter much attention that morning, choosing to busy herself with household duties which seemed to be her highest priority, no one could deny she was a good mother and a good wife, but she seemed emotionally distant from Peter. Martha had observed them over the last couple of hours. Mae was preparing some lunch for them all whilst Martha sat at the table and prepared the evenings vegetables. Mae was looking in the larder, and Peter had come up behind her and put his arms around her waist and began kissing her neck. She didn't push him off, but she didn't seem thrilled either. If anything, she didn't change. Martha thought how she would love to have that intimacy again. Maybe it's because she was there and Mae didn't feel relaxed around her? She went to check on the boys in the other room, just to give them a minute to themselves really, but she found herself listening in to what they were saying.

'God I've missed you. I've missed the way you look, the way you dress, your smell, your breasts, that bottom...'

'Oh, for heaven's sake, Peter, put me down. It's only been three weeks,' said a dismissive sounding Mae.

Martha could hear what sounded like Peter kissing Mae whilst talking in between.

'Three weeks...seems like a lifetime...d'you know what else has been three weeks...three weeks since I got to feel you...feel your warmth... kiss you all over...slide into you...'

'Right, Peter, that is enough. Martha and the boys are in the other room.'

Then there was silence, and Martha realised that maybe they knew she had been listening and began to feel rather awkward. Then she heard them again.

'Look, you dirty beggar, we will continue this later, so for the time being, keep your hands to yourself.'

Martha then realised that Mae did love Peter, but she must not like to show it in front of people. She was glad that everything was ok, if not a bit disappointed that Mae was getting something tonight that she was not.

She pretended to play with the boys in the front room.

'Oh, look, a big red fire engine,' she said, pretending to be interested and trying to ignore her feelings of arousal which was infuriating and frustrating.

She hadn't felt aroused in years, and now her friend being reunited with her husband and listening in to their private conversation was enough to fire her up. She was beginning to wish David from the garage was single, even if it was just for one night. Whilst in this somewhat frenzied trance, Charlie had been telling Martha how much he would like to be a fireman but he was interrupted by his dad.

'That's wonderful, Charlie, but perhaps Martha would like to come and play with the grownups now and leave you boys to play like boys?'

Martha looked around over her shoulder and saw Peter standing there in the door. He winked at her.

'Play?' she said feeling confused.

What did he mean play? Yes, she was aroused but suddenly not so much. Were they doing that in the kitchen on purpose so she could hear and now they wanted her to join in?

'Yes, play. I have brought a bottle back of something strong. One of the chaps from work gave it to me, thought it would be a nice way to welcome you to our home.'

He looked extremely tall from a sitting down position and really quite dashing in his work gear. She decided that Mae was very lucky, and she was happy for her friend to have everything she could want and need. She also realised that she had been staring at Peter and hadn't said anything. Peter put out his hand.

'Come on, I'll help you up.'

With that, she got to her feet and left the room. Peter put his arm around her and told her that, although she was Mae's friend, she was his friend too and that she should feel very at home, and she shouldn't feel like she must play with the boys and keep out of their way. They went into the kitchen where Peter poured them all a drink, and they all lit up a cigarette. The alcohol tingled through Martha's body. She couldn't remember the last time she had had any due to lack of income and rations. She could remember, however, the number of times she'd wished she'd had some.

Peter and Mae were in a strong financial position because of his work and family money; they still had to be careful but they were certainly more comfortable than most. They had a few drinks and caught up on old times, and

Martha relaxed and enjoyed herself more than she had in a long time. They sat around the table, and Martha was taking it all in. She was giggling at the stories Mae reminded her of from when they were kids that she had completely forgotten about.

She watched in awe at how loving Peter was with Mae and wished she could have what they had. The way he would occasionally put his arm around her whilst regaling them with one of his stories from the army, the way he would put his hand over hers on the table, the way he tended to her every need, and she wondered if Mae could see it for herself. Martha and Johnny had a very loving relationship, but the strain of him being in the lower ranks of the army and having a child meant they never had a lot of money. Even before Willy came along, they didn't have a lot of money. They had both wanted their independence and so had moved out and began renting a property as soon as they were married which was a stretch, but they didn't complain and rarely argued, they just wanted to be together in their own space.

Martha wondered if they had had the beginnings that Peter and Mae had, what their relationship would've been like. Johnny always wanted to have more. He often told Martha he would give her the world if he could, but that one day, she would have everything. He would still buy her flowers and make her little gifts which she loved, and she kept all of them although she hadn't been able to look at any of them since he passed.

After the boys had been fed, the women bathed them and got them ready for bed.

'You must be so glad to have Peter home. I didn't realise he would be back today?'

'I didn't know he was coming back today. He never tells me. Not out of covertness but, when he joined up all those years ago, we made a pact that when he went away, he wouldn't say when he was coming back just in case...You know. It worked for us anyway, and we have done it ever since, even though he rarely goes away now.'

'Yes, I know. We all hoped it would never come to that, but for some of us, it did. There was no effective way or helpful way of coping when they were gone.'

'No, there wasn't and there isn't for those still dealing with it, but that's why you are here and we are keeping each other company. Everything will be ok. I can feel it.'

'I feel it too, Mae, and I am glad to be here, although I feel like you and Peter should be allowed time together without me in the way.

Why don't you go out for the evening? I can take care of the boys.'

'Oh, we don't need special time together. He is always away and then back and away and then back. This is normal for us. We might take you up on it and go out one evening but not tonight. Although, whilst we are on the subject, I will apologise in advance should you hear anything tonight. He's on a promise, and you know what they get like if they don't get to sow their wild oats regularly.'

She winked at Martha, and with that, Mae lifted Charlie out of the bathtub with his towel and wrapped it around him. Martha didn't know where to look, and what was it with the two of them winking all the time? Earlier she had thought Peter was flirting with her, but it must be their thing, she thought. Mae had always been so open with that kind of thing and Martha never had. She wished Mae hadn't told her the plans for the evening because what if they knew she was awake? She didn't want them thinking she was listening. Furthermore, she hadn't been loved like that for over two years, and now she was going to hear her friend doing it? Once again, she felt extremely awkward and laughed nervously.

'You two do what you've got to do. I'll be asleep anyway.'

'Got to do, just about sums it up,' said Mae, and she finished drying Charlie off and left the room.

Martha told Willy to stand up and hoisted him out of the bath as well.

'You are getting too big, my boy. Soon you will be telling me you don't want me in here, no doubt, and one day I really will be alone.'

'You won't be alone, Mummy, you have me. I'll look after you.'

Martha wrapped the towel around her boy and rested her head on his belly, and he patted her hair with his wet hand. She didn't mind; in fact, she liked it a lot. She was so blessed to have a little boy like Willy.

The women put the boys to bed and went back downstairs. Martha was going to clear up all the dinner plates, but Peter had already done it whilst they had been bathing the boys.

'Where's all the washing up? I was going to do it.'

'It's all done, I did it,' Peter said with a smile.

Martha was blown away. It was unheard of for men like Peter to help around the house. She noticed how Mae didn't even acknowledge his help.

'I was going to do it,' she repeated. 'I want to make myself as useful as I can whilst I am here...'

'And I'm sure you will,' Peter interrupted, 'but it's only your second night with us, and I was able to help whilst you girls played Mummy. Now sit down and have a drink.'

Martha noticed how Mae still hadn't shown any gratitude and didn't want to step on her toes by showing hers, so she picked up her drink and said thank you. They sat around the table for around an hour or so, and Martha began to feel woozy. She very much enjoyed the way the alcohol was making her feel numb yet warm. Mae was telling Peter about something that had happened in the village that week, and Martha found herself staring at them. She looked at Mae, all glamorous and beautiful with silky hair and expensive clothes, and Peter, slicked back hair, chiselled looks and big strong arms.

'I hear you met David today,' said Peter, interrupting her thoughts at probably just the right time.

'Yes, I did. Mae and I took the boys out for a walk and she introduced me. He seemed nice, but then, as the old saying goes, the taken ones always are.' She examined her drink swirling around in her glass.

'Taken? David is not taken and hasn't been

for a while, so I believe...' Peter stopped talking because he noticed Martha glaring at Mae.

'Oh, look, alright, I know what I said, but you were being so serious, and since our chat this afternoon you have really lightened up. So, what if David is or isn't taken. You are a big enough girl to do what you want whether I influence it or not,' said Mae defiantly.

Martha knocked back her drink and said she was going to bed.

'Oh, don't be like that.'

'I'm not actually. I'm not being like that, I'm fine. Honestly. I'm tired. It's been a busy couple of days, and anyway, maybe I am off to go and dream about David.'

She gave them a cheeky smile and bid them both good night. She wasn't angry. She had had a really nice day, and Mae might have had a point. She did need to lighten up. Plus, she wanted to get to bed before they did so she could have a head start on getting to sleep and not hear their lovemaking.

'Come here, you bad girl, let me look at you.'

Martha had managed to get to sleep, but now it seemed she had been woken up and was about to hear everything. The walls weren't that thick, and she could hear muffled laughing and squeals of pleasure.

'You know what happens to bad girls, don't you. They get a good spanking...'

Martha cringed, she hoped they wouldn't take that long because she could hardly bear to listen. Then she heard the slap, groan, pause, slap, groan, pause. Yes, someone was being spanked. It was hard to tell which one, but Martha guessed Peter was spanking Mae. Then there was quiet. *Why have they stopped?* thought Martha. Again, she wondered if it was because of her. Then she heard a deep gasp from Mae. They hadn't stopped. The foreplay had, but the intercourse was just beginning by the sound of it.

'Ahhh, yes, ahhh, yes. Oh. Peter. Oh. Yes'

Mae was not being quiet in the slightest; she wasn't even trying to be quiet. Martha could hear the sound of skin slapping, Peter groaning, Mae begging for more, and she found herself extremely aroused. Mae was telling Peter how big and hard he was, and Martha found that her breathing pattern was copying Mae's. She lifted her nightdress and pulled her knickers to the side. She felt slightly surprised by her own actions but knew she was drunk. She began to pleasure herself whilst listening to Peter and Mae having sex. With every slap of skin, she would thrust, with every yelp of pleasure, she would bite her lip, with every groan from Peter she would gasp and grab the pillows. All three of them were having sex but in two different rooms. As Martha could feel herself getting wetter and wetter, the slaps from the adjoining room became quicker and quicker. Martha was picturing Johnny. She was imagining it was his fingers, not hers. She was imagining that she could feel his hot breath on her neck and that he was kissing her erect nipples. She was getting closer. She imagined rubbing her hands over his body and then grabbing hold of his lovely, pert bottom and pulling him in harder each time. She was there. She was coming. So were Mae and Peter. The release was intense and explosive. Martha bit on her pillow and squeezed her blankets as hard as she could, careful not to let out even so much as a whimper although she wanted to scream in pleasure. From what had seemed like ferocious noise in Martha's head, the house was now quiet. Almost silent apart from the odd creak. They had all stopped, and Martha calmed down with only her heavy breathing for company. She relaxed and closed her eyes and said, 'I love you,' to an image in her head. The image was not Johnny. It was Peter. She sat bolt upright.

CHAPTER FOUR

Evelyn was in the area because of Simon, her psychopathic son. He had escaped from the psychiatric hospital where he had been for the last decade and was on the loose, and as the officer had put it, 'a danger to society.' The staff at the hospital and the police thought it might help find him if she were nearby. She was familiar with the area and knew her way around the town very well now due to visiting him for many years.

She used to hate making the journey up to see him. It always filled her with cold dread. She would feel like everyone would know who she was as she walked the streets. She would think that the staff in charge of him thought she was responsible for him and his ways. Evelyn couldn't understand what had become of her youngest son Simon. From the minute he had been born, he was different to his siblings. He had a nasty way about him. His eyes were big and dark, and she felt like he would slice through you with his stare. His eyes lacked emotion. He was aggressive, cold and distant. She hadn't treated him differently to his brother and sister, yet he was the opposite to them. She hated the expression 'blame the parents,' which locals had whispered behind her in Church, behind her in the post office queue, or as they passed her on the street. She always pretended not to hear, but she would make a point of smiling and saying hello if the opportunity was there. She had no idea what she could have done to prevent his actions. He was brought up in a firm but fair household. The eldest son, Michael, had gone on to become a doctor. The middle child, Grace, was a wife and mother to two darling little boys. Simon, however, the youngest born, was to grow up to become a very dark, tormented soul who would be found guilty of murder.

Evelyn noticed very early on that he was different from his siblings. He was headstrong and stubborn from the moment he could think for himself. He didn't get along with any of the family even to the point where the children's late father accused Evelyn of having bedded someone else during a heated argument one evening saying, 'That boy is the spawn of Satan, he is no child of mine. Where did you get him from?'

Simon's ways took its toll on the whole family. The older he got, the worse he became. He was nasty to other children, abusive towards animals, and just didn't seem to have an ounce of compassion in his soul. Once he started school, things became worse. Evelyn was forever being called in and often told to take him home. No one could handle him. She loved him, of course she did. He was her son, and for years she just wished she could crack his code. She was convinced that there must be a small part of him somewhere that cared. She never found it. The real dark side of him came out at secondary school. The first major incident was concerning James Hardy. He was the son of a very good friend of hers. Perhaps Simon didn't like him because James never put a foot wrong. When the two women would catch up, they would sing James' praises. They couldn't sing Simon's because there were none to be sung. James' mother, Violet, was as proud as punch of her boy.

'James is excelling in all of his subjects at school. I don't know where he gets it from,' she would tell Evelyn. 'He's so caring and happy to help, all off his own back too. He doesn't need any prompting from me. How are your children getting on?'

Evelyn wished she could say she didn't have anything to worry about when it came to her lot. She could speak highly of the older two but not of Simon, and everyone knew it. He was the elephant in the room.

'Mine are doing just fine. They are performing as expected of their age group, so I can't ask for more than that,' she would say whilst busying herself with whatever was to hand at the time, usually a placemat or a cup of tea.

One afternoon, Evelyn got a call from the school. The lady on the phone sounded somewhat distraught whilst telling Evelyn that she must come to the school at once. Evelyn's heart sank as she put on her coat and checked her bag to make sure she had everything before leaving the house. She procrastinated, double checking she had her purse and her keys, delaying the inevitable bad news that she was about to receive.

She arrived at the school and was shown

through to the Headmaster's Office where she saw Simon looking very pleased with himself.

He saw his mother and said, 'Hi, mother, and don't you look just pretty as a picture today,' whilst grinning positively.

Evelyn started to feel hot and flustered. She knew by the look on her son's face that this was not going to be good. He was so pleased with himself, more pleased than she had seen him in quite some time that she knew it must be very bad this time. The headmaster went on to tell Evelyn that Simon had been into the store cupboard in his science lesson. They believed he had stolen a type of acid and had poured it down the back of James' shirt, immediately burning him, and that James had been taken to the local hospital. Evelyn wished she could jump into defence mode.

'There is no smoke without fire,' she could say. 'Maybe it happened in defence. Maybe James was going to attack Simon. They must have been fighting. He probably...'

And with that, her thoughts slowly drew to a halt. She knew deep down the headmaster wasn't lying to her; she was just so ashamed to be told it. She felt sick that her son could be capable of such cold violence, but she knew that he was telling her the truth.

The headmaster asked Simon to give his mother his own account of what happened, and he did. He spoke clearly and confidently and took her through a step-by-step account of how he approached James from behind, grabbed him by the scruff of his clothing, and pulled at his shirt collar, and then poured the acid he had stolen down James' back, totally unprovoked. Evelyn felt sick. Her mouth flooded quickly with warm saliva; her palms became clammy. She felt desperate and totally alone. She had been called to the school before, but most of the time it was because of good reports of her other two children and the frequent and general bad behaviour of Simon. The headmaster told Evelyn that the school would no longer tolerate Simon's behaviour. He went on to tell her that he 'did not think the school was equipped to deal with a child of Simon's nature and that perhaps she could get him into a school for children with behavioural problems.'

Simon laughed and laughed out loud, swinging on his chair. Evelyn was mortified. She couldn't believe she was sitting in a room being told her child was too violent for the school he was at. Not only that but there were no schools local to them, not of the sort he was implying, and even so, they cost a lot of money. Money that

Joseph and Evelyn didn't have. Evelyn wept silently. Small tears rolling down her cheeks, one after the other. She took out her handkerchief from her purse, wiped her face quietly, and then she folded it back up and put it neatly away.

'Very well, Headmaster, I understand what you have told me. Come on Simon...' She beckoned Simon up from his chair, nodded at the Head and his assistant, and left the room.

That evening Simon stayed in his room quite content with what he had achieved that day. Nothing scared him. He was fearless. His behaviour got him the results he didn't deserve to have such as a bedroom of his own, forcing his brother and sister to share the other room. He couldn't share a room with another person due to his temperament, persona, and unpredictable behaviour. No one would see his temper coming, but they soon knew about it. He would flip in a second, going from quiet and subdued to an almost possessed-like state. When he was mad, he had the strength of an ox. Even his father couldn't hold him back.

His brother became frightened whilst sharing a room with him, so the family made the decision that Simon could have a room of his own and the other two children would share despite Evelyn feeling that her only daughter should have her own room, but they all had to make sacrifices for Simon and his ways. The only saving grace that came out of Simon being given his own room was that, due to his apparent hatred for humanity, he would happily lock himself away and not integrate with the rest of the family.

Evelyn's husband, Joseph, returned from a hard day's graft to find Evelyn with a broken smile. He put his sack of tools down on the table and sighed. He knew that look on her face. She was trying to act normal, but her exhausted eyes told him that she was also begging to be asked. He couldn't be bothered. He didn't want to hear it. There was nothing they could do. The boy was a lost cause. He slowly took his worn and old looking coat off, sighing louder as he pulled it over his tired, weary and fed up shoulders. He then left the kitchen and walked out to the hallway to hang up his coat, the whole time feeling Evelyn's exasperation. He made the short walk back in to the kitchen in no hurry, eyes down to the ground and pulled out a chair, still not looking at Evelyn. He then put all his weight against the back of the chair, almost using the chair to crack his back in a few places and then bringing his hands up to rub his face and finally running them through his wiry grey hair before putting Evelyn out of her misery.

'What is it, now?'

As he met her tear-filled eyes with his, he didn't want to know. If anything, he wanted to know about anything else in the world apart from Simon's behaviour. Evelyn could tell him about what time she took the bins out, she could tell him what groceries she bought, she could tell him what chores she had done, anything would appeal to him more right now than hearing about what horrific thing his son had done, how much it broke Evelyn's heart and subsequently leaving him feeling utterly useless in defending his family and controlling his son. Joseph listened to Evelyn; he listened to her pour her heart out and go through the cycle of confusion. The confusion that leads to blame, that leads to hurt, that leads to desperation, that leads to the inevitable hopelessness and then back to confusion. He listened to all of it whilst feeling numb the whole time. He didn't love his son. Evelyn did. He guessed that she did because she carried him; she was more emotionally connected to him than he was. He had loved Simon at first, but the years of trauma that child had caused and watching the effect it had on his wife and other children had caused his love for his youngest to cease. The boy didn't seem like a child to him, and he couldn't make excuses for him, not when his two other children were worlds apart from Simon.

Joe knew that nothing he and Evelyn had done had contributed to Simon's despondent persona. He could no longer give love to the boy that broke his wife's heart daily, the boy that made him look weak, and the boy that frightened his siblings. Joe didn't know when the love stopped. It hadn't happened overnight; it wasn't a switch. He just knew now that he didn't love him but that he had to be responsible for him.

Joe was a hardworking man. He was brought up in a house of love, and most of the time, he was the kind of man that kept his head down. He was a respected man. He didn't have much in terms of wealth, but he had his integrity and that was something he held very dear, and he would not let that wretched boy, Simon, break him. He would just have to support his family the best he could, but deep down, he wished that his family didn't include Simon. A very small piece of him, buried deep within him, disliked Simon for making him dislike Simon. He never thought he would have a child like Simon. He thought he would be a stern parent who could control his children, but Simon could not be controlled by anyone, and Joe was ashamed of himself for that. For what he considered to be his failings.

Joe couldn't stop the way Simon behaved. He couldn't mend Evelyn's heart. He couldn't tell his other two children that everything would be fine, but there was one thing Joe could do. He could talk. He was a man of few words, but everyone that knew him thought him a decent man, and because of that he always got their full attention. People listened to him. Joe told Evelyn he would meet with the headmaster and see if they would reconsider taking Simon back.

Evelyn didn't know what Joe had said to the school, but whatever it was, it was enough for them to take him back on a managed-plan basis. They had agreed that Simon could go to school three days a week, and on the other days, Tuesdays and Thursdays, he was to be schooled at home to the best of Evelyn's ability. This benefitted everyone concerned, no more than Simon himself who once again was being rewarded for his cruelty and got exactly what he wanted – time out from normal life.

The family had hoped that this plan might work for Simon and that the time removed from society might calm his erratic and psychotic behaviour. This was not to be the case. He became more empowered when people gave up on him. He thought he was winning. As the years went on, people would pass Evelyn in the street and give her an awkward smile or a wave but always choose to not get too close because she was the mother of 'that god awful boy.'

As the time passed and Simon went from a boy to a young man, the calls from the school were replaced with calls from the police. Simon managed to escape severe punishment for a few years, only guilty of petty crime. Evelyn and Joe became more and more distant due to the shame that Simon brought upon their family. Simon's siblings distanced themselves from Simon because they couldn't be near him without fear. Then one evening, their lives were to change forever.

The knock at the door was a typical policeman's knock. They'd heard it enough times to know, and a jolly visitor doesn't deliver such an assertive knock. Joseph and Evelyn put down the books they had been reading, sitting across from each other in their dated living room and looked at each other. Joseph sighed. Evelyn's heart sank. What on earth could it be this time? Not even their biggest fears could prepare them for what they were about to be told.

'I'll go, love,' said Joe, slowly rising from his

chair and patting Evelyn on the shoulder as he made his way out of the room.

'Evening, Mr Paterson,' said Officer Clarke.

'Evening, officer, what's he done now then?'

The two men knew each other well. They weren't friends, but they had met in circumstances like this on several occasions now. Officer Clarke looked at Joe and held his stare for a moment.

'I think we'd better go inside, Mr Paterson. Let's get you seated.'

Joseph opened the door fully for the Officer and gestured for him to come in. Officer Clarke removed his hat and held it to his chest. He made his way into the living room and greeted Evelyn. He looked at an empty chair and said, 'May I?'

'Yes, of course. Would you like some tea?' replied Evelyn.

Officer Clarke knew this was not going to be easy. He did not want to have to deliver the news, and accepting tea, although he could do with it on this evening, would prolong the agony. *Best just to get on with it,* he thought.

'No, Mrs Paterson, I won't on this occasion. I think it's best we just get to the point of my visit. What I am about to tell you is not going to come easily. We've met on occasions like this many times now over the years, but I'm afraid this time it is much more serious. When I ask you both some questions following what I am about to tell you, I will need you to be completely honest with me. Do you understand?'

He had Joe's and Evelyn's full attentions, and they agreed with a silent nod and Joe taking Evelyn's hand and slowly rubbing it.

'Mr and Mrs Paterson, we are looking for your son Simon. We believe he...we believe he has been seen...we need to question him about...'

The officer struggled with what he needed to say. He knew Joe and Evelyn were good people; he knew their two other children were decent people, but he knew Simon was a different breed. He wished he could make it easy on them; he knew this was to be a devastating blow, but he also had a job to do and get on with it he must.

'Mr and Mrs Paterson...' he lowered his voice, 'we believe Simon has committed murder.'

He paused and waited for their reaction. Evelyn looked up at Joe who was sitting on the arm of her chair. Her face faded to white instantly. Her eyes filled with tears, and she began to shake. Joe stood up and walked to the window. He had his back to the others and put his head in his hands. The room was silent for a couple of minutes. The silence had never been so loud. Evelyn could hear her heart beating in her ears. It was pumping so hard it was like her head was under water. Officer Clarke broke the silence.

'Mr and Mrs Paterson, do you understand what I have told you? I'm afraid this is very serious. I appreciate it will take some time to sink in. I do, however, need to ask you some questions when you are ready.'

Joe turned around to face them, one hand on his hip and the other rubbing his forehead.

'Go on then, let's begin,' he said shakily. 'And just call me Joe.'

'Very well, Joe, when was the last time you saw Simon?'

'Um, yesterday morning, I think...' he stammered.

'Joe, it is extremely important we get this right. I know you are in shock, so please don't rush. Take your time and think as clearly as you can, ok?'

'Ok, ok. I was leaving for work, and he passed me on the upstairs landing. He was going for a bath.'

'And you haven't seen him since then?' asked Officer Clarke delicately.

'No, no, I don't think so. He comes and goes these days. We don't ask too much. You know what he is like, Officer. He's not worth talking to most of the time.'

'Ok, and how did he look to you, Joe?'

'I didn't really pay much attention. He looked his normal self, I think. We didn't speak; he went about his business in his usual manner...head looking down and despondent, you could say.'

Officer Clarke looked at Evelyn who looked exhausted and ill.

'Evelyn, what about you? When did you see him last?'

She spoke almost in a whisper. 'I couldn't tell you; I mean we can't keep tabs on him. You know what he's like...' She started to become distressed, as if the officer thought badly of her for not knowing Simon's movements, but the officer didn't think that of her at all.

'Evelyn, try to remain calm if you can. We just need to put together some pieces. We are looking for Simon as we speak, assuming he is not here, and I wanted to be the one to come and tell you myself and to...and to confirm his recent whereabouts. To confirm...'

He paused and looked at Joe and then Evelyn.

'And to confirm he...he doesn't have an alibi, do you understand?'

Joe could tell that this was something that Evelyn could not cope with. He would have to take control of this horrific situation and tell the officer the truth, get him out of the house, and let them both digest what was being told to them.

'Officer Clarke, I can tell you we have not bloody seen Simon, and if you are saying that he...that he has done this horrific act, then you must get on with your job and find him. He has no alibi here. The...boy...the man...whatever he is, must be treated in the way you people treat criminals and allow this to be dealt with. Just bloody find him and do what must be done...'

His voice was raised and assertive.

'We all know he is not right; I can't stand here and defend him. I mean, we never thought it would come to this but, what did we think he would amount to? He's not human and never bloody has been,' Joe said, exasperated.

Evelyn began sobbing louder now.

'Joe, I can assure you, we will find your son.'

'Don't call him my son... He is a bloody animal, and I want nothing to do with him. Enough is enough, that boy has ruined this family. He's ruined our lives for years now. My children's lives. He's tested our marriage...just get him locked up and throw away the bloody key.'

Evelyn fled the room in tears.

Officer Clarke went on to tell Joe that Simon was believed to be responsible for the murder of a local man who was younger than him and who had special needs. They believe he went for him because he was vulnerable. Both families knew each other. They weren't friends though. They weren't friends with anyone anymore because of Simon. Everyone thought he was a monster, and so the locals isolated the family. Officer Clarke told Joe that they believed Simon had stabbed the man to death; the man was known as Stephen Donald. He told him that the attack was unprovoked and that Simon had mugged his victim, it was an act of sheer brutality, and that the body discovered was one of the most shocking things he had seen in his career. Officer Clarke warned Joe that life may become difficult for them as a family due to this horrific crime and they should think about their options as to staying in the village. He suggested if they had somewhere else to go then they might want to do that. Everything Officer Clarke said was heard by Joe in an almost dream-like trance. He could hear him, but it sounded echo-like. He tried to take it all in, but he was struggling with it. He could hear the keywords loudly, ringing in his ears;

'Murder. Horrific. Unprovoked. Revenge. Move away.'

How could they move? he thought. He didn't earn much these days, and they had inherited the house they lived in. They just couldn't afford to up sticks and leave, but he, of course, understood why Officer Clarke had recommended it. Officer Clarke was in the Paterson's house for about three hours, but when Joe saw him out and closed the door, time stood still. He put his back to the door and slid down to the ground with bended knees.

That was an evening Evelyn would never forget. For a long time, they were shunned by the local community. Their other two children found new paths in life and left the village; their parents didn't blame them. Joe and Evelyn struggled on, but Joe was to die of a heart attack and leave Evelyn on her own a few years later. She always believed that Simon caused the death of him. He was never the same after that night. He was broken, defeated, crushed and with no life in his eyes. On the day he had the heart attack, she found him in his chair. It was too late, and nothing could be done. They had a funeral; the two children attended, and much to Evelyn's surprise, some of the locals came as well, mainly people Joe had worked with or had done DIY jobs for, but they didn't speak to the family. Evelyn knew they had come to pay their respects and that was it. She wasn't going to beg for their friendship or understanding. After the funeral, she rarely saw the two older children, and with Simon being locked away, she was completely alone. Doctors believed Simon to be mentally disturbed and had him locked up in a secure hospital for life.

The only bit of luck that Evelyn had was another lot of inheritance came in, and so she was able to buy a house somewhere else and start again. The new house was closer to where Simon was being kept and quite some distance from the town she had spent most of her life in.

For the next several years, her life became more pleasant as she could hide her dark secret from her new neighbours, and she began to feel happiness again. She would visit Simon once a year; that was all she could manage. It was too distressing for her and would take her weeks to recover, but she was incapable of abandoning him completely, despite his complete lack of care or even respect for her when she visited.

CHAPTER FIVE

Martha woke up to clattering noises coming from the kitchen. It sounded like everyone was up apart from her. She took a minute to sit upright and accept the new day ahead of her. Her head felt fuzzy; she could tell she had a drink last night. She rubbed her forehead and thought how disgusting her mouth tasted after too many cigarettes and alcohol from the night before.

These were trivial thoughts. She was trying to block out her main thought, and that was Peter. She couldn't ignore it any more. She couldn't ignore what had happened in bed the night before. What she had done and who she had thought of? He was going to stick around in her thoughts, and she needed to figure out why. Martha wasn't the sort of person to ignore something like that. She would enquire and enquire again and again into her own mind until she could figure out what was happening. She would torment herself looking for a rational explanation and the hope that it was a one-off. *It was the alcohol*, she told herself.

In her mind, she had betrayed her husband and her friend with her illicit thoughts last night. Two of the most important people to her and she betrayed them both. Her mind was going wild with questions.

Maybe it was the alcohol, maybe it was loneliness, maybe it was because I could hear them having sex, yes, maybe hearing them having sex made me think I was having sex with Johnny but I was interrupted by their noise which is why I pictured Peter, she told herself, desperately trying to find an answer that she was happy with. The truth is, if she was completely honest with herself, there was one clear and bold as day answer. It was screaming out to her, and she was trying to bury it with other questions in her mind to avoid it.

Her question was *Why did I picture Peter whilst I was doing that to myself, to the sound of him and Mae having sex last night?* The answer was because she felt there was a spark between the two of them. She knew it was wrong, and she didn't want a spark. Mae was all she had for crying out loud. But she knew it, and she knew that he felt it too. The feeling she got from him, however, was that the guilt belonging to their desires didn't reside in him. He loved Mae, Martha didn't doubt that, but the two women were very different, and all three of them knew that Mae didn't love Peter like she used to. Mae had probably grown bored of him in true Mae fashion. She would never leave him, but she loved him on her terms. It could be turned on and off like a switch. Mae was like that with everyone, and sadly, her own husband was no exception to the rule. Most women they knew would bow down to their husbands. They would care for them, appreciate them, cook for them, keep the house a home for them, make love to them on their say so, and most women would be happy to be a wife, but Mae had always been overconfident and didn't need anyone. Everything was on her terms, and although she would carry out her wifely duties, it was normally because there was something in it for her. All that aside, Mae didn't deserve the thoughts that were going on under that roof.

Although Martha hadn't asked Peter, she

knew she didn't have to. He felt it, just like she did. He was overconfident, just like his wife, so he would assume naturally that Martha would want him, desire him, and respect him, but she was certain that he desired her also. It hadn't been that clear at first — she had only been there a few days — but even within those short hours she spent in Peter's presence, she now knew that he had had improper thoughts about the two of them. Martha sighed. This just wouldn't do. The house move was meant to make life easier for them all, and now everything felt more complicated than ever.

She took her hands under her blankets again and began exploring her body once more. The troubling factor was that although she knew it was very wrong for her to have sexual thoughts about Peter, she now realised that she longed to be intimate with a man. As she stroked her breasts, she longed to be held by strong arms. Her nipples became erect. She craved soft kisses on her neck whilst moving her hands down her soft, smooth stomach. She longed for her hair to be stroked during an embrace, and so, she ran her fingers through her own hair. She longed for hot, passionate kisses. She inserted her fingers. She longed for the weight of a man on top of her and began to pleasure herself. Imagining how much she longed to be thrown about in bed, she began to fantasise. What she wouldn't give for that intense passion! Her body became warmer. She longed to feel a hard man inside of her, and as she did so, she became wetter. She longed for the thrusting, so she created her own, rocking her hips gently. She longed for the heavy breathing. She was heavy breathing now. She longed for her nipples to be sucked. Her body was tingling all over. She longed for big hands around her tiny waist pulling her closer towards him. She gently pulled her own hair. She longed to let him take the lead and for her to be powerless. She was very much in the lead. She longed to hold him tight with her legs wrapped around him. She brought her knees up whilst her fingers caressed her clitoris. She longed to kiss him heavily. She wanted to scream now. She longed to scratch her nails down his back. She was getting very close. She longed to tell him she wanted more. She did want more. She longed to whisper how hard he was in his ear. She really wanted that. She longed to move her hips with his. Her fingers would have to make do. She longed to tell him she was almost there. She whispered that bit out loud. She longed for those last few final hard thrusts. She longed to tell Peter she had come.

Martha lay there silently in ecstasy. She felt alive. She hadn't felt like this for what seemed like forever. She was blocking out her conscience whilst lying there just trying to enjoy the euphoria for a moment. Her breathing had calmed down and temperature slowly went back to normal. She had better get up, she thought.

It was kind of Mae to allow her to have a lie in and get the boys up. She probably wouldn't have been so generous if she knew Martha was masturbating over her husband in her good bed sheets, thought Martha. She had forgotten about Mae for the last few minutes. The last few minutes she had been imagining she was having sex with Mae's husband, Peter. Martha began to panic. What if Mae could tell how she was beginning to feel? She realised that whilst she had been consumed in her own debauchery, the clattering noise from downstairs had escalated into what sounded like a row between Peter and Mae. Martha tried to listen in, but she couldn't make out what was being said.

'Now, I really must get up,' she said, trying to break her own nervous silence.

She would have to get up and face them. 'It'll be ok,' she said quietly to herself. 'They can't possibly know what's been going on in this room.' But Martha knew she was not very good at keeping secrets. She had a guilty face for crimes she hadn't committed, let alone ones she had. She decided to bite the bullet and throw on some clothes.

She went in to the bathroom and freshened up. She looked at herself in the mirror. Her big eyes were sad; she felt so guilty and had a horrible feeling that things weren't going to get better anytime soon. She topped up her flicks of eyeliner and put on her favourite crimson red lipstick. She tidied up her victory rolls and then took one last look in the mirror.

'You are not a bad person, Martha. You haven't done anything wrong. Oh, for God's sake.' She covered her face with her hands and sighed.

With that, she went to make her way out of the bathroom. Someone was coming up the stairs; it sounded like Peter. Her heart fluttered. She opened the door, and Peter came right at her. He put his hands at the top of her arms and manhandled her out of the room so that he could get in.

'Sorry, Martha, in a rush,' he said as he picked up his toothbrush.

'Oh, uh, no bother. Sorry if I took too long, I... I... seem to have slept in.' She blushed and tucked her hair behind her ear.

'Not at all.'

He was drying his mouth with the towel. He looked around at her, and she realised she was just standing there.

'You look lovely today, Martha; the sleep must've done you good. You've got a glow about you.'

Martha blushed. She knew her face could not hide a lie. *Did he know? Could he tell?* she thought. He smiled and moved past her and skipped down the stairs. She was still just standing there watching him go down the stairs.

'Bye, darling, give us a kiss,' she heard him say to Mae.

'Oh, clear off and leave me alone,' said Mae.

'You really are a piece of work,' Peter said back to her, and with that, he left the kitchen, stormed up the hallway, and slammed the front door.

Martha stood at the top of the stairs, wondering what had happened. Had they argued about her? Did Mae think Peter was attracted to her? Was she going to ask her to leave? Martha's panic was in full steam.

'It's ok, Martha, you can come down, you know.'

Martha made her way down the stairs into

the kitchen to find Mae at the table smoking a cigarette and looking slightly peeved.

'Morning', said Martha gingerly. 'Sorry I was late up today, I...'

She was interrupted by Mae.

'Men. They think they are God's bloody gift sometimes. Why should we have to bow to their every beck and call? So, what if I can't be bothered to wake him up with sex.'

Martha gulped and began to make a pot of tea.

'One day, Martha, one day you will see that we will live in a world where we are equal. More and more of the women I know are now out working. Women. Working. Who would've thought that twenty years ago? But what I say is if we have to work like a man, then we get the same rights as a man.'

But you don't work, thought Martha as she got out two cups and saucers.

'He comes and goes as he pleases in this house, quite literally sometimes...' Mae went on, although Martha wished she wouldn't because it wasn't helping her current predicament.

'You know, so what if I don't want to have sex with him.'

Martha dropped a plate on the floor and smashed it.

'Oh god, I am so sorry. Where's the dustpan and brush? I'm so sorry, Mae, I will replace it.'

'Don't worry about it, Martha, it's not one of my favourites. I have about five other sets in the larder. This is the set Peter's mother, the old witch, don't tell him I called her that, gave us, so I don't care what happens to these. Break them all for all I care. In fact, I might help you.'

She handed Martha the dustpan and brush she had got out of the cupboard and sat back down and finished her cigarette. Martha swept up the broken crockery and placed it all in the bin. She looked out of the window and saw the two boys playing in the garden. Martha's heavy heart lifted when she saw how happy her little boy was. She took the teapot to the table, placed a cup and saucer down, and sat to face Mae.

'Look, don't worry about Peter.'

'I'm not,' Mae retorted. 'He should worry about me. I am capable of looking after myself...'

You are not, thought Martha, *not without his money anyway.*

'...Oh, I don't know, men. I suppose I shall have to bounce his balls this evening and make amends.'

They both giggled. Mae was so outspoken compared to Martha. The words she used, the way she talked. If it wasn't for Peter, she would be no more than a common fishwife, but the exclusivity that Peter brought to the table allowed her potty mouth to be excused, and some people loved it, men mainly. It made Martha feel uncomfortable.

'Well, I've been thinking, you and Peter need to have some quality husband and wife time, and I'm here getting in the way, so why don't the two of you go out for an evening and I'll stay in with the boys? It might be just what you need to get that lust back.'

Martha was smiling encouragingly at Mae.

'What if I said I would rather Peter looked after the boys and we went out for the evening? That would be more fun to me,' said Mae dismissively.

'Oh, look really, we are alright. I just get fed up with him being around sometimes. You know, he is away for days at a time and I get the house to myself. I have gotten used to being by myself, and I like things the way I like them, and then he comes back and everything has to be his way. Sometimes I wish he just didn't bother coming back.'

Mae huffed and picked up another cigarette. *Some women would give anything to have their husband around,* thought Martha. Martha was jealous of what she had with Peter and thought her friend was ungrateful and unappreciative.

'You don't mean that, Mae. I had that one day. That one day where Johnny didn't come home. You really don't want that, believe me,' said Martha calmly, thinking it would make Mae feel bad for being so insensitive.

'I don't know, try me,' said Mae with a face so straight and cold that it caused a wave of anger in Martha.

Mae put out her cigarette and got up from the table. She went to the back door and called in the boys.

'Charlie. Willy. Come on in now. Let's have some lunch and maybe we can go for a walk to the pond.'

The two boys raced each other in, and Willy hung off his mother's arm. Martha picked him up and put him on her knee.

'Oh, you are almost getting too big for Mummy's knee now, darling,' as she smoothed down his hair.

'I love you, Mummy,' he said and rested on her chest.

Willy had calmed the scene once again. She wouldn't think of anything when she cuddled him. She would just feel love.

Charlie started laughing and chanting, 'You love her. You love her.'

Willy got embarrassed and jumped off and chased Charlie. The boys would be starting preschool soon, and she worried that the other children would toughen him up too much. She liked him being a Mummy's boy.

After lunch, the women got the two boys ready and ventured out for a stroll. Mae still seemed a tad irritable, so Martha hoped the fresh air might do her some good. She was, however, relieved that the attention was not on her and realised that her earlier fears about them discovering her growing crush on Peter was silly. The two ladies walked to the end of the road, which should've taken a couple of minutes, but with the number of people that Mae knew and stopped to speak to, it took them about twenty minutes.

'Right, then,' said Mae. 'If we go left we can swing by David's garage and say hello, but I know how upset you get about being introduced to new and somewhat attractive men, so we can go right and walk past the factory, and gaze in awe at the women doing the jobs of men and paving the way for a new world where men and women are equals,' she said jokingly.

'Well, Mae, I think your certain 'je ne sais

quoi' could be rubbing off on me. Let's go left,' said Martha as she glided along with her back straight and shoulders pulled back.

'Ooooh,' scoffed Mae, 'I think I like where this is heading. So, the lady wants to see David. Maybe all of that talk at the breakfast table this morning got you all fired up.' She beamed at Martha.

'Not everything is about that, Mae, but I do think you have a point. Johnny is gone. He is not coming back. It's been two years now, so maybe it's time to move on. I'm not sure I am ready, mind you, but I am happy to start talking to strangers, you could say.'

Martha had decided in her mind that perhaps if she started talking about David it would distract everyone, including her, from her growing feelings for Peter. She had no intentions of anything happening with David; she just wanted to talk about her feelings and use someone else's identity to cover up her secret. Martha noticed that Mae's mood had improved significantly as they walked along the street and knew that this was probably because she had a plan up her sleeve.

'Mae, I know I said I am happy to walk this way, but that doesn't mean I want to rush into anything, ok?' said Martha, trying to be as assertive as she could be.

'Martha, I can lead a horse to water...let's just go and say hello, ok?'

Martha nodded but wasn't convinced. As the two women approached David's workplace, they could see his head under the bonnet of a car working away. Martha noticed he had quite big arms, not huge but more muscled than the average man. He was wearing some overalls that he only had his legs in with the top half tied around his waist revealing his grease marked white vest. On his head, he had a very worn flat cap that had seen better days.

'Hi, David,' Mae cooed.

David pulled away from under the bonnet and removed his hat. He took a cloth and mopped his brow. 'Afternoon, ladies, you both look lovely today. How are you?'

Martha noticed he had a boyish charm about him. He had a nice smile which she hadn't noticed before. The two boys found some tyres in the corner and used them as seats and began bouncing on them.

'Willy, don't bounce on those. They're not for children,' said Martha and motioned for him to get off.

'They're alright,' said David. 'Probably the

safest thing for them to play with in here. I don't mind if you don't.'

Martha met his eyes and smiled sheepishly.

'Ok, boys, but just the tyres. Don't touch anything else.'

Mae piped up, 'So, what are you working on here then? Looks nice.'

Before David could answer, Martha chipped in, 'That's a Morris Minor. Well, it is, isn't it?'

David laughed and said, 'Yes, it is. So, you like your cars then?'

Mae stood behind him smiling and raising her eyebrows rather animatedly.

'Oh, I don't know much really; I just recognise that one, that's all.'

'I'm impressed,' said David, and Martha suspected he actually was.

'This little lady isn't in too good a condition though. Well, she wasn't when she came in, but with a bit of work, I'll have her back on the road in no time. Should be working again by tomorrow, I think.'

He rubbed the side of the car with what looked like genuine love and care. Mae piped up again. 'So, you'll have to take it out for a test drive when you think it's fixed again, won't you, you know, to make sure it goes ok?'

Martha knew exactly what was coming next.

'Yes, I will, just a quick jaunt around the block just to make sure she is ok,' replied David.

'Well, you could take Martha out with you seeing as she likes them so much. Swing by my place when you're done and take her out for a spin. You'd like that, wouldn't you, Martha?'

Martha wanted to say, 'No, not really,' but she remembered her earlier plan to keep the distraction going and agreed that it would be nice. David was shocked.

'Really? You would come out with me? Ok, then, I'll pick you up. We won't go out for long, you know, in case...well, I won't keep you is what I mean.'

'Perfect.' Mae squealed. 'That's agreed that then; we'll have Martha waiting for you looking all pretty.'

Martha hated the way Mae was talking as if she were her mother but agreed, for the time being, this was not a bad idea.

The two women arrived back at the house with two exhausted boys who had run all the way home.

'Right, boys, wash your hands, and I will get you some water and start dinner,' Mae called after them as they ran through the house.

Peter was back, and instantly Martha's heart fluttered and began to race.

'This is ridiculous,' she said softly.

Mae began to busy herself in the kitchen, which Martha noticed she had become quite accustomed to. She hoped Mae didn't think she was allowing her to do everything, but at the same time, Mae seemed happier in charge of everything, maybe happier in charge of everything and happier busying herself away from Peter. She didn't even acknowledge him when they came in. Martha did.

He was sitting at the table smoking a cigar. He had his shirt sleeves rolled up and his top button undone. Also on the table was an open bottle of scotch with almost a quarter of it gone, of which only a tiny bit of that was sitting still in a crystal tumbler on the table. Peter picked up the expensive-looking glass and knocked back the remainder of its contents.

'Pull up a chair, Martha, and tell me about your day.'

Peter beckoned her to sit.

'Oh, I should really see if Mae needs some help with dinner...'

'I'm fine, thanks. Sit,' Mae interrupted Martha.

Martha wanted to help; she was almost sweating at the thought of sitting with Peter.

'See, the Führer said you can sit.' He laughed to himself.

'I heard that,' Mae sneered.

'You were meant to,' Peter called back jokingly. 'Grab a glass and sit.' He beckoned Martha again.

'Oh, I shouldn't drink; I normally wait until William is in bed.'

Peter got up and got a glass from the cupboard, took it to the table, sat down and poured a drink, and slid it across to where Martha should sit, right in front of him.

'Young, beautiful Martha.'

Her heart fluttered.

'You need to relax a little. We like to have fun in this house, don't we, darling?'

Mae clattered about. Martha was sure she heard, and that the pots and pans being clattered was an act of defiance on her part. Peter leaned over to Martha.

He whispered, 'Miserable goat,' and leaned back grinning. He winked at her.

His breath smelled strongly of scotch, and she found that it lured her in like a moth to a flame. Martha pulled out the chair and sat down gingerly. Her skin tingled into goosebumps all the while she tried to pretend that everything was normal.

'I like your blouse, you look pretty in it,' Peter said whilst sipping on his scotch, not taking his eyes off her.

Martha's heart was pounding. She was certain he was not being 'just polite.' He wanted her, and she knew it and, somewhat ashamedly, she wanted him too. Mae came to the table and joined them. She took a glass and poured herself a drink.

'Doesn't she look pretty, Mae?'

Martha began to feel extremely awkward, nervous, and on display.

Mae looked at Martha and looked at Peter.

'Yes, she does rather, I suppose.'

With that, she knocked her drink back in one. Martha sat there in silence. Was Peter flirting with her or was he deliberately wanting Mae to bite? Was she a pawn in their dwindling relationship? Perhaps Peter didn't want her after all. Perhaps he just wanted to feel real love from his wife again, and to get it, he would flirt with her friend. It might not get him the reaction he wanted, but it would be a reaction and that was good enough for a breaking heart, right? A flare of jealousy would be enough to reassure him, Martha pondered. It suddenly became clear that they were all sitting in silence, and it was too loud for Martha.

'Well, anyway, David certainly thinks she is pretty. He is taking her out tomorrow.'

Mae broke the silence with this new information to Peter and poured everyone another drink.

'Is he?' Peter said, swiftly sitting up straight. 'Well, that's great. Good for you, girl. Get back out there, get back in the saddle, as it were.'

Martha didn't believe Peter was genuinely happy about it. If anything, she thought his response seemed quite unnatural despite his best efforts to hide his dismay.

'I don't know about getting 'back in the saddle," shrugged Martha nervously.

'Oh, shush, Martha, you like him, he likes you...who knows what could happen. The back of the car looked quite roomy to me.'

Mae joked causing Martha to blush and feel a surge of anger. Peter fixated his eyes on Martha, and she could tell that the two women in the room began to feel not quite happy with the way this conversation was going. Peter clearly thought things weren't awkward enough as he probed Martha with more questions.

'Do you like this man then? Is this what you want in the next man? Are you attracted to him? A mere mechanic? I thought you had better taste.'

Martha saw that Mae was getting more agitated.

'What the hell is that supposed to mean?' Mae raised her voice to Peter.

'Shut up, woman. Do not speak to me in that tone. If I want to question the girl, I will; and I will not be spoken to like a fool by you. Sometimes you'd do well to remember your place, god damn, I let you get away with it most of the time.'

Peter finished his drink and slammed his glass down on the table. Mae's face burned a crimson red. She got up and left the table, leaving Martha and Peter alone. Peter was getting drunk, and Martha hadn't seen him speak to anyone like that before, although she wasn't surprised. Mae always did push the boundaries. He was normally so jovial and chivalrous, but things always do go on behind closed doors, thought Martha, and she was caught in the thick of it.

'I'll go and see if Mae needs anything,' said Martha sheepishly, and she got up and left the table.

Martha found Mae in the front room picking up toys. She was doing it frantically as if she was being timed in a competition.

'Mae,' said Martha quietly.

Mae acted surprised. 'Martha. I didn't see you there. I was just clearing up.'

Martha put her hand on Mae's arm. 'Are you ok? Is everything ok?' she asked.

'Oh, yes, everything is fine. Take no notice of that idiot. He's had too much to drink. I hope he didn't upset you,' she said as though the wind had been knocked out of her sails.

Martha thought it was odd that Mae thought Martha would be upset; if anything, it should be Mae that was upset. *Unless she is trying to deny what was happening at that table,* thought Martha. The two women got on with dinner and didn't talk about the table conversation any further. Peter didn't join them for dinner. He sat in 'his' chair and listened to the wireless whilst the women played 'Mum' with their two boys.

Later that evening, after the women put the boys to bed, Martha decided to try and avoid the crossfire and went to bed early to read and leave Peter and Mae alone. Although she tried to read, her mind was racing. Peter had made it clear he had feelings for her. Was he just trying to make Mae jealous? Martha couldn't tell. Whatever he was doing, Martha couldn't tell.

Is he jealous because I am going out with David tomorrow, or was it just the alcohol? Does Mae trust me? Is she going to ask us to leave?

Where would we go? Oh, I'm probably reading too much into it. Stop thinking, Martha. Shut up. She smacked her book against her head to try and quieten her thoughts. She realised she had read about three chapters and hadn't taken any of it in. She wondered what time it was, and then she heard them coming up the stairs so she realised it must be later than she thought.

There was muffled talking. She couldn't make out if they had resolved their earlier spat or not. Someone went into the bathroom. It sounded like Peter. The toilet flushed. The tap ran. There was the spitting of toothpaste. The tap went off. The door opened. There were a few footsteps. They had stopped outside Martha's door. Silence. Martha's heart pounded. Then there was the creak of the other bedroom door opening. Her visitor had left. Who was it? Was it Mae? Was it Peter? Shortly after, Martha then heard what sounded like Peter and Mae having sex. There was no noise from them, just the sound of the bed creaking. It didn't last long and ended with relief noises from Peter but not a single sound from Mae. Compared to how vocal they had been the other night, that was not an act of love that had happened next door. It sounded like a wife fulfilling her marital duties. Martha couldn't sleep. She lay there for what seemed like ages just staring. Her mind was racing with so many thoughts that she just couldn't sleep. She didn't even want to go out with David. She agreed to it to keep everyone else happy, and now they had all argued about it.

She needed to go to the toilet. She didn't want to get up and disturb anyone. If anything, right now, she wished she could be invisible in that house. She felt like there was a bright light shining on her wherever she was. She couldn't hold it in; she must go to the loo. She crept out of bed as quietly as she could and tiptoed into the bathroom. When she returned to her room, Peter was in there, standing right in front of her.

'Don't go out with David,' he said, staring right into her eyes.

Martha's heart felt like it was a racehorse and it was going to burst out of her chest. It was beating so loudly she was sure they both could hear it.

'Don't, I don't want you to go out with him,' Peter continued.

Martha tried to find the words to say but was speechless. Peter stepped closer towards her. She gulped. He put one hand on her chin and stroked it whilst looking at her up and down. Then, he moved his hand under her hair and cupped the back of her head and pulled her in.

They began kissing passionately. Their hands were going everywhere, exploring each other's bodies, and then Peter pulled away. He held Martha in front of him and looked right at her.

'Don't go out with him.'

He stroked her hair away from her eyes, kissed her on the forehead, and then left the room. Martha collapsed on the bed.

CHAPTER SIX

The next morning, Martha was up before everyone. To put the previous evening's events to the back of her mind, she thought she would get up and prepare breakfast for everyone. It was a lovely day with the sun shining bright and a warm breeze blowing. She opened the back door and had the windows open and set about laying the table for them all to eat together. She could hear movement upstairs and knew it wouldn't be long before she was faced with her betrayal. She didn't know who she wanted to see the least but had hoped that today was a new day and that last night was the result of Peter having had too much to drink; despite the feeling she was trying to rid herself of that, she had actually enjoyed kissing Peter. Mae was the first to appear.

'Morning, Martha, that early night did you good.'

She appeared in the kitchen looking as glamorous as usual. Martha felt panicky whilst filling a teacup for Mae.

'Did you go straight to sleep? You're not normally up this early,' she said, sitting down to the cup that had been poured for her.

'Do you know, I think I must've done,' she replied nervously with a slight laugh.

The first lie had been told. That was it now. The web of lies had been created. Mae was the spider, Peter was the web, and Martha was the helpless fly destined for a slow death.

'I'm sorry about last night, Martha. Peter can be such an arse when he's had a drink. Now that you are living with us you will get to see a different side to his personality. Just ignore him, that's what I try to do.'

She had got away with it. Mae was none the wiser. Martha felt relief followed by grief followed by shame.

'Just be grateful you don't have to sleep with the buffoon.'

They both giggled. Mae's was a genuine laugh and Martha's was of sheer panic. The two boys came bounding down the stairs like a small herd of elephants bringing the whole house to life which calmed Martha's nerves. She could concentrate on them now and not be forced into talking about things she wasn't comfortable with.

'Mummy?' Willy piped up, staring at her with his big blue eyes. She couldn't believe she had created something so beautiful.

'Yes, darling?'

'Mummy, can you take me to the park today? Just us?'

Martha looked at Mae and then back at Willy.

'Yes, of course, angel, that would be lovely. We can go out after breakfast if you like.'

He nodded and stuffed a piece of toast into his mouth. Martha felt like her little hero had just saved the day. He hadn't asked to be alone with her since they moved house, but she was glad of it. A few hours out of that house would be a welcome break today. Her short spell at happiness was short-lived as she heard Peter's footsteps coming down the stairs. All she could do was to carry on what she was doing, shuffling about pretending to organise breakfast. *Act normal, Martha,* she thought. *It meant nothing. He was drunk. It was a stupid mistake.*

As Peter reached the bottom of the stairs, he

was whistling and came into the kitchen, beaming.

'Morning, lovely ladies and charming chaps.' The boys giggled and Mae ignored him. 'Isn't it a beautiful day. The sun is shining. I have two beautiful women living under my roof, a young son destined for great things with a good friend by his side. What a glorious life it is sometimes.'

The kitchen remained silent.

'What? God, can't a man do anything right these days? Anyone would think this house had been bombed. We are some of the lucky ones, you know. Well, I think I'm lucky,' he said as he kissed Mae's neck, and again, she ignored him. 'Ah, well, never mind. Is this fresh tea? Thank you, Martha. How are you today? Did you sleep well?' he asked her, seeming positively full of himself without an ounce of guilt about him.

'Yes, thank you, Peter, I did.'

Willy had finished his breakfast, and so she seized the opportunity to take the boys upstairs and get them dressed. She got out their clothes in autopilot mode whilst being completely baffled and somewhat dumbfounded by Peter's actions just then. Was he honestly that happy? Why? Was it because of their kiss? Was it because he had realised he had made a mistake and had decided to move on and make it work with Mae?

She hoped so. She picked up Willy's top. It was quite dirty. It would have to do for today, and she would hand wash it tonight. She didn't have any spare money for clothes at the moment, but her sister was due to send her some in the next couple of weeks. Hopefully, they would have a nice sunny day where Martha and Mae could go shopping together with the boys. She had moved to Mae's because not only the space and the offer itself, but Mae's village was considered safer than where she had been living. She had been quite close to the city previously. Moving to the countryside made her feel much more at ease. It was comforting to be somewhere safer, but they were living in uncertain times, and theoretically nowhere was safe.

'Right, there you are, my boy. Don't you look just as handsome as ever. I still can't believe how big you are getting,' Martha said as she slipped on his shoes.

'I'm not that big, silly Mummy, I'm still little,' said Willy, patting her head as he leaned on her.

'Well, I guess you are still a bit little, *and* you will *always* be my baby.' Charlie had been getting dressed as well and began laughing and taunting Willy.

'Baby. Baby. Baby.'

Willy looked annoyed. She could see his personality developing; he didn't like being mocked, and she could tell that Charlie was destined to be the class clown.

'Come on you two, let's go downstairs.'

The two boys raced ahead. They very rarely moved at a normal pace; that was reserved for when they were tired or being forced to eat something they didn't want to. Any other time of the day seemed to be a race for them. They were always buzzing about, and it was nice and just how boys should be.

Martha walked into the kitchen. Peter was still sitting at the table, and Mae was out in the garden emptying the bin. Peter was reading the paper but made a point of lowering it to stare at Martha. There were no grey areas this time. He was staring right at her. Thankfully, Mae came in.

'You two off out then? You and Willy?'

Martha's heart was up and down like a yo-yo. She didn't know how she was going to cope with this. Every question seemed like it began as an accusation but then ended with relief.

'Yes, I'm going to take him down to the river. He obviously wants some Mummy time. He won't for much longer, so I had better make the most of it.'

She said it in a jovial way, trying to ignore the feeling of Peter's eyes staring at the back of her.

'Oh really? Down to the river and past David's garage by any chance?' she enquired.

'No, I won't take Willy down there. I think maybe he is a bit insecure with all the recent changes. No, I think what he needs is to have me to himself for a couple of hours like how we used to be.'

'Yes. Children do pick up on everything, don't they. Sometimes I think they see things even adults can't. They're very, oh, what's the word, you know, like a sponge. They soak everything up like a sponge. Oh well, he doesn't need to know you are seeing delicious David later. Time for him this morning and some time for Mummy this evening,' she said, winking at Martha.

Peter put down his paper, went to the back door, and lit up a cigarette.

'Well, yes, perhaps,' agreed Martha, somewhat against her will.

'I'll have some lunch for when you get back then.'

With that, Mae began to busy herself again. She always seemed genuinely happy when she could busy herself. It was almost as if she wasn't comfortable in her own skin and her apparent abundance of confidence was a façade. Martha went to the back door and called Willy in and then reluctantly made contact with Peter's eyes. He stared right at her and mouthed 'Don't.' She gulped, took Willy's hand, and said goodbye to them all.

She was glad to be out of that house. *How on earth could she have let this happen?* she thought. Everyone who knows her would be so disappointed in her if they knew what had been going on. She never thought she would be the sort of woman to get caught up in something like this. She decided not to let it spoil her morning with Willy; he didn't deserve that. He deserved her full attention. She loved that little boy for many reasons and one of those reasons was he could make her forget all her troubles. The two of them walked down the street hand-in-hand, him in his little cap and her looking dainty and elegant. To look at her, she looked like one of those women that had it all together, but she was a nothing but a confused mess inside.

That morning, Martha had quality time with her beloved son, Willy. He was like anaesthetic for her unhappy mind. They blew dandelions. They watched ducks in the river. They made daisy chains. They lay together in the long grass.

They cuddled. He stroked her hair with his chubby little hands. When she was with him, she was at peace. He distracted her from anything bad in the world or in her life.

Sometimes she would look at him and just want to cry. Sometimes it was because he made her heart ache with love. Sometimes it was because he had no idea how much she needed him, let alone him needing her. Sometimes it was because she couldn't see very far ahead in the future, and she didn't know if she could be the best mother to him. She didn't have a lot to offer him, and she felt he deserved the world. She really couldn't have asked for a more special little boy. He would be at school soon, and although a lot of families were struggling due to the war, she had almost nothing materialistically for him. Thank goodness for her sister Jane's financial support.

She wished she could give him the world but what if she never could? What if life got the better of her and she became bitter and took it out on him? What if he grew up not to like her? What if he wished he had a different family? She wished John was there to help her through it. Many of her friends had told her she was so strong. A lot of them had said they wouldn't have coped as well as she did. They were being nice and supportive, she knew that, but what choice did she have? All she could do was carry on. All she could do was try and keep it together for Willy. God, it had been so hard. There were many times she wished she could give up. If it hadn't been for Willy, who knows where she would be now? He was a blessing for her mental state, but on the other hand, he gave her more responsibility than she thought she could handle at times. She hated herself for even thinking that. He didn't ask to be here.

He was the child that they had both wanted so much, and she physically winced every time she had a thought about how hard life was. He was her beautiful, blue-eyed boy. He never gave her grief. He was just a sweet little boy without a dad and with a mum just trying to do her best. He never judged her. He always wanted to see her in the morning, and he always wanted her to tuck him in at night. She would tuck him in and tell him not to worry about the boogie man, she would always protect him, but it was Willy who was saving her at the moment.

After they had played together for a couple of hours, they picked up their things and made their way back to the house. Willy needed feeding. The fresh air had tired him out, and Martha could feel herself getting distracted and not giving him her full attention, so she decided it would be best to get him back to his playmate. As they walked back, Willy was very talkative about the clouds in the sky. He was trying to count them all as he walked.

'There are two big ones and three small ones. Oh, there's another big one, so there's three big ones, Mummy.'

Martha looked up at the sky and counted with him.

'You're a clever boy, there are three big ones and three smaller ones...'

They were both looking up when a familiar voice said, 'Boo,' and Willy burst into fits of giggles. It was David from the garage. He had walked straight into them and was tickling Willy under his chin.

'Hello, Martha, you look beautiful today,' he said, staring right at her.

She blushed.

'Thank you, David. I wouldn't say beautiful, but thank you.'

She looked down at the ground. The meeting was quite awkward.

'So, uh, so...are we still on for this evening?' David enquired, sensing that Martha was not relaxed, 'because we can do it some other time if you prefer. Well, I don't know if I'll still have the car you like next time, but I get a different car to fix every few days, so I'm pretty sure I'll have something to take you for a spin in.'

He looked at her, and she was still staring at the ground.

'Unless it's not the car. We don't have to go out ever if you don't want to. I know Mae put us on the spot, but I just thought you did want to, but like I say...'

Martha cut him off. 'Of course I would like to. I said I would and I do. It wasn't Mae's decision; it was mine, and yes. Yes, I would. Very much so. Shall we say 7.30pm?'

David's face lit up and a smile spread across his face. She realised he really liked her. Mae had pushed her into seeing him, but it had only just occurred to her that he didn't need pushing. He *really* liked her. *Oh great, just what I need,* she thought. She could tell he was a nice man, but he wasn't exactly her cup of tea, and with everything that had happened between her and Peter recently, she just didn't feel like getting involved with anyone. It was a big mess, but she also knew she had to go out with him to keep Mae off her back; and she could go out with him once, and then she would tell Mae that there was no spark so that Mae would leave her alone. At least she could say she tried. That is what she would do. She would go out with David tonight. Peter wouldn't be happy, but then she would tell Mae they were not compatible. Then she could tell Peter that she did it to keep Mae off her back and that she had no intention of seeing him again. But then Peter would think she did it for him. If she goes, Peter is unhappy. If she doesn't go, Mae is unhappy. If she does either, then she is unhappy.

David walked with them back to the house. He was very good with Willy, and in the short, walk she had discovered that he very much wanted a family and she knew he would be good at it. She could tell he was dependable. He wasn't a risk. He also wasn't in the army, so theoretically she knew he would come home. He had been dismissed on medical grounds because he had problems with his breathing. He had done all the talking. She hadn't said a word apart from the odd acknowledgement and the odd giggle here and there. They arrived at the front door, and the awkwardness crept back in.

'Well,' she said, 'I will see you this evening.'

She looked down at Willy who was staring across the road. She had looked at him so that she didn't have to look at David. She opened the door and told Willy to go in. David took her hand and kissed the back of it.

'Yes, you will, Martha, see you at 7.30.'

He took his cap off and gave a slight bow and walked off smiling. He had spring in his step and wanted her to see it. She watched him for a few seconds and then brought her gaze back to find Peter across the road staring at her. He was just standing there, smoking and watching. She looked behind her, looked around her and then back at him, and he was still there just watching her. He then put his cigarette out with his shoe, the whole time, just staring at her. She hastily turned and went into the house, closing the door behind her without looking back.

Willy had already run off to play with Charlie, and Mae was sitting out in the back garden. Martha sat down and joined her.

'Hello, darling, beautiful day, isn't it?' Mae said, basking in the sun.

Martha agreed, sitting back and closing her eyes.

'Did you two have an enjoyable time?' Mae asked, eyes still closed.

'Yes, we did. We just played by the river, blew some dandelions...'

But Martha was interrupted by Willy. He had come over and put his hands on her knees

and said, 'Mummy, where is Uncle Peter?'
Martha became uncomfortable.

'I don't know, Willy; he has gone out I think.'

'He was outside, Mummy. Why didn't he
come in?' Martha's heart began to race. 'Was he?
I didn't see him,' she said, hoping Mae wouldn't
think too much of it and feeling guilty for lying
to her son.

'Yes. He was. He was staring at you when
you were talking to that man by the front door.
He was across the road staring. I waved at him
but he didn't wave back at me. Why didn't he
come in?'

Martha needed to stop the questioning.

'You must've seen someone that looked like
him. I didn't see him. Never mind, I'm sure he
will be home soon and you boys can play
cowboys and Indians.'

She laughed it off and looked around to Mae
for reassurance. Mae was still basking in the sun,
eyes closed. *What was Mae thinking?* she
thought.

She had become a paranoid wreck over the
last 48 hours and now she was lying to her son.
This situation needed to end and it needed to
end soon. She couldn't cope with the dishonesty,
the lies. *Why did he stare like that? What did it
mean?* she pondered. She had really hoped the

other night was a mistake. *Was he staring because he wanted her to see him? If so, what point was he trying to make? He didn't want David around? He wanted to be David? Why was he angry?* She hadn't done anything wrong apart from kiss him, she thought, but he kissed her. He plied her with alcohol and then he kissed her whilst she was weak. She would never have done that if she was sober.

Mae still hadn't said a word. The two women sat in silence, both soaking up the sun in ignorant bliss. The bliss was short-lived as Peter came bounding in. He was whistling loudly and making more noise than usual. It was as if he wanted his presence to be known. This time he didn't come out and greet the women. He banged about in the kitchen. He didn't even say hello to his son, which was not normal for him. Well, Martha hadn't been with them long, but in the brief time she had been there, he always greeted everyone when he came in. Martha was panicked. Mae was still silent. The boys continued to play, the women continued to sit quietly, and Peter continued to keep himself to himself.

Martha was sure something was wrong. *Perhaps they had another row,* she thought. *Nothing has been said about me before now, so surely, I'm worrying about nothing.* she said to herself, trying to rationalise how uncomfortable she was feeling.

Mae broke the silence.

'So, you've got a date tonight. What clothes have you got with you?' she said still staring ahead.

'Well, I hadn't really given it much thought. I wasn't really looking at it as a date,' Martha said nonchalantly.

'Don't be so ridiculous.' Mae took off her hat and got up from her seat. 'Come on. I've got something in mind for you.'

Martha didn't argue. She suddenly felt like there was something in the air and that it would be easier just to do what Mae said. They went back into the house. Peter had poured himself a drink again. That worried Martha. This time, however, he didn't even acknowledge them.

'I'm just taking Martha upstairs to dress her up for her date. Watch the boys, please.'

Again, he didn't make a remark. Martha began to feel like a pawn in a game of chess for the second time this week, and who knew who would win?

CHAPTER SEVEN

There was a knock at the door at 7.25pm. David was five minutes early.

'Someone's keen to make a good impression,' Mae said to Martha whilst grinning from ear to ear.

Mae seemed heavily interested in this evening's events whilst Martha was dreading it and wondering why on earth she agreed to it. She just wanted to get it over with and wished that Mae wouldn't make such a big thing of it. She was making Martha feel like a child with her constant goading. Martha was a grown up, but suddenly it felt like Mae was the older, more mature one and everyone wanted silly little Martha to get a boyfriend. Martha hated how patronising and short-sighted Mae could be at times. She knew that Mae genuinely wanted her to be happy, but she was happy. She didn't need a man to make her happy. She wasn't Mae. It started off as that anyway, but now Martha suspected that Mae was cottoning on to Peter's wandering eye. *Maybe it will be a good thing to get out of the house this evening,* she thought, *better than being played by Mae and Peter.* She wasn't a piece of meat and was rapidly becoming uncomfortable about being caught up in their game.

Martha said her goodbyes and pretended to be excited about going out. She asked them to wish her luck as she headed for the door.

'Luck won't come into it, in that dress' remarked Peter.

He was not happy, and Martha couldn't get out quick enough. David was at the door and, much to Martha's surprise, looked very dapper. She had only seen him in his work clothes, but tonight he had his hair slicked back and looked clean shaven. She could even smell aftershave on him. They kissed each other on the cheeks.

'You look...' they both said at the same time.

Martha giggled and David apologised.

'No need to apologise,' said Martha. 'You didn't do anything wrong.'

'Well, I was just going to say that you look beautiful, Martha, and it is my pleasure to have your company for the evening.'

He opened the car door to let her in. Martha thought he was very sweet. She imagined that he had probably had his heart broken before, with a soft nature like that.

The pair made small talk for the first fifteen minutes or so. They drove off in silence, so Martha broke the ice and started asking David about his interests. Even if she wasn't interested in him, the ride would be easier to endure if they spoke a little. She was worried about talking too much in case he she could be accused of leading him on, but at the same time, she didn't want him feeling rejected. She was a sucker for always trying to make people feel better, even to the detriment of her own happiness. David talked about his first love, cars. As the conversation flowed, she realised cars were his only love.

'So, there's never been a Mrs David?'

She was sure she wasn't this direct with people a year ago, but she was changing. Her independence was growing. That, and a lack of not caring so much about what people thought of her these days. She surprised herself with her direct questioning and was instantly riddled with nerves and guilt because she was worried he would think she was more interested in him than she was. David smiled at the question and replied;

'No. Nope. Not a Mrs David yet. Never anyone that special that has caught my eye yet. A few that I wanted but wasn't in their league, mind. But I haven't given up.'

He was staring right at her. She gulped and reminded him that he needed to watch the road. His eyes suddenly looked sad, and he turned his head to focus on the road. Again, she found herself feeling guilty, and she felt the strong desire to make him feel better.

She said, 'I'm sure there is a Mrs David out there, and she would be mad not to want you.'

He blushed a little and carried on driving. He didn't dare take his eyes off the road. The couple had been driving for about half an hour. David had driven her through a couple of neighbouring villages. Martha sat back and enjoyed the ride. She felt free. Free from being a Mum. Free from Mae. Free from Peter. Free from life. She couldn't remember the last time her mind was this clear. She felt happy. So happy. All because she was doing nothing but being in a lovely car, being driven around and taking in the views on a beautiful, light evening. She had the window down, and the warm breeze was blowing through her hair. She wished this moment, this feeling, could last longer than she knew it would.

They passed through the next village, and David had begun talking again. He told her he knew this spot where it might be nice to pull up and watch the sun go down. She felt like the suggestion was a bit more romantic than what she wanted, but he had been so lovely to her, and she had surprisingly enjoyed herself so far; so, she thought he at least deserved to pull over and watch the sunset with her if that's what he wanted. They cruised through the village, and Martha noticed a lady. An elderly woman with a frail frame. She felt like she recognised her but couldn't think where from or how. She didn't have any friends apart from Mae, so she must've just looked familiar. Whoever she was, she looked troubled and in need of a hug, but she couldn't say, '*Stop the car. I don't know if I know that woman or not, but I feel like I do and she looks down. I have to see her and give her some comfort.*' Martha felt frustrated. She hated seeing people looking down; she had always wanted to help others. That's just the way she was. Strangers or not.

They drove past and exited the village with Martha feeling in a quandary. David drove a little further and pulled over in a secluded spot. He turned off the ignition and the two sat silently. He realised that maybe taking her here wasn't a good idea. It screamed romance, and he didn't even know if she liked him like that.

'I've always loved this spot,' he said and broke the silence. 'When I come here and I look at the views... I worry about nothing. You ever feel like that?'

He looked at Martha. He didn't know that she had already been feeling like that on their little trip out that evening.

'Yes.' She looked down at her lap. 'Yes, sometimes I do.'

Martha looked out of her window and gazed. It was very quiet. You could hear a pin drop. David thought she was wonderful. It had been so long since he had had female company like this, one on one. He couldn't detect how she felt but he knew he didn't want to miss his chance. He had let the love of his life slip through his fingers once before. He couldn't let that happen again. He wasn't sure if he was in love again but it damn well felt close. He was mesmerised by her looks. Every little detail of her. The way she dressed. The way she smelled. Her eyes. Her hair. She was just beautiful, and he knew that she didn't know quite how beautiful he thought she was. He also knew that if he told her how beautiful he thought she was, she would just hush him. She was a modest, classy woman and that was another thing he loved about her. He stared at her staring out of the car window. He looked at her jawline, her small dainty ears. He didn't think he had ever studied someone's ears properly before but hers...the way they folded...the neat little creases. She was just beautiful.

He raised his hand and reached out to stroke her face. His heart was pounding. It was all or nothing. He wanted a good woman, and he decided not to be the wimp he had been in the past. She needed to know he liked her. Martha didn't even flinch. She knew it was coming at some point. She continued to stare out of the window. Her mind was in turmoil. She wasn't really interested in David. He was a good-looking man — she could do a lot worse — but the spark just wasn't there. If everything had been ok at home, she would have had the confidence to tell him it wasn't going to happen, but what with everything that had been happening with Mae and Peter, she just felt all out of sorts. She felt like she didn't know who she was anymore. She hadn't been the kind of woman to lead men on, lie to her friends and play games. Everything she valued and believed in had been tarnished.

She lifted her hand to meet David's and pulled it away from her face; she held it on her lap. She needed to be straight with him. She couldn't change Peter, but she could control what happened next. David was lovely and sweet and thoughtful, but she needed to not play with him. If Peter and Mae wanted to play a game, then that was up to them. Martha could make sure she wasn't contributing to the mess, and so she would tell David she didn't ever want to be with anyone apart from her deceased husband. That wasn't entirely true. She loved Johnny, and she missed him and she was beginning to feel like she could love again, but not with David. She would have to tell him now. It would be better to disappoint him now rather than break his heart later. She sighed deeply and turned to look at him.

He was staring right at her. He looked helpless like he needed rescuing. She went to speak, but he leaned in and kissed her, and she hesitantly reciprocated. She knew it was wrong. She should stop. This couldn't end well. But she kissed him back. She began kissing him more and more. His lips were so soft. *My god, can he kiss,* she thought. He held the back of her head with one hand whilst the other held her face. He ran his fingers through her hair. This was a man who knew exactly what he wanted. This wasn't a 'back of the school bike shed' kind of kiss. This was a 'I want you in my life' kind of kiss.

The pair became short of breath. Martha felt her nipples harden. She didn't even think about who she was kissing, she just knew she liked it, and her body was crying out for passion. She hadn't had sex for almost four years now. She missed the feeling of being overpowered. That sensation of succumbing to the man. The pleasure she got out of feeling that appreciated. David's hands started to explore her body, and she didn't stop him. His hand was smoothing her thigh, inching closer and closer. The kissing got heavier. She ran her hand along his thigh and found his very hard erection. *God, I want you to take me.* she thought. *Just take me to bed and enjoy every bit of my body,* she fantasised. The kissing slowed. David took his hand away from her legs and ran it back up her body until he got to her face. He cupped her face and pulled away. Then he gave her two gentle pecks.

'You are one fine woman, Martha. I just can't believe you like me back. I am one lucky guy.'

Martha was still panting gently, completely caught up in the moment.

'Well, I had better get you back. I said I wouldn't keep you out late,' and he turned back to face the road and started the car up.

The pair drove off with David telling Martha how much good care he was going to take of her and Willy and that everything was going to be great for them all. Now, she knew why he hadn't been successful with the women; he was quite full on. He wore his heart on his sleeve so low that it was grazed from being dragged along the ground. She didn't have the energy to disappoint him, and although she knew it was wrong, she just let David talk and lay out his plans for them both as they drove back.

They pulled up outside the house, and David gazed at Martha. He looked like a lovesick puppy which made her regret the fabulous kiss.

'I can't thank you enough, Martha. I've had such a lovely evening. Shall we say same time again tomorrow?'

Her heart sank. She felt so tangled up inside.

'I can't tomorrow evening, I'm afraid...' David instantly looked broken, and Martha knew she was in too deep. 'But I can do the evening after that. How does that sound? We could do the same again?'

His smile lifted, and although she could tell that he was still disappointed, he was at least a little happier with her sub offer. He leaned in and began to kiss her again, and she kissed him back.

Peter was watching the pair from the upstairs window. They hadn't seen him. He had slightly twitched the curtain and had been popping into that room regularly for the last hour so that he could do so. He couldn't bear the thought of her being with David and was extremely tormented by the idea that she wanted to be with David and not him. He watched as David got out of the car and walked around to her side to let her out. He gave her his hand to help her stand and then he held her. It had begun to drizzle slightly, and so David shielded her with his coat until she got into the house. Peter heard the door go and watched as David got back into his car and drove off.

'That little bitch,' he said quietly to himself. He could hear the women downstairs talking and rolled his eyes at the thought of what was being said between them.

He made his way downstairs quietly and listened in to what they were saying.

'Ooh, Martha, you naughty devil. I didn't have you down to be putting out on the first date,' Mae cackled.

Peter felt his blood boil and clenched his

fists. He had to calm down. Mae knew he wasn't happy with her right now, but he couldn't push his growing affection for Martha too far. He composed himself and walked into the room.

'You didn't put out, did you?' he laughed nervously.

'No, I did not,' retorted Martha. 'We just... kissed. You know, nothing serious, just a...kiss...' and she began to blush brightly.

'Well, good for you, Martha. It's about time you had some happiness. David seems like a nice chap, so what harm can it do?'

He stared at Martha, and a huge knot of confusion was being conjured up within her, she didn't know if he meant it or not. *Maybe he has realised that he was in the wrong. Maybe seeing me with someone else makes him want to improve things with him and Mae. Maybe everything will work out in the end,* Martha thought, trying to unravel the ever-growing knot.

'Well, let's have a drink then,' squealed Mae. 'A celebratory toast.'

Martha thought she looked nervous. She began to think that her being with David meant more to Mae than it did to her. Maybe she would have to keep seeing this David, if only to keep the peace for a while. The three of them sat around the table drinking scotch and smoking. It was just like her first night there, and everything seemed relaxed again, for now. The wireless was on in the kitchen and the news reporter told a story of how they believed that the madman that had escaped a mental institute, Simon Paterson, had murdered again. A woman's remains were found close to the factory where she worked, and he was the main suspect.

'Jesus Christ, what is the god damn world coming to,' Peter said angrily. 'Haven't we been through enough as a nation without madmen running loose. If anything happened to either of you two, well, it doesn't bear thinking about, but the police would be better finding him before I did. His story wouldn't end in a cell if I caught up with him.'

Peter was visibly shaking. The news had rattled most folks in the town. It was a quiet town where nothing ever happened. The war was a big enough worry for everyone, but Martha thought she was safe living with Peter and Mae.

'You both need to be extra careful, do you hear me?' Peter said to the two women. 'You need to stay in numbers. Don't go out alone. You just don't know where this freak might strike next.'

They all sat quietly for a moment.

'Does anyone know who the latest woman

is?' asked Mae quietly. 'Maybe we know her or her family?' she said, not really looking at anyone.

'They haven't mentioned any names, but apparently, they have brought the animal's mother to town to help with the search for him. How she can help, I don't know. Why would you even show your face if that was your son? Surely you would be ashamed and want nothing to do with the disgusting creature. Mind you, we don't know anything about her. Maybe she made him that way,' Peter said.

'Oh, I don't know,' Martha chipped in. 'It's a tough situation. Surely an animal is an animal? I don't think I could abandon Willy whatever he did. I mean, I might not understand it but I just don't know if I could ever disown him. He's all I have.'

'I would feel the same, Martha. If Charlie ever did anything like that, I think I could never forgive him but I couldn't stop loving him,' Mae said, looking at Peter.

'If our son was ever capable of anything like that, then he would be no son of mine, Mae.' Peter had the last word.

Mae didn't answer him back on this occasion. He knocked back his scotch and poured them all another. Eventually, they decided to go up to bed. Martha cleared the table and took the glasses to the sink whilst Mae bid them all goodnight and went straight up. She began to rinse the dishes off when she felt Peter's hands on her hips. He nuzzled into her neck and started kissing her softly. Her heart began to pound, and she had goosebumps all over her body. She said nothing. He began kissing her neck harder and sucking and biting. Then he began kissing his way down her back until he was low enough to get his hands up her dress. He then began to rise again whilst running his hands up her legs, still kissing her the whole time. He was standing upright now and didn't try to turn her. He just kept kissing her, getting rougher and pulling her hair to move her head from side to side. Now his hands were running over her bottom, occasionally touching her around the front. She didn't want to stop him. She couldn't bear how awful this was, but the passion she was feeling right now was far more than what she had experienced with David only a few hours back. If he slipped inside her now, she didn't think she could say no. He lifted her pants with his fingers and worked his way in. She flinched and let out a gasp. He put a hand over her mouth and whispered, 'Sssshhh.'

He continued to pleasure her with his

fingers. He could feel her heavy breathing on his hand, and it was making him harder with every breath. He could tell she wanted him. She was getting wetter and wetter. She felt good. She was tight, and he knew how good it would feel to be inside her. He imagined he was inside her now, slapping against her perfectly pert bottom, his hands on her breasts, each thrust more euphoric than the last. Her heart was about to burst out of her chest. Her breathing was pushing hard against him as he continued to get her wetter. She was about to climax, and he was in total control.

'God, I want you,' he whispered in her ear; with that she came on his fingers, and he came in his trousers. He collapsed on her back, and the pair of them hunched over the sink. They were both panting heavily, and he nuzzled into her neck again. He kissed her a few more times, little, soft, sweet kisses, and then whispered into her ear, 'Good night,' and took himself upstairs.

What the hell! she screamed to herself in her head. She picked up a glass tumbler from the sink, walked over to the scotch, poured herself another one with very shaky hands, and sat at the table. She knocked it back in one and stared into the distance, heart still pounding.

CHAPTER EIGHT

'Mrs Paterson...Can I call you Evelyn?' said the police officer.

'Oh, yes, Evelyn is fine', she said agreeably.

'Mrs, sorry, Evelyn, I have asked you to speak with us in the hope that your knowledge of your son, Simon, might be able to help us locate him. I understand that this might be difficult for you. However, with your help, you might be able to prevent...well, to prevent another murder.'

The officer felt sorry for Evelyn. She looked like a nice elderly woman. She was well turned out but she looked frail and had that 'lost' look in her pale grey eyes. He wondered if those eyes once glistened and sparkled with life before now.

'I'm more than happy to help, Officer. We all

want the same outcome. We need Simon back at the hospital, and no one wants to see another murder, but let's just be clear, we don't know for sure he is guilty this time.'

She smoothed down her skirt with both hands in a defiant way in the dimly lit, greyish room. The likelihood was that it was Simon, but as his mother, she had to give him the benefit of the doubt. Innocent until proven guilty. No one else would give him that, so it was the least she could do. Or was it hope? She wasn't sure. Officer Pembrooke didn't mind her optimism. In fact, he understood it to a degree. He had done this job long enough to know when someone was saying something for their own benefit. The amount of times he had interviewed a family member of a horrendous criminal, the majority would all respond the same. It was like if they said what they wanted to hear, then maybe their own denial would become true and they wouldn't feel so guilty about being related to that person. They wouldn't hold themselves responsible for what the criminal had done. They wouldn't feel like everyone thought they must be a criminal too if they were related to one. The truth is Officer Pembrooke would know when he was sat in front of a good person or not. It saddened him when he could see one of the good ones in a blind state of panic or desperation for peace again.

He would also say some of the nicest people he interviewed were guilty of some of the worst things he had dealt with because, ultimately, a lot of criminals were actors in his mind. They would put on an act to lure their victims in to a false sense of security. They could be charming, enigmatic, light-up-the-room sort of people, and in his mind, that was what made them so dangerous. He could look into someone's eyes and know if they were guilty or not. He could see that Mrs Paterson was one of the good ones and, if anything, a victim herself. Her son Simon wasn't an actor. He was down and out crazy. There were no false pretences with him. He was wired up wrongly, or at least that was how Officer Pembrooke described him, and that was why he took pity on Evelyn. That son of hers was beyond help. There was nothing she could have ever done to prevent him from being the way he is, but he understood the heartache that must have caused for Evelyn.

'Before we begin, would you like a drink, Evelyn?' asked Officer Pembrooke.

'Yes, please. A glass of water would be nice, my dear.'

'Very well.'

Officer Pembrooke went to fetch a glass of water for the old lady, and as he exited the room, he released a big sigh and rubbed his forehead. The biggest satisfaction of his job was catching criminals but the hardest was dealing with the innocent and broken. He would normally wait to be offered a drink in someone else's house, but she was alone, elderly and frail, and he didn't mind. He poured them both a glass of water and returned to her living room. It was a quaint little room. She had matching crocheted doilies dotted around and the ornaments placed evenly around the room. Her tiled fireplace looked like it had never been used, it was so clean, but it must have been because she had a poker and a small metal dustpan and a little brush on the hearth. *She must spend a lot of time cleaning,* thought the officer. Another one of Pembrooke's theories was that the state of someone's home was a good interpretation of the state of their mind. If it was a mess, they were a mess. If it was immaculately clean, they were controlling and obsessive. If it appeared tidy but inside the cupboards were messy, they were putting on an act. He had always stood by that and hadn't often been wrong.

'So, Evelyn, where should we begin? What I want is to get to know Simon the best I can. I want to get inside his mind. I want to know his mood patterns. I want to know the things he likes, the things that make him mad. I know you don't see much of him, but the better picture we can get of him, the better hope we have of getting him back and...' he paused.

He had to be delicate with her.

'Getting him back and getting him the help he needs.'

'Well. I don't know really. He's my boy and... oh, I don't know what's useful and what's not.'

She looked helpless and took a sip of her water.

'Ok, well, let's just try and break it down, bit by bit. What sort of things made him happy? What made him mad? All of this is to try and help me and the other police officers figure out where he might be hiding, and who he might be looking for next.'

Officer Pembrooke was leaning forward in his chair so that he could be closer to her. So that he could analyse what she was saying. She might come out with something useful and not even know it's useful.

'He liked to be alone. That was always the thing that was different between him and his siblings. He was happiest alone whereas the other two were always together or with us in the kitchen or playing with friends as children. But not Simon. He always wanted to be alone. If he was happy, he would be outside, and if he was mad, he would be in his room alone. He wasn't the same every time, mind you. I couldn't say for matter of fact what he would be doing each day, but generally, if he was happy – outside, if he was unhappy – inside. But then, oh. I don't know. I don't know what he was up to when he was outside. Maybe he was mad and doing dreadful things.'

Officer Pembrooke was scribbling down notes.

'Take your time, Evelyn, try not to get upset. There's no rush. I've got all evening if you have. I'm just trying to figure out where he could be.'

Officer Pembrooke was one of the nicer policemen. He really knew how to be understanding and how to make people feel comfortable. Evelyn patted down her skirt and looked around the room.

'He was a jealous boy. The first time he got in serious trouble was for pouring acid down a boy's back at school. He must've been, crikey, I can't remember now. He must have been twelve, maybe thirteen? That was a terrible day. I was good friends with the boy's mother up until that day.'

'And why do you think he did what he did that day, Evelyn? Had anything happened that you know about to spur that on?'

Evelyn racked her brain for something worthy, but what was worthy of that sort of behaviour?

'I wish something had spurred it on, Officer, but actually, I think it was just pure jealousy. The boy he attacked, James, well, he was a well-rounded achiever really. His mother used to come around and we would talk about our children, and James was always doing so well in everything and everyone liked him. He was a good-looking, popular boy. I think Simon was jealous because people didn't talk about him in a good way. He was always the child everyone had to stay away from. People would cross the street and look the other way if they saw us coming. People said he had the devil in him.'

'Ok, can you think of any more instances where he lashed out but for a reason? I know he was a difficult boy, but is there anything you can remember when he did something but for a reason?'

Evelyn slowly looked around the room again, racking her brains for the right thing to say. She wanted to help the officer as much as she could, but she couldn't think of anything in particular.

'Well, I don't know if this is useful or not, but he always had an eye for the girls.'

Officer Pembrooke began to look a bit awkward. *We know that. He's murdered and assaulted, maybe raped three...* he thought but he didn't want to say it out loud. He didn't want to upset her when he knew she was trying.

'One year he went after the prettiest girl in the town. She was seeing one of the prettiest boys in the town, so she was off limits, but it didn't stop Simon. He followed her around. He would pick her flowers from down by the river and try and give them to her, but she would run away screaming. Her boyfriend spoke to him about it a few times and asked Simon to leave her alone. He wasn't nasty to Simon; he knew he wasn't a threat, and actually, he was a nice boy. I think he felt sorry for Simon. Well, anyway, Simon wouldn't leave her alone and one day he had handpicked some wildflowers from near the riverbank, and he waited for her where he would normally see her with her friends. The story goes that he saw her approaching, and so he pretended he had hurt himself whilst she was walking past. He pretended he had hurt his leg and couldn't get up. Well, the girl went over to help him...after an initial hesitation...but she went to help him, and she got him up from the ground. He gave her the flowers he had picked which were on the ground where he had been lying, and she threw them down. Then he grabbed her and dragged her down the grass verge and under the bridge. Apparently...'

'Go on, Evelyn...'

'Apparently, he assaulted her. You know...in a sexual way.' She looked down at her lap and was examining her hands and nails.

'You say 'apparently,' Evelyn. Why do you say apparently?' Pembrooke was still making notes.

'Well, I say apparently because nothing was ever proven. No one caught him red-handed. She screamed for help, and he scarpered off. He admitted to everything apart from the assault.'

Pembrooke put down his notepad.

'And what do you think, Evelyn? Do you think he was guilty of that crime?'

He picked up his pad and had his pen poised ready to go.

'Well, yes, Officer. I'm afraid I do.' She looked down at her lap again.

Pembrooke made a note: Mother thinks he's GUILTY.

'You know, Evelyn, one of the things that fascinates me with this job is the psychology behind crime. Yes, I want to catch the criminals, but there is so much more to crime than the crime, if you know what I mean. I think in years to come, medical science will have vastly improved, and I hope it does because that means that people like Simon may get the help they need earlier on and can be prevented from committing such awful acts. You know, I've been reading up on something recently. The Americans think there is an emotional and social disorder affecting children called 'Autism.' It refers to children who don't interact like other children and they are isolated. The things you have told me about your Simon, about him being insular as a boy, well, maybe in time, in the future like, maybe there will be help for people like him.'

'He doesn't have that. We know what he has. He is schizophrenic,' Evelyn snapped.

'I'm sorry,' said Officer Pembrooke, and he genuinely was. She knew that.

'It's ok, Officer. Sorry for snapping. I'm just tired and all of this talking upsets me. There is no help for my boy. Do you really think someone could do what he has done and be fixed with treatment? No, that boy is beyond help. There's something not right with him, but he's my boy and he always will be. You can't go around saying that all children who are different will end up as murderers. That's not right.' Evelyn looked at the clock.

'I wasn't suggesting that, Evelyn, and I'm sorry if I upset you. I didn't mean it. I just like my studies and got a bit carried away. I haven't dealt with many Simons in my time, but yes, he is still your son and you deserve a bit of dignity. Do you want to carry on or shall we try again another time?'

A crash of a plate breaking on the floor came from the kitchen. Evelyn jumped out of her seat. Officer Pembrooke darted out of the front room and in to the kitchen. There was no one in there, but the back door was open. He looked outside of the door and out into the garden. It was pitch black. He turned on his torch and skimmed his eyes around, but there was nothing, not even a sound. Officer Pembrooke closed the door and returned to the living room. Evelyn was still sitting there which surprised him. He half-expected her to be cowering or watching over his shoulder.

'Well, I can't see anyone out there,' he said, puzzled. Evelyn didn't even look at him.

'Must've been the wind; perhaps I didn't close it properly,' she said.

'Maybe,' said Pembrooke, looking around.

'Will you be ok here on your own, Evelyn? Have you got anyone that could stay with you?'

'I'll be fine,' she said. 'I've been on my own long enough now.'

Officer Pembrooke was thinking. Something didn't seem right. An older lady on her own would normally be nervous about strange goings on in a house. *Perhaps she is too broken to even care,* he thought.

'Well, perhaps we should leave things there for tonight, but I would still like to talk to you some more if that's ok with you, Evelyn?'

She got up from her chair.

'Oh, yes, anytime. Well, I had better get on and clear up that broken dish.'

She proceeded to go through to the kitchen and get out the dustpan and brush. Officer Pembrooke found himself looking around for clues.

Old ladies don't leave doors open. There isn't a wind tonight. Wind wouldn't have knocked that dish off the side anyway.

This wasn't sitting right with him. Evelyn came back into the room.

'Well, I suppose you had better get on, Officer. You must have a family waiting for you to get home,' she said, smiling up at him.

'That I do, Evelyn, but crime never sleeps, unfortunately.'

He picked up the glasses they had been drinking from and took them through to the kitchen and placed them in the sink. He rinsed his hands quickly and picked up the tea towel to dry them off. As he put the tea towel back, he noticed a glass on the side half-filled with water. He looked back in the sink to where the two glasses were and then back at the worktop. He then looked at the dishes on the side. One knife, one fork and one glass. There would've been one plate had it not been smashed on the floor. He went back out to see Evelyn, who was hovering around in the living room.

'Thirsty work all this talking, eh?' he said to her in a gentle quiz-like manner.

'Well, I guess it can be. I drank all mine. Did you drink yours?'

His mind started ticking over. 'I didn't finish mine, no. Never have been good at keeping hydrated.' 'You could have finished mine instead of pouring another one. Save on the dishes,' he said, waiting with bated breath for what she would say next.

'I'm afraid I don't know what you mean, Officer.'

'Well, I just noticed another glass on the side

in the kitchen and it's half-full or empty depending on which way you look at it.'

Evelyn looked confused.

'Is there?' she said, walking off to have a look. They both stopped and stared at the glass.

'Well, so there is,' she laughed nervously. 'I must have made another one. I probably did it before you came.'

She turned to look at Pembrooke. His face had hardened a little.

'Evelyn, did you make that drink yourself, or is there a chance someone else could have been here?'

The colour drained from Evelyn's face. She began to stutter and looked frightened.

'Mrs Paterson. I think you had better come with me, to the station.'

Evelyn began to get upset. 'Why? I don't understand.' She was shaking and became teary.

'It's for your own safety more than anything else.'

Evelyn looked troubled and began to pace up and down the hallway. Officer Pembrooke felt helpless. Normally speaking, she could be holding a prisoner; therefore, she should be taken into custody. But she was, as far as he could see, an elderly lady who really didn't have a bad bone in her body. He wished he could make it better for her, but his primary role was to protect the public and, in this case, find Simon and get him back into a secure unit. Evelyn looked up to Officer Pembrooke with pleading eyes.

'I know what you think. You think I'm housing Simon. I'm not,' she tried to assure him, begging for his belief in her. 'I promise you I have not opened up my home to him.'

Her posture changed now, and she went from pleading to being assertive.

'If he was here... if he was in my home tonight... then surely we are better off with me being here. He might come back once you've gone. And, if he does, then we have a better chance of... of... getting him back in that place where he belongs.'

She looked at the ground in a state of defeat. She wished she could help her son. She wished she could wrap him up and tell him it was all going to be ok. Nothing would ever change that he was her son, and she wanted to believe in him and wish it was all one horrible, awful dream. Officer Pembrooke placed his hands gently on Evelyn's upper arms.

'Evelyn, that is what I am concerned about. You know Simon is dangerous. What if he comes here and puts you in danger? I don't want that. I want to protect you and get Simon off the streets again.'

She didn't respond to his affectionate touch, and he felt awkward, so he removed his hands but didn't know what to do with himself next. She had him in a puzzle which was not something that happened to him very often. Normally he would have a clear hunch, and it would just be a case of proving it, but this time he really wasn't sure if she was being honest or if she was covering for her son. All he knew was that he had to take the right action to get the best possible results. He needed to be on the same side as her. He needed her to cooperate with him. If she was hiding him, it would be easier if to catch Simon if he was on good terms with Evelyn. If he pushed her too far, it might push back the enquiry.

'Evelyn, I wouldn't normally do this, but I can see where you are coming from. I would normally take you in because I am worried about your safety, but to be honest, all I can offer at this time of night would be a cell, and that doesn't sit well with me. A decent woman like yourself can't be in a cell this evening. No, that's it, I've decided. You can stay here, but if anything, and I mean *anything,* happens that concerns you, you call this number right away. This number will be picked up by the station master, and if you call it, I will be around here in a flash.'

Evelyn's demeanour improved drastically.

'Oh, thank you, Officer Pembrooke, that makes me much happier,' and this time she reached out to him and touched his arm. 'I think I will be fine. I don't believe that anything will happen here, tonight, but I appreciate everything you have tried to do.'

Officer Pembrooke went on to thank her for her time that evening, reassured her that he was there if ever she needed him or thought of anything that might be useful in the investigation, and then bid her goodnight. He left the property feeling frustrated. He was more confused by the time he left than he had been when he arrived. It didn't sit well with him, the way the evening had panned out. He decided to do a quick walk around the property and up and down the street, just to see if he could find anything at all that seemed suspicious, and to give him time to collect his thoughts.

CHAPTER NINE

A few days had passed since Peter had made his move on Martha in the kitchen that night. The morning after, he had acted like nothing had happened again. He wasn't dismissive of Martha – he was quite pleasant – but he didn't make any more moves. He didn't stare for a second too long; he didn't strike up any unnecessary conversation. In fact, he hardly gave her any attention at all. Initially, that pleased Martha; the elephant in the room that had been expected was nowhere to be seen. Martha was more confused than ever.

Luckily, Mae still seemed to have not noticed a thing. She was obsessed on keeping Martha and David together. Her interest in their relationship was a welcome distraction from the guilt that Martha was feeling. Martha had barely stepped a foot out of line in her whole life. She prided herself on being a good person with her morals intact, but over the last few weeks, she had become embroiled in one of the biggest sins possible for a person to commit.

Occasionally she would wonder what would happen if Mae found out what had been going on right under her nose. Obviously, Mae would be upset, and Martha didn't like the idea of getting on the wrong side of her but she couldn't help but wonder what Peter would do. Martha would have nowhere to go if Mae threw her out, but then, would Peter let that happen? Maybe he would seize the moment and say that it was Martha he wanted. But then, where would Mae go? And Charlie? No good could ever come of what had happened. A family would be ruined and someone would be out on the streets. Martha was glad that Peter had left her alone the last few days. She was seeing David tonight, and she was, surprisingly, really looking forward to it. He lived with his mum and dad and younger brother, and from what she could gather, he was the man of the house. His parents were getting older, and although they were still mobile, they relied on him a lot for his help and to keep the property running. From what she had heard of his younger brother Michael, David was very proud of him and loved him dearly, but it sounded like David was more of a guardian to him than a big brother.

Tonight, Martha was going to meet all of them. David had invited her over. He was going to pick her up at 6pm which meant Mae would be putting Willy to bed, but she was more than happy to do so because she was so keen for their relationship to develop. Mae had planned an afternoon of pampering to prepare Martha for her date. She was going to give Martha a makeover.

'He won't be able to resist you,' she beamed.

Martha wasn't there yet. She was very taken with David, and she knew she could do a lot worse but she wasn't ready to give herself to him, she wasn't bothered about the marriage side of things. She had already been married once; it didn't seem the same to her now, to wait and do it all again. She couldn't imagine marrying again but she did crave intimacy and passion. She wasn't in a rush with David, but she could imagine them being together soon. Tonight was about meeting his family, and she was pretty sure she wouldn't feel sexy by the time Mae had finished with her. She had a feeling she may end up being a little tartier than she was comfortable with, but Mae had this way of just making Martha go along with her plans.

The night before, Mae had washed Martha's hair with water mixed with baking powder followed by rubbing raw eggs into her scalp.

'This will give you that salon shine,' she squealed in pure delight.

She was in her element. Martha was sure Mae would have loved a daughter. Martha didn't mind being Mae's guinea pig; she enjoyed being pampered. She had no one to take care of her, and it was nice to have Mae's attention. Mae was much better at the glamour side of things than she was. Martha was very beautiful anyway, so she didn't need much work; neither did Mae for that matter, but Mae knew all the latest tips and tricks. The women that Mae was friends with would share secrets with each other on how to be glamorous during the tough times of rations, and to give credit where it was due, they always did look *very* glamorous. After Mae had washed Martha's hair, she spent a good hour wrapping it up in rags to create those perfect curls. The two women sat on the bed in Martha's room.

'We'll make a 'Rosie Riveter' out of you in no time,' she said, carefully selecting locks of hair and tying them up in neat little sections.

'Women. Taking the power back. Men might think they rule the world, but when you step outside tomorrow and David takes one look at you, the power will be all yours, my girl.'

Martha never felt like she needed to be in control. In fact, she preferred to be guided. It was easier that way, but Mae was the opposite. She enjoyed power and she enjoyed having her own way.

'You know, this is like the time you took me to that rugby match,' Martha said to Mae. 'Do you remember? You told me about it perhaps a week before and you said you were going to find me a man? We spent the whole week trying to make ourselves pretty and then I met Johnny.'

The room seemed very quiet.

'I remember, Martha. Those were wonderful times. Oh. What fun we had. But...you can have that fun again. Why do you think I'm doing all of this? I just want to see you happy again, and I know you can be.'

Mae had almost finished wrapping up her hair which she had done with great precision and finesse. Martha's eyes were fixed on the wall and had glazed over. Her face was blank and looked as if she was daydreaming.

'I know you miss him, Martha. We all do. It's a terrible shame. But look at it like this, you have the chance to have all that excitement again. Not like me. I'm stuck with Peter.'

They both let out a slight laugh at Mae's joke, although it made Martha's heart flutter with fear. She felt compelled to say all the right things to cover her guilt.

'Peter's not bad really. Look at the life you have together. This beautiful house, you have more than most. A beautiful child together. I can see Peter can be moody at times, but you both love each other and that's more than some have.'

Martha smiled at Mae and didn't know whether if she blinked she would look guilty or whether she was ok to blink. *How does my face look when I am a good person? Can she tell I am hiding something?* she thought to herself. She couldn't remember how to act when these conversations cropped up. Mae had finished her hair and looked at her.

'I don't know if Peter does love me anymore. He has changed recently. His moods seem different. Normally he is either at work or with us, but lately, he hasn't been spending as much time with us. He doesn't touch me much anymore, and when he does, he seems rougher or less interested.'

Martha could feel her temperature rising.

'Really? You both seem happy together,' she

said but wished they could talk about something else.

Her guilt was rising to extremely high levels now.

'I think we are happy but I think this is it now. He has finally lost interest. He's bored. We've been together for almost 20 years, and he just doesn't fancy me anymore, I think. Take last night, I tried to have sex with him, and he wasn't interested. He said he wasn't in the mood. So, as much as I couldn't be bothered really, I tried to get him in the mood. I went down on him, and he instantly got hard and I thought I was doing the trick. I had only been at it for a couple of minutes I think, and you know...he...well, he finished. I didn't do it for that. I did it so that he would have sex with me. He finished and just rolled over and didn't even say thanks. Oh, I don't know.'

She began to become teary, and now Martha really wanted the ground to swallow her up there and then. The guilt resided within her as if a stone had been tied with a piece of string and was hanging off her heart. She put her arms around Mae and soothed her.

'Sssshhh, there, there. I'm sure you are reading too much into it. Perhaps he was just tired. Don't upset yourself. I'm sure he will be back to normal soon, maybe he has things on his mind.'

Martha decided from this moment on nothing would ever happen between her and Peter again. She had been so selfish up until now, and now that she thought about it, she didn't think she had ever seen Mae cry before. Well, not real tears anyway. This reminded Martha of how human Mae was. When she had been with Peter, it was as if Mae didn't exist. She didn't enter her brain at all. She was consumed with excitement, passion and desire. It was as if she was in another world when he put his hands on her, a world that only they knew existed. Martha had never felt worse and didn't get much sleep that night. Her mind was racing with a magnitude of thoughts.

She was racked with guilt and didn't know how she could have ever got wrapped up in something so sordid. She was immersed in curiosity and wondered what was happening between the three of them. *Why was Peter rejecting Mae? Does he want me? Is he making advances at me because his relationship with Mae is breaking down? Am I nothing to him? Just a floozy who happens to be under his roof that he thinks he can have? Or does he like me? Oh, shut up, Martha.* She pulled her pillow over her head as if it would work to suffocate her thoughts. The only thing that would put a stop to her thoughts would be a bullet to the head. This situation couldn't continue. She was worn out with pretending all the time.

She was exhausted by her treachery. Life simply couldn't continue this way. How she was ever going to get out of this tug of war of love, she didn't know. Her state of desperation was interrupted by a knocking next door. She listened carefully and realised Peter and Mae were having sex. Her turmoil was soothed by the sound of their lovemaking. With every knock and every gasp, she could hear it was like a little bit more of her anguish was being released, like a pressure cooker. The noises were becoming louder, and it sounded like Peter was determinedly making up for his behaviour the night before. Martha felt like she had had a close escape, again. She listened to the two of them until she fell asleep.

A new day and a fresh chance to start again and today the house seemed like Spring had sprung. Everyone rose around the same time. The boys were in a good mood and playing together joyfully, running about like little bees. Peter and Mae were making breakfast for everyone like two lovesick puppies. He had his hands on her at any opportunity, and they giggled each time they touched as they navigated their way around the kitchen without separating their bodies. He looked dashing in his trousers and braces and his tight white vest. He was only half-dressed, and Martha kept finding herself looking at his arms and his body. She tried to busy herself with laying the table. Mae was positively blooming. She looked radiant, and Martha hadn't noticed that Mae had been down before, in truth. It was only this morning that she realised how happy she seemed that made her notice she hadn't been herself lately. Normally she was very good at picking up on things, but she had missed it recently. She had been an awful friend and didn't even know how awful until now. Although, the way they were carrying on this morning was as if she wasn't even there. They were so wrapped up in each other, and Martha didn't know where to put herself.

'You two seem in very good spirits today, it's nice to see,' she said awkwardly, not knowing if she should distract them or not.

'We are in good spirits, aren't we,' said Mae looking at Peter. 'Can I tell her? Please. I know we only just talked about it, but please, she's my friend.' Mae was looking at Peter like a love-struck teenager.

'Go on then, my dear, but no one else, not until, well, you know.'

He poured himself a hot drink. Martha wondered what the news could possibly be and waited in suspense.

'Well, come on then, what is it?' she said, looking at them both.

'Well, I think I...' she looked out of the window to make sure the boys couldn't hear, 'we are having a baby,' and she shrieked with sheer delight.

Martha didn't say anything. She looked at them both and realised she owed them a reaction.

'Well, that's great. I mean, are you sure? How long do you...' she didn't get to finish before Mae interrupted.

'Well, I think it's not long. I just feel different, and I'm sure that's what it is, but even if it's not, after what this one did to me last night I could be,' she said, sitting herself on Peter's knee and kissing him.

'Oh, ok, so you don't actually know if you are, but you are going to try anyway?'

Martha didn't feel that happy about it. She wasn't sure why but she felt angry. She felt jealous. She felt annoyed. Peter and Mae could both see that Martha didn't seem that happy.

Peter looked around the room, feeling equally unsettled, and Mae looked at him with sadness that her friend didn't seem happy for her.

'Martha, I thought you would be pleased for me, for us.'

Mae was disappointed in her friend.

Martha knew she had to stop being so selfish and give her friend what she wanted, but she wasn't happy for her because Peter had been a creep recently. A bastard. She was unsettled by the news. She wanted to scream out and tell her it was not ok. She wanted to tell her she was making a mistake. She wanted to tell her that she needed to work on her relationship first before patching it up with another baby, but, well, maybe it would get them back on track, unlikely, but maybe.

'Mae, of course I am happy for you. I'm just surprised, that's all. I didn't realise you were trying, but of course I am happy for you.'

She leaned over and gave Mae a kiss on the cheek, then she leaned in to Peter and kissed his cheek whilst taking in his scent. She was aroused by it. She sat down again, and the atmosphere was a little tense.

'Martha, I think I know what this is about. You're worried about what this means for you and Willy, aren't you? Well, it will be fine. A baby doesn't take up a lot of space at first, and you will undoubtedly be a great help to have around when Peter is not here. Plus, who knows what will happen in the next year or so. I'm pretty sure David is in love with you, and what happens when two people are in love? They get married, live together, and have babies.'

She snuggled into Peter, and he placed his hand on her stomach.

'Yes, they do, and it's wonderful when it happens,' added Peter.

Martha felt sick. A rage boiled up within her, and she wanted to smack Peter around the face. She was beginning to see him for what he really was. A cold, nasty, and utter bastard. A typical man of his power.

He thinks because he comes from a wealthy family and, as a result, he now has a good amount of money that he can have whatever he wants. Money might have got him everything he wanted in life, but you can't buy good morals and that's what he lacks, she rambled silently. Then, that internal dialogue she constantly had these days quickly reminded her that her morals weren't what they used to be either.

'Well, I had better let you ladies get on with day two of your pampering, in preparation for the date with David tonight. Things seem to be going well with him, Martha. It's nice to see you smile again.'

He squeezed her shoulder whilst mopping his mouth with his serviette. Mae cleared away the dishes and took them to the sink. He followed her and put his hands around her and nuzzled her neck. Martha found herself staring at his muscly back that was exposed through the shoulders of his white vest. She began to daydream and then remembered that not so long ago she stood at that sink, and he nuzzled into her, amongst other things. She became jealous and flustered and realised she had probably been staring too long and that she ought to busy herself before they caught her staring at them both. Peter put Mae down and went upstairs to finish getting dressed. Mae had a couple of bunches of tea leaves in muslin cloth in her hand and looked pleased with herself.

'Hopefully, there is enough here for both legs,' she said smiling brightly.

Martha looked at her with confusion.

'Legs?'

Mae rolled her eyes because of how clueless her friend was with this kind of stuff.

'Yes. Legs. We will use these to make your legs look tanned. I know we would normally paste gravy on, but I was talking to Elsie, you know, she lives a few doors down. Well, she said women are not using gravy anymore. Everyone is staining their legs with used tea bags now.'

She looked quite pleased with herself and tottered off out of the room. Martha felt totally and utterly deflated, confused, used, and angry. Her eyes began to prick with tears. She was angry with herself more than anyone else and began to regret moving in. A short while ago life was better. Was she lonely? Yes. Was money tight? What money, more like. But she was coping, and she had morals and dignity and friendships that were valuable instead of tarnished.

'Martha, is everything alright?'

Mae had come back into the room and was shocked to see Martha standing there gazing into space. *Great, this is all I need,* thought Martha. She struggled to hold back the tears. The lump began to rise in her throat, and she knew if she opened her mouth to talk she would burst into tears. Her breathing became heavy, and Mae stood right in front of her and put her hands on her shoulders.

'Martha, what is it?'

She pulled her in and embraced her. Her kindness and softness were too much for Martha to take and the tears came tumbling down. Mae did her best to soothe Martha whilst being taken aback as to what it was all about. After a few heavy sobs, Martha managed to control herself and took a step back out of Mae's arms and looked at her.

'Martha, what is this all about? Is it the baby thing?' she said, whilst fetching a handkerchief for her friend.

'Oh, I don't know,' lied Martha. 'I just feel a bit overwhelmed, and obviously, I am completely happy for you. I think it's wonderful news. I guess I did wonder what it meant for Willy and me, and it makes me wonder where we will be in the next few years and if I will be with someone. Oh, I don't know. I am just being silly.'

'Yes, you are being silly, and now you are going to have puffy eyes when I am trying to get you ready for David,' smiled Mae.

'Sorry,' Martha said with her big reindeer-like eyes, all glassy from the tears which accentuated her eyelashes.

Her eyes were so big that her teardrops sat on her bottom lashes like a raindrop on a rose petal.

'Don't be. You are going to have a nice life ahead of you. I can feel it. Hopefully, David will show you that. You two seem to be getting on. How do you feel about him now?'

Mae began to prepare another pot of tea and looked out of the window to check on the boys playing.

'Well, I wasn't sure at first, but actually, I'm beginning to think he might be perfect. I'm feeling like...' she paused and then said, 'I think he is exactly the sort of choice I should be making.'

Not only did she just tell that to Mae, she was telling it to herself also.

'Yes, I really think I ought to give him a chance,' she said and smiled at Mae.

'That's more like it. And a smile too. How wonderful. Well, by the time I've finished with you he won't know what's hit him. You might want to think about giving him the goods tonight as well, I wouldn't keep him waiting too long,' she said as if she knew best.

She didn't realise how offensive her assumption was that Martha was incapable of holding a man's interest without her trusted and experienced guidance. Martha scowled with disapproval but had known Mae long enough not to be shocked at this. Mae wouldn't talk to anyone else like this. She liked everyone to think of her as a lady, but when it was just the two of them, she could talk with a smutty mouth like a man.

'Seriously, Martha. Come on. You've been married, you have a son. You're not a virgin. He's not going to pop the question to get his leg over. I would give him what he wants, and you never know, you might end up getting what you want.'

Martha didn't even know what she wanted.

'Think about it,' said Mae, and she went out the back to round up the boys.

Martha began to wonder. Mae and Peter were obviously making more plans together for their future, so Peter had no intention of being with her at all. He just wanted to see if he could have her. She felt so stupid. And guilty. And angry. Maybe she should give David a chance. She hadn't even considered him before now because she was clouded by what was happening with Peter. She had been a fool and almost lost her best friend and ruined a marriage. In fact, David was her chance at a new beginning. If she let him in, then she might fall in love with him and then they could be together rather than being stuck under the roof of Peter's false love. The only person he was in love with was himself. Martha *had* to make it work with David. She couldn't continue to live in this tormented world. Maybe tonight they would make love, seal the deal, give him a night to remember, and the thought of that, surprisingly, aroused her.

CHAPTER TEN

'Well, what do you think?' Mae paraded Martha in front of Peter like a handbag she had handmade at school.

'Doesn't she look...hmmm...I was going to say divine, but that isn't the look we are going for... she looks...irresistible.'

Martha blushed and felt far more exposed than she was comfortable with. Her make-up was heavy, her legs stained with tea bags, and a line drawn down the back to create the look of stockings. Her breasts were pushed together and lifted and had gone numb with the tightness of her underwear. Mae really had gone to town and excelled herself this time. Peter stared at Martha. He looked her up and down. He then returned to look at his paper and picked up his cup of tea. The room was silent. His slurp seemed loud. Martha felt as though she was breathing too loudly, and she could see Mae's chest rising up and down in the corner of her eye. Peter put his cup back down and, supposedly, continued to read his paper.

'I don't like it.'

Mae huffed like a child.

'What do you mean, you don't like it? I put a lot of effort into that.'

Once again Martha felt like an object and wished she wasn't being spoken about in such a way.

'Mae, stop behaving like a brat. The woman is going to meet his family, God damn it. Holy shit, she looks like a woman of the night. What will his family think? You wanted to help her make it work with him, and the only thing you are doing is guaranteeing he gets his leg over.'

He shook his paper as if to re-read it and pick up where he left off, although they all knew he wasn't reading it a minute ago. Peter was irate. He very rarely swore, especially not in front of women, but he was agitated and both the women knew it.

'She looks like a victory girl. You've seen those posters that are brandished everywhere.

Warning the soldiers that these women are not clean. That they are riddled with disease.'

Peter lit a cigarette. Martha was mortified. Mae was insulted.

'That is quite enough, Peter. I think it is quite clear you don't like it. I was just trying to make the woman feel good, and make sure David would make her feel good too. There is no need to take it that far.'

Peter gave a look of sheer disgust at Mae. Martha wondered if he had ever hit her, he looked so mad. Martha decided to speak up. She had bit her tongue for long enough. She was fed up of being everyone's new toy. She just hoped she could do it eloquently and not as a quivering wreck.

'As much as I appreciate you both looking out for me, I am capable of looking after myself...'

Peter snorted a laugh, and Martha went crimson with rage. She had had just about enough of these two.

'No more,' she said with a raised voice and looking at both of them. 'I have had it. Can't you see how you are treating me? I am a grown woman. A widow. A mother. Mae, I don't mind you dressing me but see it as that and only that. I don't mind but, sometimes I am happy with the way I am, and, Peter, I don't need you to protect me. I appreciate it, I really do, but you two arguing over me is ridiculous. Now, I am going to go upstairs, get changed, and kiss my son. David should be here any minute.'

She looked at them. They were both looking in opposite directions like spoilt children. Peter was staring at the ash tip growing on the end of his cigarette. He was probably wondering how long he could let it grow, how long he could control it before it would eventually fall off and into the ashtray and become a little pile of ash. He would have to inhale a few more drags before he could daydream and ponder that thought again. Mae was probably seething. She did not like being put in her place. The only one that got away with that was Peter. Martha had spent most of her life avoiding confrontations with Mae. She imagined that Mae was probably annoyed that her 'work' hadn't been appreciated. Her taste wasn't up to scratch. She wore it well, but ultimately, it wasn't Martha's cup of tea, and if anything, Martha was glad the row had happened because she got to get changed and wear what she wanted. Something plain. Something simple. Nothing too flashy. Nothing that exposed too much chest.

Martha turned on her heels and went upstairs. She looked through the crack in the door and watched the boys play. They were so good, and tonight they seemed more angelic than normal. When all was strange in her life, she had her boy. As always, he calmed her. He made her feel normal when everything else was a quagmire of emotional mess and moral wrongdoings. She then went into the bathroom and looked at her face. Mae had done a good job with this bit actually. She looked very glamorous. Martha could cope with the extra make-up. In fact, it was nice to look this good, but the make-up combined with the dress and breasts was a tad too much. She gazed at her face in the mirror. She liked what she saw.

'You're not too bad, Martha Henderson. Tonight, you have scrubbed up ok,' she said to herself.

Then she went into her room and looked at her dresses in the wardrobe. She wished she could embrace what Mae had put her in and wear it with style and confidence, but the reality was that she would shuffle out the house in it and keep an eye on her boobs all night. It wouldn't look sexy at all.

'No, the face I can live with, but the boys are going back in the barracks tonight. Sorry,' she said, holding her boobs and looking at herself in the mirror.

She realised she had made a joke. She realised her personality came out. It seemed a while since she had been that way. She realised she felt good. Great in fact. She came out of her room in something much daintier. She still looked fashionable and classy but just not as racy. She went in to the boys to kiss them goodnight. She sat on the floor next to Willy and hoisted him up on her lap. He was almost too heavy for this now, she thought. He obviously didn't think so because he tucked himself into her and curled up.

'You look nice, Mummy.'

She cuddled her boy and squeezed him tight.

'Thank you, William. What do you think, Charlie, will I do?'

Charlie blushed and picked up his toy and pretended to play with that.

'Well, you boys be good. I am popping out this evening so, Willy, be good for Aunty Mae.'

She stood him up and got to her feet. She stroked his hair across his head, and he leaned in to her thigh and wrapped his little arms around the top of her knees. She wondered what he thought about at times. Did he worry about her going out and not being across the hall from him? Did he worry about having a 'new dad'? Does he even think about who his dad was? How would

173

he cope if she did settle down with someone else? She lowered down to his height and gave him one more squeeze and a kiss on the head.

'Goodnight, darling, Mummy loves you.'

She went downstairs and was glad to hear Peter and Mae were talking normally again. She couldn't make out what they were saying, but they were talking, and, boy, was she glad. She made her entrance in the room and they both stopped. They were back to silence again.

'Oh, come on you two. I heard you talking as I was coming down the stairs. Mae, I like what you did, but I am more comfortable in this. This is more me, but I love the make-up. I never have the patience for all that stuff, but I really love it, so thank you.'

She decided not to acknowledge Peter's outburst because she was afraid of where it would lead, and right now, the most important person was Mae where feelings were concerned.

'I think you look better,' Peter said, having taken a quick glance and then looking away again. 'I think you're right. My Mae looks beautiful in her dresses. The bee's knees. But you look better as you are, a plain Jane.'

Martha felt hurt by that last statement but decided not to react. They had gotten enough of her in the last hour or so, but she did wonder

what he meant. *A plain Jane? I'm boring?
Nothing special? He said I looked like a tart
earlier and now a plain Jane? Why is he being so
cruel? Perhaps he is jealous over David and me?*
Her thoughts were stopped by the knock at the
door.

'Well, that's me,' she said awkwardly at them
both.

Mae got up from her seat and patted down
Martha's hair whilst looking her up and down.

'You'll knock him dead, whatever you wear.'

Martha looked down and blushed.

'Thank you.'

She turned her back to them both and made
her way to the front door.

'And, Martha,' Mae called.

'Yes?' she said, turning to look at Mae.

'If you don't want to come back tonight, you
don't have to. I can sort the boys out.'

Martha nodded and smiled and turned to
open the door.

David and Martha pulled up outside his
house. He switched off the engine and the lights
went out. It was almost dark outside. David
leaned in to Martha and pulled her face into his.
His soft lips kissed her gently. His hand cupped
her head. She felt so relaxed. She wanted to kiss
him harder. He pulled away.

'You look beautiful, Martha. More make up on than you need, mind, but you look beautiful.'

He was about to open his car door, but she grabbed his shoulder. He turned back in his seat to face her again, and she kissed him. He had always made the move before, but this time she kissed him. She planted a small, soft kiss on his lips. Then she put her hand on his thigh and leaned in closer to him. She kissed him again. He felt as though he had surrendered to her and kissed her back at her beck and call. She kissed him harder, but this time she didn't pull away. She opened her mouth, and he did his. He teasingly offered her his tongue, and she accepted. They began kissing passionately. Her heart was racing, and she was becoming increasingly aroused. Her nipples were on end and his erection was huge. They knew they had to go inside, and so they stopped, both still holding each other with their lips locked, holding it there for a moment. Just one more little moment. They then pulled away simultaneously whilst staring into each other's eyes.

'What did I do to deserve you, Martha? You really are a fine woman.'

She smiled from ear to ear and genuinely felt happy. She had opened her heart to him, and it wasn't as scary as she thought. Now that she had tried David, she wanted more. She wanted all of him. She wished he could take her right now, but that would have to wait. *God, I'm turning into Mae.* she thought. David got out of the car and walked around to her side to open her door. She couldn't believe how much of a gentleman he was. He didn't have much materialistically, but his manners were impeccable.

'Mum and Dad are going to love you. Just watch out for Michael; he will probably love you like I do.'

David had meant to be funny but had quickly realised the enormity of his words. He looked for the ground to swallow him up. Martha took his hand and entwined their fingers.

'I'm sure I will love all of them, just like I love you.'

He smiled at her in a goofy way, and she realised suddenly that she could do a lot worse. This man wore his heart on his sleeve, and she was the one he wanted to give it to. They walked hand-in-hand, and she felt the most at ease now than she had in the last couple of days.

It was hard to see what the house was like as it was starting to get dark, but it seemed pleasant. It was just outside of their local village, only a few miles from Peter and Mae's house. It looked like an old farm. It seemed as though it could benefit from a bit of tidying up but it looked ok. The pair went inside, and Martha was surprised to see the house was very nice. It could have done with a proper clean, but apart from that, it looked homely. She got the impression his family must have been quite comfortable before their health had started to deteriorate. It was decorated nicely with lots of family photographs and lots of light throughout. Martha could smell something sweet. Something like apple pie or a crumble or something. David had told her they were old and needed looking after, but she didn't know how old or how much looking after they needed. He spent most of his time working down at the garage, after all.

David's mother came out of the front room to greet them in the hall. She was delighted to see them. Her smile lit up her whole face, and she moved slowly towards Martha to welcome her. The two women exchanged pecks on the cheeks, and David's mother held Martha's hands and took a good look at her. Martha could tell instantly that she was a lovely woman. She had kind eyes. Eyes that could tell a thousand stories. Grey hair neatly pinned back in a small bun. A few loose strands fell down and framed her face. Martha could see that she would have been an attractive woman in her youth.

'Well, David, she's a beauty. This is the one. I can tell. You keep hold of this one, boy.'

She hadn't taken her eyes off Martha, and she was still holding her hands.

'Don't worry, Mum, I don't intend to. I know this one is special.'

Martha spent the next couple of hours getting to know the family. David's father was in a far worse condition than his mother. He didn't talk. He just nodded from time to time. Martha didn't want to ask what was wrong with him; she didn't want to seem rude. At one point in the evening, whilst at the dinner table, she made eye contact with him, and he stared at her. He didn't smile but she got the feeling he couldn't. She got the feeling he gave her his blessing. David's younger brother, Michael, was a darling. He was slightly taller and slightly leaner than David, and he was cheekier than David, but you could see he idolised his older brother. Martha was very happy with the family. They were all lovely. They all made her feel quite at home. They were salt of the earth kind of people.

She compared them to Peter and Mae. Peter and Mae were comfortable because Peter was born into money. Mae wasn't born into anything. The two of them acted rather high and mighty compared to this family. Martha would put money on it that David's family made their own money and that's why they were so normal. They didn't gloat or act like they were better than anyone. In fact, they invited her in; fed her wonderful, tasty food; and all asked her lots of questions about her life. They were interested in her. She didn't feel like she had much to tell, but they were hanging off her every word. David and Martha insisted that everyone could go and sit down and that they would clear up. Michael sat in the back room with his parents, and Martha and David danced around each other in the kitchen. Love was well and truly in the air. They put away the last of the dishes and David blew out the last candle at the dinner table.

'Come on, I'll give you a tour,' he said, and he took her hand.

She had only seen the hallway and the kitchen since she arrived. Martha hadn't realised the place was as big as it was. Every room was nice and well kept apart from a bit of dust. Some of the rooms hardly looked lived in. There was the kitchen where they had been tonight, a front living room which David said didn't get used too much, a back dining room which was used more in the height of summer, and another living room at the back. There was even a downstairs toilet. The back living room was where his parents spent most of their time. His father had a bed made up in there and they had a small sofa, two armchairs, and some furniture dotted around. His dad wasn't mobile enough to get up the stairs anymore. Once back in the large hallway, David looked at Martha.

'Shall I show you upstairs? Nothing funny-like, just give you the grand tour, you know.'

He laughed nervously.

'Yes, of course. Why not. I can't believe how big this place is. It's huge. It can't be easy trying to keep it clean and tidy,' Martha said, genuinely surprised.

'It's not easy, but Mum still manages a bit and I do some when I'm not working. Michael tries but he's just not that way inclined. He makes things untidier than they were so we let him off the housework.'

'I heard that,' Michael shouted through.

They smirked at each other and went upstairs. Martha was shown four bedrooms, a bathroom, and a couple of laundry cupboards. She realised his mother must have been very house proud. The place still looked great, but you could see it was a bit tired in places. For a moment, they stood in the hallway not knowing what to do next. Martha asked to use the bathroom and told David to wait for her in his bedroom. She had another look at herself in the mirror. She dabbed her eyes for any smudged make-up and blotted her lips. She ran her finger under the cold tap and used the water to wet her lip and use the lip stain as blusher. She didn't know what was about to happen. She felt nervous yet excited. Then she thought about Johnny and it took her by surprise. She hadn't thought of Johnny for a few days. She felt a pang of guilt. She stared at her eyes in the mirror desperately looking for answers but she wasn't going to get any. She was a big girl now and she was in charge. She looked up at the ceiling.

'Johnny. If you are there...I love you. I miss you terribly and think of you all the time. No one will ever replace you.'

She closed her eyes and pictured his face. This time she remembered it clearly. She hadn't seen it like that for a long time. He smiled at her and that told her everything she needed to know. She blew a kiss up to the ceiling and took a deep breath.

She went back into David's room, and he was pacing around it slowly. They smiled at each other and then she sat on the edge of his bed. He bit his nail and looked at her. She patted the bed and gestured to him to sit down.

'I can't sit down, Martha. I would love to, but

I have to be honest with you, I just can't sit there.'

She looked at him as he continued to nibble on his nails.

'Why can't you, David?'

She asked, although she was pretty certain she knew why.

'Don't ask me that, Martha. You will think I'm just like all the other men and I'm not. My mother brought me up better than that.'

He began to pace again.

'David, I really like you.'

She reached her hand out to him, but it was just a little too far away to touch him.

'I like you, Martha. That's why I can't sit there. If I sit on that bed, I won't be able to keep my hands to myself. Don't think I'm always like this because I'm not. It's just you. You are beautiful. You're intelligent. You're funny. You're a great mother. My mother loves you; my whole family loves you.'

He turned to look at her.

'I love you.'

Martha gulped.

'If I lay on that bed with you, I will want to make love to you, and the fact that I can't, well, I couldn't bear it, and so I have to wait. You are a lady, and so you will be treated like one.'

Martha couldn't quite believe her ears. She never thought she would find a man who was so respectful. He wanted to treat her right and not take what he thought was his.

'I understand, David.'

Martha stood up.

'I am actually blown away by how wonderful you are, and I...'

Her heart began to pound as she felt herself let go.

'I am falling for you, too. I didn't, however, realise how irresistible I was.'

She let out a slight giggle.

'But it is important that we do this right. I assume your parents know I am a widow and have a son, but still, tonight is the first night we have met, and I don't want them getting the wrong idea about me.'

David gave her a soft kiss on the lips and then held her head.

'Firstly, my mother knows everything about you, and she knew about you the day you arrived in the village because that's when I first set eyes on you. She knows about Willy, and she can't wait to meet him. She was sad to hear about your husband and has told me I must take extra care of you, and as for what happens between us, that is our business and no one else's.'

Martha felt light-headed with pure elation. All her worries disappeared. Her barriers dropped, and she wanted to give him everything she had and for him to take all of it. She let out a sigh and leaned in to kiss him. She almost wanted to collapse into his arms. It had been years since someone had made her feel this way and made her feel good and made her feel safe. The two began kissing passionately again like they had in his car earlier. The passion between the two of them seemed to pick up where they left off. It was a deep passion. Peter's recent affections had been intense and selfish, but David's were deep and meaningful, and he was sensual just as her late husband, Johnny, had been with her.

He kissed her and lowered her onto his bed. The kissing became even more animated, passionate and desperate, and they began to explore each other with their hands. He ran a hand up her long slender leg. She had a hand on his chest, feeling his strong physique. He kissed her all over her neck and then her chest and as low as her dress would allow. He rose to his feet and removed his top to expose his naked torso. He looked much stronger and more rugged than she had expected. He removed her shoes and lifted her skirt. He kissed up her legs. Every single goosebump on her delicate skin rose. Her soft hairs stood on end. He kissed her thigh and caused her to tremble. He sat her up and tenderly removed her dress. He took a minute to stare at her body and take in her beauty. Whilst keeping his eyes fixated on her, he removed the rest of his clothes down to his underwear. He climbed on top of her and they kissed for the first time, skin on skin.

Martha felt like she was in heaven. One of her favourite things was just two bodies touching, naked skin on naked skin. The two of them became immersed in each other, and David couldn't hide his hard erection. It was big and prodding against her. She couldn't wait to feel it inside of her. She had been living a life of celibacy for so long. That sensation of him sliding in and taking her breath away, she could only imagine the euphoria she would experience. Those sensations had been lying dormant within her for years. She was tingling with passion in her knickers, and if she knew him better, she would just take over right now and take him. Get on top of him and sit on him and take every inch he had to offer. He was kissing her all over her stomach. Even though she had carried a child, her stomach was smooth and taut. She was slight and slender. He pulled her bra down to expose her breasts and sucked and nibbled on her erect nipples. Her body was writhing in pure ecstasy. He got up and quickly removed his pants.

'Sorry,' he said, 'I can't wait any longer.'

She sat up and removed her bra.

'Don't be. I want you.'

With that, he pulled down her knickers and straddled her. He gently pushed her down on the bed, kissing her continuously, stroking her hair down to her chest and then her breasts and then finally dragging his index finger down her torso to her navel. He wet his finger, never taking his eyes off her, and stroked it down and around her and then inside to make sure she was ready. She bit her lip. He pushed her legs wide and brought himself up to her.

'Are you sure?'

She nodded back at him. He slid his large, hard erection inside of her, and she gasped. She wrapped her legs tight around him and pulled him in close. She was in heaven.

CHAPTER ELEVEN

David pulled up outside Mae and Peter's house. It was dark and the street was barely lit. There was soft drizzle floating gently down; you could just make it out in the soft lighting of the street lamps.

'I really wish you would've stayed,' he said, looking at Martha like a lovesick puppy.

He stroked her face; she held his stare and bit her lip.

'This evening has been wonderful, and you, well, you were wonderful,' she said blushing slightly. 'I have to get back to Willy. I haven't left him on his own overnight before. So much has changed for him recently, I don't want him to think I am abandoning him. He's probably asleep anyway, but he needs a goodnight kiss from his mum. He needs to know I am home.'

She let out a gentle sigh.

'Why don't you bring him over next time. My mother would love to meet the little guy, and Michael is great with kids too.'

Martha looked at him but didn't say anything. Her mind was racing with several thoughts all at once.

'He will have to come over one day. If you keep liking me and keep wanting to see me, then I guess the next step will be you and Willy coming to live with me.'

Martha was shocked. She hadn't thought that far ahead, but what shocked her even more was that the idea didn't scare her. David made her feel whole again. He made her feel comfortable in herself. Being at his house tonight, she felt at home. She hadn't realised at the time, but she had moved around that kitchen with more ease than she ever had at Mae's. It all just felt so natural. She broke into a sheepish smile.

'Yes, I suppose that would be the next step. One step at a time, but yes, one day. Your family would need to get to know me better first.'

She reached down to pick up her bag.

'They will get to know you because you'll be

coming around more and you will bring Willy with you too. I'll never be his dad, and I would never try to replace him, but I promise you I will look after you both. You'd never want for anything. I could teach him things. He could come to the garage with me. You and mum could make the house all pretty, however you wanted it, and do the things you girls like to do. She would like another lady in the house, and I know she likes you.'

David was grinning from ear to ear, and she believed everything he said. He was one of life's gentle souls. She knew he meant the things he had just said.

'I wish you didn't have to go back in there. I wish you were staying with me and I wish I was holding you until you fell asleep in my arms.'

They both embraced each other tightly and then kissed each other goodnight. David got out of the car and walked around to let Martha out. She stood up, and he kissed her again.

'And another thing, Martha Henderson, you were incredible tonight,' he whispered into her ear.

He walked her to the door, and Mae opened it, making it clear she had been waiting on the other side.

'David, darling. How are you?' Mae was

looking at them both and then eyed Martha up and down.

'I'm very well, thank you, Mae. In fact, I'm grand. I'll let Martha fill you in on the details. Goodnight, ladies.'

He kissed Martha on the cheek one more time whilst holding her hand. He started to walk back, still holding her hand for as long as they could reach until their touch finally separated, but never taking their eyes off each other. The two women stepped inside and closed the door with David waving them off. He stood on the pavement for a moment taking it all in. He couldn't believe how lucky he was. She was the most beautiful and perfect woman he had ever known. He was on cloud nine. He looked up to the sky. It was a clear night and there were lots of stars out.

'A beautiful night for a beautiful woman. Thank you, God,' he said quietly to himself.

Then he noticed Peter in the window upstairs. David gave a coy wave, embarrassed that he had been caught in cloud cuckoo land. Peter looked at him and closed the curtain without giving a wave back. David thought it was a bit strange, but no one could dampen his mood right now. He opened the car door and joyfully got in, still shaking his head in disbelief at how his life was shaping up. He started up the engine and drove off with Peter watching him through the net curtains the whole time.

'So, come on. Tell me. You did, didn't you. I can tell. Look at you, you're glowing. How was it?'

Mae finally sat down after almost jigging about in the kitchen. The women took their normal seats at the table and Mae got some brandy out. Martha swirled it around in her glass watching it, almost in a daze, but smiling the whole time. She dipped her finger in and tasted it. She then ran her finger around the edge of the glass, still smiling and thinking back over the last couple of hours. She looked up at Mae.

'Well, it, or should I say he, was...'

'He was what? What have I missed?' A disgruntled Peter had entered the room.

Martha's heart sank slightly. She didn't want to talk about this with him. She had felt wonderful a moment ago, but she knew he would make it awkward. She was beginning to see him for the complete arsehole that he was. She had had a wonderful evening with David, and she was not about to let him spoil it. If he hadn't been there, she would have told Mae the details, and so she decided not to let him spoil it for them both.

'He was incredible,' she said, holding Peter's stare.

'So, you did it then?' Mae squealed, but waiting for more, she was hanging on, begging for Martha to give her more detail.

'Yes, we did it,' said Martha, oozing with confidence.

Peter didn't have a hold on her anymore, and she had now found someone who genuinely cared for her and she did him. She had the whole room in her hand with her audience feeding very different emotions into the mix. She knocked back the brandy and poured another one. She was completely calm. Mae quickly gulped hers back to keep up. Peter looked at her with sheer disgust.

'I see. Drink like a man, fuck like a man.'

'Peter. What in heaven's sake has gotten into you?' Mae scowled.

He didn't retaliate. He just sat there swirling his drink around slowly as Martha had done just moments before.

'I don't care, Mae. No one can take away from me how I feel right now. I feel just wonderful. They were all lovely. I met his mother, father, and brother, and they were all so kind and just so lovely. We had a fantastic meal that David had cooked himself and then they left us to it.'

Mae was staring at her like a child being read a scary story, desperate to find out what happened next.

'And?' she begged.

'And we went to his room, and well, you know, we made love. Oh, Mae, he was incredible. I can't ever remember feeling like that. But it isn't just what we did, it's all of it. The way he makes me feel. I want more. I feel so relaxed and comfortable with him. I never thought I would feel this way again, but he somehow makes me feel complete. I feel like I've always known him.'

Her face was beaming with a huge smile, and she had chosen her words deliberately to aggravate Peter, but why? Why did she care what Peter thought? she questioned herself.

'Well, Martha, it would seem that you are in love. My work here is done.'

Mae had decided the success was down to her, Martha realised.

'And what about you, Peter,' Martha said, picking up his cigarette packet and helping herself. 'I disgust you, do I? I'm done with playing by the rules. I know what I wanted and I took it, so what?'

She lit the cigarette and a plume of smoke travelled up her face. He couldn't take his eyes off her. This new-found confidence of hers made him want her even more. The way her lips sealed around the tip of the cigarette made him imagine them around his penis.

'Well?' Martha broke his train of immoral thought.

'Well, what? It's your life, Martha, you do what you want. Just don't come crying to me when the village starts referring to you as the local bike.'

CHAPTER TWELVE

Martha came downstairs the next morning to find Mae sobbing at the table, and Peter pacing the kitchen like a caged and hungry tiger.

'What's going on? What has happened?' she asked completely confused and concerned.

'Oh, Martha.'

Mae put her head in her hands and let out a wail. Peter went over to her and rubbed her back and then began pacing again and smoking his cigarette with purpose.

'Well?' begged Martha. 'What the hell has happened?'

Mae sobbed and sobbed.

'It's that bastard madman that's on the loose,'

Peter said whilst still pacing, looking as though he was ready to pounce at any moment.

Martha looked at them both.

'He has struck again. A woman from this village. A friend of Mae's.'

Martha gulped.

'How bad is it?' she said, already knowing the answer.

'The sick son-of-a-bitch raped and murdered her. She was found late last night in an alleyway. Just a few streets away from here. Apparently, the scene was pretty horrific.'

Mae began to wail again.

Martha let out a sigh and rubbed her forehead. She was speechless. What was there to say in a situation like this? She pulled up a chair next to Mae and sat next to her and comforted her. Mae began to compose herself.

'She was young. She was due to get married. It's just awful,' Mae sobbed.

'How did you find out?' Martha enquired, feeling as though she ought to say something but not knowing what.

'One of the neighbours came to the door a couple of hours ago to let us know. I think the idea was to make us all vigilant. I'm calling a community meeting with the police this evening. Something needs to be done before someone else gets hurt. I'd like to find him myself...I'd really make him suffer.'

Peter clenched his fists.

'I don't want you girls going out anywhere on your own, you hear me? This sick bastard is on the prowl in our neighbourhood and you need to be careful.'

The two women nodded in unison.

The morning passed and the house was moody. The event hung over them like a dark cloud. Peter was the only one who sparked up a conversation from time to time, but that was mainly to break the silence. They didn't feel as though they could enjoy themselves; they didn't feel as though they could eat. They couldn't do anything knowing the pain and suffering that young girl's family was going through just a few streets away. It was at times like this having young children in the house was a blessing.

All the adults acted as if nothing had happened in front of the boys. They didn't want them to be worried, and ultimately, they were not at risk. Having them there gave them all something to focus on. Martha wanted to see David but didn't feel as though she could say that. She felt guilty and selfish for thinking of him on a day like this, but if anything, she just wanted to be in his arms and feel safe. After

Peter's reaction last night, she knew if she dared mention his name today, he would most likely rip chunks off her. No, she wouldn't say a thing. She would just think about him quietly in her private mind. The silence was broken with a loud knock at the front door. The three adults looked at each other, and the visitor knocked again.

'Alright, alright,' said Peter, getting up to answer it.

Martha and Mae looked at each other wondering what on earth it could be now, begging for it not to be more bad news. Peter opened the door to find an unsettled David on the other side.

'Is she here? Is she ok? Can I see her?'

Peter didn't say anything; he just opened the door wider and let his love rival in. David went bounding into the kitchen, and the relief was clear on his face when he saw Martha. At that moment, she saw how much he really did care for her. She stood up to greet him and the two embraced tightly. David inhaled Martha's scent and held her close to him.

'Oh, God, I'm glad you are ok. I was so worried about you.'

Peter's face turned crimson.

'What were you worried about, you fool. You

knew Martha was fine. It was the Smith's girl a couple of streets back, you imbecile.'

Mae began to cry again. David looked confused. Martha felt incredibly awkward.

'I know who it was, Peter, but I was just worried about my girl. It's a horrible thing, and I didn't like to think of her being upset on her own. That's all.'

Martha's heart melted. She couldn't believe how sweet he was, but she knew that would rile Peter even more.

'Your girl? For heaven's sakes,' scoffed Peter. 'She's not on her own; she's here with us. Her friends. Christ, we are basically her family.'

David looked disgruntled but was far too polite to say how he really felt to Peter. He hated the way Peter spoke to him. He looked down on him, and he knew it. David would give anyone the time of day but not Peter. No, you had to be a certain breed to get Peter's respect. If you had less wealth than him, he didn't want to know you; and if you had more wealth than him, he wanted to be your best friend.

'Well, I am glad she has you all to care for her, and I can only hope there is a little room left for me to care for her as well,' said David, placing his arm around her shoulder.

Martha took his hand and looked up at him

and smiled. The more time she spent with him the more she was learning that he just didn't have a bad bone in his body.

'Shall I make us all some tea?' she said looking around the room.

Mae nodded, seemingly unable to speak yet. Martha stood up, patted down her skirt and began to move about the kitchen. The men stayed silent. As Martha pottered around, she kept trying to take a glance at the room and see who was doing what. Peter was stood with his back against the side, casually puffing on a cigarette. He was so confident. Sometimes she thought he was a total arse, but still, at times, she was drawn to him. Mae was staring into space, her face drained and pale from all the upset this morning. David was fidgeting about; he had both hands in his pockets. She caught his stare, and he gave her a sheepish smile which she returned. The only thing breaking the silence was the whistle of the kettle on the stove and the faint giggling of the boys playing in the back garden. Martha poured everyone a cup of tea and sat down. She wished that making tea took longer as it gave her something to do for a moment, and now they were all sitting around awkwardly again.

'We're holding a community meeting

tonight, David. Well, the men of the community are, with the police, to try and get this psycho caught and locked up. Did you want to come, seeing as you fancy yourself as a local hero here to our beloved Martha?' Peter said smirking. He was so full of himself at times, and most of the time, it was only he that found himself funny. Martha tutted and scowled at Peter.

'Actually, I was hoping that Martha might come and stay with me tonight.'

David looked at her with desperate eyes hoping she would accept.

'I...well...um...' Martha stuttered. She felt like she was a girl again and had to seek permission to do her own thing. Mae finally spoke up.

'I think you should. Willy will be fine here. Today can't get any worse. Go and be with David. It will help take your mind off things.'

The room fell silent for a moment.

'Actually, I thought Willy could come with us. I can make him up a bed, and he has to meet my family at some point.'

David waited again, hoping she would agree. Martha's heart was racing. She could feel Peter's stare burning into her.

'Oh, I don't know; it does sound lovely. I

wouldn't want to put your family out,' she said, unable to take control of the situation.

Her mind was racing, knowing she had to decide, but whatever her decision was, someone was going to be upset. Go with David and know that Peter wouldn't be happy, or stay at home and crush David's kind-hearted spirit. She looked around the room trying to find the answer in someone's face, anyone's face. Mae looked as if she had lost the will to live. Peter pretended not to look like he cared but it was clear that he did. David looked like a hungry little puppy desperate for his next meal. Martha let out a sigh, and with an awkward smile said, 'Ok, why not. I guess I can't do anything here. Mae, you will be ok, won't you? Peter will take care of you.'

She looked to Mae for confirmation that she was doing the right thing. Mae took her hand.

'Darling, go. It will do you good. I will be fine. I will probably be in bed by seven. I feel drained and exhausted.'

Peter put out his cigarette and looked like he was hatching a plan. 'Actually, tonight is not a good night for you to stay out. As I have already explained, the men of the village are having a meeting with the police. If you stay out, that means Mae will be on her own, and I can't have that. You will have to pick up your romantic love affair another time,' he said victoriously.

David looked as though the wind had been knocked out of his sails.

'I didn't think of that, actually,' said Mae in a voice that was oddly quiet for her.

Martha hadn't seen her so downbeat before and realised she really ought to be there with her friend, despite wanting to be as far away from the house as possible. She wished David would whisk her off her feet and take her away now and out of Peter's claws. She was beginning to realise that Peter was not going to make it easy for her and David. She realised she liked David. She knew he was safe. She knew he was sweet. She could already tell he was going to adore her for as long as she would let him.

But then there was Peter. Sometimes she felt like she could hate him, but at other times she felt drawn in by his arrogance. He was handsome. He was confident. He was manly but a different type of man to David. He wasn't an engine-oil-and-workshop-grease-kind of man. He was arrogant, educated, and a captivating man. She couldn't figure her feelings for him out. She thought he was an awful person at times, but shamefully, she fantasised about him taking her.

She knew instinctively that he would be

good. She knew with the two of them it would be passionate. She knew it would be hard and just the right amount of rough. She also knew that once he had her, the light he burned for her would probably go out. She was just a target for him. She was the match that lit the candle. The match that brought the candle to light, and once he had his way she would be thrown in the bin. Disposed of, not to be used again.

At times, she thought she could handle being the match just to see how bright the flame would burn with him. In the right conditions, the flame could burn for a very long time, heating up the wax and slowly melting the once powerful and erect candle. She didn't think of David in the same way. David was more of a light bulb. Reliable. There whenever she needed him. Ask for it, flick the switch, and there he would be. Not like Peter. Unreliable. Not able to provide much apart from a desire to have something different. The candle and the bulb. Two very different men. She knew what the right choice was. The sensible choice, but if only sensible had a bit more passion.

'Ok, so why don't I stay here tonight with you, Mae, and then Willy and I will come over to yours for the weekend, David? It's Thursday now. Why don't you pick us up on Saturday morning, and we can have the weekend together, and your family can get to know the two of us?'

David smiled. He was disappointed he would have to wait to have some time with Martha again, but he was happy that she had agreed to come and stay. He was fidgeting on the spot because he was happy but didn't want to show it too much, not in front of Peter, at least.

'Good, then we are agreed,' said Martha with a surge of relief. 'Shall I do us some lunch? I know you won't feel like much, Mae, but you should have something. I could do us some soup. I think we have some tins in the larder. There should be enough for all of us.'

Martha was realising that she was only comfortable around Peter if she was busy these days.

'I'm just going to freshen up and then I'll be back down. Just give me five minutes.'

She smiled at the three very different faces: Peter looking agitated, Mae looking distraught, and David looking like a teenage schoolboy on his way to the prom. She made her way up to the bathroom. She went in, shut the door, and sat on the edge of the bath and let out a large sigh. It had been a stressful morning. The murder of the local girl had spooked them all, but selfishly, she was consumed with confusion and guilt over her triangle with David and Peter. It occurred to her that most of the time she was trying to fathom out her feelings, she rarely spared a thought for Mae. She didn't know when she had become so selfish. She had never been this way before. *Is this what hardship does to a person? Is this what death, poverty, and war does to a person?* she thought.

She had always been decent, but the older she was getting, the less she seemed to care about certain things. *The heart wants what it wants,* she surprised herself with that thought. It was like someone else was taking over her internal dialogue. She began to reason with herself.

The heart does want what it wants. No, Martha. The heart can't have what it wants. The heart must choose wisely. Don't let the heart be foolish. She got up and splashed her face with some cold water in the sink and looked up to see herself in the mirror. Little beads of water clung to her face, and she watched as they slowly lost grip and began to roll down her cheeks, off the end of her nose and dropping off her chin. She picked up the hand towel and began to pat her face dry in the mirror. She realised she didn't know who was looking back at her.

'Who are you these days, Martha Henderson?'

It had been a while since she had an image of Johnny pop into her head with a reassuring message. *Even Johnny doesn't like me anymore,* she thought as she put the towel back and left the room. As she opened the door, she was instantly greeted by Peter who grabbed her arm whilst gesturing 'shh.' He pulled her into her room.

'What on earth do you think you are playing at? Staying at David's for the weekend? Why are you doing this?'

He wasn't angry. He was staring at her with pleading eyes, eyes that said, *Show me you want me.* The room was deadly silent apart from the sound of their beating hearts. He watched her chest rise and fall. He wanted her to be his and they both knew it. They knew it couldn't be that way, but in this room, in this moment right now, neither of them wanted anyone else. It was like when they were alone, they forgot about the real world that existed. They forgot about their partners. They forgot about the children. They forgot about their morals. They forgot about their responsibilities. She held his stare for a moment and then leaned right in and kissed him hard on the mouth. She kissed him and kissed him. He opened her mouth with his tongue. His hands were in her hair. He was kissing her neck. She was touching him everywhere. He began to undo her blouse and pushed her back so she fell on the bed. He was on top of her, and she felt his hard erection press against her groin. She felt instantly ready. She pulled his top off and ran her hands over his incredibly toned torso. Her heart was racing frantically. She wanted him and didn't think she could say no.

They kissed passionately and let out quiet whimpers of passion. He undid his belt, and she bit her lip. He hoisted up her skirt and started kissing her inner thighs. He pulled her pants down to just above her knees and began teasing her between her legs with his tongue. She wanted to scream, she wanted to scratch her nails up his back, but knew she couldn't. She pulled at his hair and put a pillow over her mouth. He was incredible. His tongue was everywhere, soft and hard. Gentle and wet. He came back up and looked at her.

With their eyes fixated on each other, he pulled down his trousers to reveal his very large penis. His heart was racing now. He hadn't been with anyone different in years, and she was different to Mae alright. She was petite and delicate. He came in closer and lowered himself onto her body. She was panting. The tip of his penis teased her; he was about to go in, and she already felt like she could explode at any second.

'Peter. Peter. Quick.'

Mae shouted from the bottom of the stairs and the two froze in horror. Peter jumped up and pulled up his trousers. He looked at Martha and then left the room in a panic. He left her there, pants down to her knees, breasts out, hair a mess and with a heavy heart. She quickly redressed herself but was shaking like a leaf. She paced her room. Once again, the real Martha was back in the room and she knew a serious line had been crossed. This couldn't carry on. A silent tear rolled down her cheek, and she sat down on the bed and began to sob.

CHAPTER THIRTEEN

Peter ran down the stairs to find Charlie sitting at the kitchen table with a big gash in his head, blood trickling down his face and grazed knees. He didn't seem too upset by his run-in with the concrete garden path, but Mae was a mess. She always did overreact, and he had told her several times not to do so in front of their son. He didn't want him growing up to be a 'pansy,' as he put it. There wasn't much chance of that. Charlie was as tough as old boots. He was as tough as old boots or knew better than to show any emotion in front of his father; one or the other.

'Oh dear, another bop to the head, young man. How have you managed that? Who were you at battle with? The Romans? A German soldier? An alien?'

Peter wet a cloth, knelt next to his son, and began to mop his head.

'Here you go, hold that against your head. It doesn't hurt, does it? It would take more than a little scratch like that to bother you, wouldn't it, boy? We are made of tougher stuff, aren't we?'

He squeezed his little chin and gave a rough rub to his ash blonde hair and stood up and turned to face Mae who had lost all colour in her face. David was leaning against the kitchen counter, getting in the way and being no use at all as Peter could see it.

'Mae, you really must stop getting like this in front of the boy. He is going to hurt himself. He is going to get cuts and bruises. That's what happens to little boys. Get a grip, woman, for heaven's sakes.'

Martha came into the kitchen looking a little flustered.

'Everything ok? Oh dear, someone has been in the wars.'

She gave Charlie a sad face by looking at him and frowning with a down-turned bottom lip.

'Don't you start. He's already got his mother in a tizz,' Peter remarked.

Peter was from a stiff-upper-lip-type of

family. Show no emotion. Men, not boys. Mae hated how tough he was on him sometimes. He was her little baby boy, and she would always mollycoddle him, but these days it would be mainly when Peter wasn't looking.

Peter and Martha hadn't noticed, but Mae was watching them both. She was observing them. It had occurred to her suddenly that the two of them were behaving in an odd manner. Martha was restless and fidgety. Peter was more engaging, as if he was trying to distract the whole room from thinking. Mae just sat and watched them. The two of them were so focused on busying themselves, they hadn't even noticed she hadn't spoken for a while. Martha was pottering around the kitchen and talking to David. Peter was patching up his son's head, and Willy was pretending to be an aeroplane in the back garden. Not one person had noticed that Mae wasn't talking. At that point, Mae began to wonder how long Martha and Peter had been upstairs. It dawned on her that they had been up there for about twenty minutes. Then she started to think about all the times the two of them would 'disappear' for twenty minutes since Martha moved in a short while back. All the times she had gone to bed, and Peter would stay down for a bit longer. He never used to do that.

He couldn't wait to get into bed with her before Martha moved in. Then she remembered a night when she had woken up and Peter wasn't next to her but she fell back to sleep before she had found out where he had gone and how long he had been gone for. She analysed the two of them a bit more. Martha was edgy around him, almost as if she feared him brushing against her. Peter was cocky and confident. David was oblivious, but not Mae. No, something was very wrong here. She felt herself get very hot and quickly became very nauseous.

She leapt out of her chair and ran upstairs to the bathroom and threw up. She had been very sick, and after she had got it all out, she clung on to the toilet whilst trying to regain her composure. 'Was Peter taking advantage of Martha?' she pondered, terrified that her husband was a sexual predator.

She had seen how nervous Martha was around him. That would explain a lot of things. Mae knew Martha hadn't been that interested in David, but almost overnight she had leapt in to a relationship with him after making such a fuss about not wanting to rush into anything, about not introducing Willy to more change than she had to, about taking her time. She was using him to get Peter to back off. She sat up and leaned against the bath and began to cry quietly. She didn't care anymore if Peter didn't want her, but Martha was her best friend. She would not allow him to drive a wedge between the two of them. He already controlled how she was to mother her own son, but he was not about to get in the way of the one true friend that she had. The door creaked open slowly, and Martha popped her head in.

'Can I come in?' she said, and Mae accepted with a smile.

Martha sat down next to her friend. Close enough so that their bodies were touching. Martha wanted to touch Mae but didn't feel like she could put her arm around her. She wanted to comfort her friend, but knowing she might be the cause of her friends upset made her feel like she couldn't comfort her as she normally would. She positioned herself next to her and almost slid her back against the small piece of bath that remained between her and the floor. As she did, Mae began to sob heavier. Martha was torn. She had been bad, she knew that, but she wasn't going to be so bad that she would comfort her friend for the misery she was causing. She had to be quite strategic with her behaviour now. She didn't know what surprised her more; the tangled web she was caught up in or how good she was at handling it.

'I know what he's doing, Martha.'

Martha stared ahead not saying a word but feeling like her pounding heart was filling the awkward silence.

'He is a pig. I didn't see it straight away. I must've been so happy to see you here that I didn't see what was happening. What was unfolding right in front of my own eyes.'

Martha sat in silence, as she had been, continuing to stare in front of her. She could feel tiny beads of sweat appearing on her top lip. She was keen to mop them away but didn't dare move from the spot she was frozen to. A million thoughts were rushing through her brain as to what Mae knew, what Mae was about to say next and as to what would happen from here. Her whole world was about to be turned upside down. Any minute now Mae was about to go mad. The two people she trusted the most. Her husband. Her best friend. The two people she could rely on. Under her own roof. Under her own very nose. Martha tried to imagine what she might say. How was she going to react? Would she be homeless within the next five minutes?

'The trouble is, I suppose I deserve this. Karma has a funny way of catching up with you.'

Martha was alarmed by what she was hearing. Mae wasn't going to scream at her. Mae was about to confess to something. Something that could potentially reduce some of Martha's guilt.

'What do you mean? What karma?'

Mae began to fiddle with her fingernails, picking at her cuticles and examining her tips. Martha was desperate to know what she had done.

'Come on, Mae, it can't be that bad.'

Mae snorted.

'Bad? Bad doesn't even come close. I have always been insecure over Peter's wandering eye. I used to think he was a predator, that's what I would tell myself. I tell myself he can't be trusted. Sometimes I wonder if he knows and that's why he torments me so. Then other times I wonder if it is my guilt imagining the torment and that he isn't actually doing anything wrong, it's just my guilty mind playing tricks on me.'

Mae continued to look into her hands and down at the floor. Martha was eager to know more but too afraid to seem keen for answers.

'Look, Mae, whatever it is, you can confide in me. We are best friends, and whatever you tell me won't go any further. You know that. It might even help to tell me rather than bottling it all up. I bet it isn't even that bad.'

Mae turned to look at Martha.

'Charlie isn't Peter's son.'

The two women held each other's stare, but Mae couldn't hold it for long as her bottom lip began to quiver and a tear rolled down her cheek.

'What? How?'

Martha was gobsmacked. She was not expecting that at all.

'Peter was sent away with the troops as the war began. He was hardly here for the first couple of years. Probably the best part of three he was away for. He has only been around in the last year. He was able to visit occasionally, but I think it was four times in almost three years. Whilst he was away, some American troops were here for a while. It was one of them. It went on for months. After he had gone back to America, I realised I was pregnant. He wrote to me. I never told him.'

'But Charlie is the image of Peter.'

'Jim was the image of Peter. That was his name. James. Jim. Jimmy.'

Martha pulled Mae in closer to her and stroked her head. She felt numb. The two of them sat on the floor leaning against the bath.

Martha stared at the pipework under the sink. She followed the pipes that ran along the bottom of the walls and out of the rooms. She stared at them with intent, taking in every detail. She looked at how they had been painted and how there was chips in places revealing old paint underneath the top coat. She noticed that the room was dusty and could do with a good clean. She looked at the little flecks of mould and mildew on the walls. Finally, she began to think about what Mae had just said to her. She didn't want to think of her friend harbouring this secret for all that time.

She would keep Mae's secret. Knowing this new information didn't make her feel any better about what she had done. She felt sorry for Mae. She tried to imagine carrying that burden for that long. Then she realised she would carry a burden of her own. Her escapades with Peter. She didn't know if she wanted Peter. Something was going on, and she was curious as to how far it would go. She knew it was wrong but she was in it now, and she didn't feel like she could get out or even want to get out. She would have to find a way to try and stay away from him.

'You promise never to repeat this, don't you. Peter must never know. I think he would kill me. And Charlie. Charlie must never find out. They love each other so much. I don't know how or why it happened. I was just lonely and desperate for attention. When I was with him, I never spared Peter a thought. I'm going to hell, aren't I.'

Mae leaned into Martha a bit more and sobbed.

'No one is going to find out, Mae. I will keep your secret, and I understand why you did it.'

'That's why I think you should move out. You should move in with David.'

Martha jerked from her slouched position to an upright one. 'What. Why?'

'There is too much going on here. Peter is being a sleaze around you, I can see it. I can't handle it. I'm afraid if I challenge him then my secret might get blurted out and I can't have that. Anyway, David is crazy about you. He would be thrilled.'

'But I wouldn't be. I'm not moving in with him; I have only just met him. You are panicking. Just relax, as I said, no one is going to find out.'

CHAPTER FOURTEEN

There was a good turnout for the meeting with the local police that evening to discuss the capture of Simon Paterson. The capture of the escaped convict, the murderer, the rapist, Simon Paterson. The men were up in arms about the safety of their women. Their wives, their daughters, their sisters. Emotions were running high. The room was filled to capacity with testosterone. Peter had made David go along with him whilst the two women stayed at home with the boys. David wouldn't have gone if he hadn't been forced into it by Peter. He was not one for confrontation, and as much as some of the men were there out of genuine concern, there was an element of bravado from about a third of the room, in which Peter was included. They were all trying to talk the loudest. Firing questions at the police officers and not giving them the chance to answer. Dumbing down their abilities, belittling them in order to make themselves look better, like 'real men.'

David felt agitated. These men were not his kind of people. *What the hell do they know about policing?* he thought. He was sure they were doing what they could, and he was sure they could do with support and any useful information anyone might have rather than taking time out to be bullied, branded fools, and verbally assaulted by the locals. He stood at the back of the cold village hall taking it all in. The room smelt damp. There were masses of cobwebs in the creases and hinges of the double entrance doors. David took his cap off and listened to the anger. He could understand it; if any harm came to his Martha, he didn't know what he would do or what he would be capable of. He noticed the officer attempting to quieten the crowd and gain their attention but to no avail. The boisterous men were all talking over the officer, shouting and demanding answers. David began to feel hot and clammy. His heart began to beat faster than normal. He was irritated with these men who thought they could throw their weight around.

'They came to listen but aren't,' he muttered quietly under his breath whilst shaking his head at the morons.

'Let the man God damn speak!' he shouted out of nowhere.

The noise slowly hushed and each man took a look at the quiet, little mechanic in the corner. Some acted out of offence and were not happy to be put in their place, but before anyone could do anything, Peter, not to be outdone by David, possibly, had the last word.

'David is right. We must let the officer speak.'

He looked around the room, proud and overly confident like a peacock, and gestured to the officer to begin. The officer thanked Peter for his assistance, which was the story of David's life, he felt.

'Good evening, gentlemen. It was recommended to us by some of you that we hold this meeting to discuss the concerns around the escaped convict, Simon Paterson. I am Officer Pembrooke, and this is my colleague DC Harper. The situation is a grave and a very serious one. As you all know, last night another victim was found, and it is believed that Simon Paterson is the culprit. A young woman was found in an alleyway not far from here, naked from the waist down and with serious neck injuries. We don't know why she was out at that time of the evening, but we are talking to her family to try and put together a timeline of events. Although we are yet to catch Simon and question him, this most recent murder does resemble two others carried out in a thirty-mile radius over the last two months. Having spoken with police officials in those villages, we believe the same person is responsible for these heinous acts of pure wickedness. We are continuing to carry out enquiries and follow up on some leads we have received, but we need your help. We need you to be vigilant. Let us know if you see someone acting suspiciously, if you see someone acting out of character, if you see any new faces that seem to be behaving oddly. Any piece of information, big or small, may be just what we need. Keep an eye on your loved ones. Don't go out in the dark. Be careful. We will catch him. We are getting closer, but as I say, any information that you have that you think could be useful, please tell us and we will follow up.'

'He's been to my house,' said a tired, frail, and elderly voice from the back of the room.

Not everybody heard it but some of the men turned to see what the noise was.

'What did you say?' said Peter in a louder and more assertive voice than was necessary.

The elderly lady slowly walked forward with the help of a stick. David instantly pulled himself up from slouching against the door frame and went to help her. He put one arm around her shoulder and assisted her towards the two policemen. He noted how well presented she was. Her clothes were immaculate, and her dark grey hair had been pulled back neatly into a bun. He could see she was proud, but he could see she was tired. In fact, he wouldn't be surprised if she keeled over now, she looked utterly drained and exhausted. The crowd of men parted the group to allow her space to walk through. Officer Pembrooke recognised her instantly once he saw her face.

'Evelyn. What are you doing here? I don't know if you should be here.'

He looked around at the room, concerned. He moved towards Evelyn and linked arms with her and slowly walked off to the side of the room to get her away from the locals. As they slowly moved, she could be heard telling Officer Pembrooke, 'I said, he's been to my house.'

He realised she had given up, and it had aged her dramatically. She had given up the fight of protecting her son. She had caved, and the release of emotions was clear not only in her mental state but also her tired face. Her eyes looked sad. Officer Pembrooke instructed DC Harper to adjourn the meeting and clear the hall.

The men became very unsettled. Questions were flying around as DC Harper tried to calm them and get them to leave.

'What does she mean, he's been to her house?'

'Who is she?'

'What aren't you telling us?'

'You've been told everything you need to know, gents, now clear the building. As soon as we have more information, the public will be advised. Just go home to your families and keep them safe, and for God's sake, tell them you love them.'

DC Harper's son was missing in action, as were a lot of local boys and men. Tensions were running high.

Peter and David returned to join their women back at the house. In true form, Peter hit the bottle. He opened a new bottle of brandy that someone had given him recently. He was always being given gifts despite most people living off rations. He poured a decent shot for everyone.

'They won't all be like that,' he said, knocking his back. 'Just thought we could all benefit from a stiff one.'

As he said it, he squeezed Martha's shoulder. Mae had seen. She had been watching him like a hawk from the minute he stepped foot in through the front door. She wanted to know she wasn't going mad. She looked at Martha and gave her a reassuring smile. A smile that said, 'Don't worry. It's him, not you. I know you wouldn't betray me.' Martha reached out and held Mae's hand.

'Yes, I think something to lift our spirits is a good idea.'

Peter lit up a smoke and offered them around the table.

'Mind you, David doesn't need a livener. Mr Calm over here. Nothing seems to bother him. Didn't really get involved at the meeting, did you, old chap? Each to their own, I suppose, but I couldn't keep quiet, not when my girl could be in danger.'

David wasn't as stupid as Peter thought he was. He would not be provoked by the fool. His patience was wearing thin but he wouldn't be provoked. That would just be playing in to his hands, and David had more pride than that.

'I thought you did a grand job speaking on behalf of all of us, Peter.'

He gave Peter a boyish smile and raised his glass to him. He would play the game alright, just not the way Peter wanted him to. He wouldn't trip up that easily.

'Well, how did the meeting go?' asked Martha.

'Those bloody fools don't know what they are doing. Just wasting everyone's time, that's what they are doing. Trying to make it look like they are doing something when, in actual fact, they haven't got a single bloody idea. What was odd, however, was that the meeting was called to an abrupt end because this woman walked in and said the madman had been staying with her. It was most bizarre.'

You could see the cogs turning in Peter's head, trying to make sense of it all. David chuckled to himself, as he imagined Peter's slow brain looking for answers. David did think Peter was as stupid as he looked.

'What woman? What do you mean he's been staying with her?' said Mae on behalf of everyone.

'Well, tensions were running high. Everyone was shouting questions at the policemen, myself included. No one could really hear properly.

Then, just as the room had quietened down to listen to the officer in charge, an elderly lady appeared saying he had been at her house. They seemed to know who she was. I think the policeman called her Emily.'

'It was Evelyn.' David corrected Peter with a small sense of victory. If he wasn't good for much else in Peter's eyes, at least he could remember detail from twenty minutes ago.

'Oh, yes, that's it, Evelyn they called her. Then Officer Pembrooke ushered her away from the crowd and told DC Harper to get rid of us. It was rather odd. I haven't seen her in this village before. She must be a relative of the lunatic.'

The room all pondered the facts, but no one could come up with anything. Martha felt as if she knew the name Evelyn but she couldn't place it. If she did know someone called Evelyn, she can't have known her that well, if she had forgotten who she was. It was more than likely someone from near her last house and not someone she had met around here, she thought.

'Shall we play a card game?' David suggested. 'It's been a tough day. Let's take our minds off it.'

Everyone agreed that this would be a good idea, and so the four of them played cards. David happened to be very good at card games much to

Peter's dismay, but as they played, the atmosphere softened and they all enjoyed themselves. They even shared a few jokes. For the first time, the four of them sat around the dining table in the dim light, having an enjoyable time together. Sitting under a fog of cigarette smoke and getting a little bit giddy on alcohol, Peter started paying more attention to Mae, and David relaxed and even put his arm around Martha at one point. If someone was looking in from the outside window, they would see two couples enjoying themselves playing some card games and having a drink. Both women looked as glamorous as ever, the two men looked dashing and pleased to be with their women. If someone was looking in from the hallway door, they would see that Peter had his hand on Martha's leg under the table and was stroking her thigh. If you looked under the table, you would see that Martha was playing footsy with Peter's calf. On this evening, cards were not the only game being played.

CHAPTER FIFTEEN

A few weeks had passed, and Martha had not brought up the house move to anyone. At times, she had felt it was the elephant in the room between her and Mae. The truth was she didn't want to leave. As much as she knew what was happening between her and Peter was wrong, she still felt like she needed Mae. She knew that was selfish but she didn't know who she was anymore. She was lost, confused and dangerous. She used to be so sure of herself. She used to be so judgemental of Mae, but it seemed that Martha wasn't quite the woman she thought she was. Life had changed her. You could say the same for Mae. Perhaps Mae was the one with blurry morals previously; however, she was loyal to her husband and her friend.

Martha used to be. Perhaps she had never recovered from her husband's death. Perhaps being a single mother was harder than her conscious brain had realised. She thought she had been doing ok. She thought she was the same person just getting by, but her behaviour said something very different to how she saw herself.

Peter had backed off since the night of the meeting at the village hall with the police. Martha had wondered if he had experienced a wakeup call. Perhaps the realisation of his wife being in danger made him want to protect her. Too late for that, she thought. Perhaps it was because David spent the night with them, and he had discovered a new-found respect for him. Unlikely. If anything, he had given up the ghost. He had chased and, almost, had his way and now he had lost interest. That was the most logical explanation she could think of. After all, he hadn't demonstrated much compassion for others so far, so the most likely reason would surely be down to his own greed and desire. She didn't mind. In fact, it was easier if he had moved on. She would never go for him. She would never make the move. For her, it was just a chance to experience affection that she had missed, or at least, that is what she told herself.

He caught her when she was in a desperate, lonely state. He caught her when she was vulnerable. She didn't have the strength to say no. She realised now it wasn't Peter. It could have been anyone half-attractive. Anyone half-intelligent or interesting. She just missed being touched. She missed feeling wanted. She missed the pangs of love. She missed having someone. Someone to whom she could surrender her desires.

After Johnny had died, she had been alone for so long. She knew Mae would never understand if she found out. How could she? Why would she? She knew she had been an awful friend, but she wasn't ashamed. She was too weak to care. Someone offered her something that life had so cruelly taken from her, and she had given up the fight long ago to care about what was rightfully hers or not. She knew the right thing was to leave. Mae had been right about that but Mae didn't know *how* right she was. She just wished she didn't have to now.

Things had been a lot better the last couple of weeks. Peter had been normal. Mae had been more relaxed. In fact, she seemed happier than normal. The boys' friendship was growing stronger every day and they were becoming like brothers to each other now. The two of them were as thick as thieves, and Martha's heart would burst like a firework display when she watched them play together. Willy had been a quiet boy but being with Charlie had brought out a wonderful character in him that she didn't know he had. He was far more confident now than she ever thought he would be. Sometimes she would watch him and be amazed at how much stronger and resilient he was compared to her, and she wondered if she had been like that as a child as she struggled to figure out who she was now.

Mae announced her pregnancy to Martha over dinner, with Peter and David at the table. After her last announcement, her period arrived shortly after, and Martha had consoled her sad friend whilst secretly being pleased. However, she knew it was only a matter of time. Mae always got what she wanted.

David coming over for dinner had become a regular thing. Martha had become quite comfortable with that but was still in no rush to be with him completely. She sought comfort and solace in being together as a group. She could manage that quite easily. David was no danger to her, she knew that. She just didn't always want to be on her own with him. For some reason, she was holding part of herself back. She didn't know why because she was so desperate for peace in her sad mind and David offered her everything to get her there, to that place of peace and mental tranquillity, but for some reason, she couldn't be with him completely. She couldn't figure it out. Was it because she was scarred from Johnny's death and couldn't get that close to someone again? That would be an honourable reason, she thought. No one could argue with that. It would be perfectly understandable. The other part of her mind goaded her with another reason. Could it be Peter? She didn't want that to be the reason. That made her feel ashamed, disappointed in herself. What frustrated her even more was that she just didn't know. She hadn't seen clearly for the last several weeks, possibly longer.

Mae's news cut through her like a paper cut: not that bad at first, but once she had digested it, the sting lingered. It wasn't a horrendous pain, just a niggle that made her feel uncomfortable. She had hoped that her celebration had been convincing because she didn't feel it. The four of them had been sitting around the table. The two boys were asleep upstairs. Peter was smoking. Mae had seemed more joyful than normal but that hadn't stood out particularly to Martha until she thought about it after. The table had been more jovial than normal. Peter had been more relaxed with David. It must've been because his masculinity had been proved once again. Martha had begun to clear the plates when Mae told her to sit down because she had some news. When she had said that, various thoughts ran through Martha's mind, but looking back on it she knew the whole time what it was going to be. Martha played coy and went along with the 'big surprise' and sat down at the table.

On this occasion, she took David's hand under the table and squeezed it. He had noticed straight away that this was not normal behaviour for Martha, but he didn't know what it meant. He was just grateful that she had reached out to him. She hadn't done that previously. Something inside told him that he was missing something, but he couldn't put the pieces of the jigsaw together.

They sat around the table once again in the dim, moody lighting under a plume of smoke. The wireless was on and then Mae announced her news. She was pregnant. Martha knew what Mae was going to say before she had even said it and was planning her response. Before Mae had finished the sentence, Martha was going through a role play in her head. Coaching herself step by step, when to smile, when to clasp her hands together in sheer delight, when to leave her seat to go and cuddle her friend, when to kiss Peter on the cheek and congratulate them both, when to start asking all the questions of how long and what are they hoping for.

Her mind was racing; all the while she could feel her heart break a little more than it already was. The pain was physical. She didn't want Peter, she knew that, but the news just made her realise how far away she was from what she wanted out of life. As Mae ended her announcement, Martha stood up in autopilot and went through the motions she had just been thinking of, acting each section out perfectly. She believed it was convincing. She believed that Mae had bought every second of it. The two friends embraced and shared excitement over the news. Martha was excited. She was excited for Mae and Peter and she was excited about new life coming to them again. This new life could cement Peter and Mae's cracked love, she hoped, and allow her to move on with her own life. This news was a wake-up call. She needed to get the true Martha back and stop allowing the harshness of life dictate who she was now. If she got a grip now, then no one had to know what her and Peter had been doing, and then no damage would be done really – well, not to Mae anyway. That's what she hoped for.

The men had a toast to Peter's virility, and the women cooed over names and the prospect of a new baby. Mae couldn't be sure exactly how far she was gone, but she thought it was about ten weeks. She told Martha she hadn't noticed at first, but looking back, her last period had been lighter than normal and then there was her meltdown in the bathroom upstairs a couple of weeks back, which she had put down to hormones. Martha reassured her that it was ok and that she would be on hand for any meltdown, big or small. Mae took Martha's hands and clasped them within hers. She looked at her and as their pupils met. Martha felt like she knew. Martha felt like behind Mae's camaraderie, she was more attuned than people gave her credit for, and as the two of them sat there, holding each other's stare, Martha knew that Mae knew something was amiss.

'I'm so excited to be having my second baby. I feel like it will help Peter and I get back on track, and I want you to be a big part of his or her life, but you need to leave us now. Do you understand?' Mae had said this quietly.

The men hadn't heard the two of them talking, but Martha received the message loud and clear. She still didn't know if Mae knew or what she knew exactly. She couldn't quite understand if her friend was asking her to leave because she thought her husband was having elicit thoughts, or if she knew the finer details of their betrayal and was giving Martha an opportunity to do the right thing. All Martha knew was that she understood the request, and now, despite how much she didn't want to, it was time for her and Willy to move on. She continued to hold Mae's clasp and mouthed, 'I know,' and the two women embraced. As they did, Martha let out a silent tear. She was afraid of what was around the corner, but she knew she had to do this.

David stayed with her that night, as he had been doing recently. They lay in bed, and he stroked her constantly, which she found irritating on this particular evening. She didn't normally, but she was not relaxed at all. The evening's events had her head in a spin. She felt aggrieved about being pushed into living with David. She wished she could go back three years and be with her Johnny. She didn't know why, or how, her life had become so messy and when it became so self-pitying. She didn't know what she had done to deserve any of it. The whole time she was beating herself up, David was stroking her hair then her face, then her arms and then her stomach talking about his own excitement at being a dad one day. At this moment in time, she couldn't care less. She just wanted happiness. She didn't want to be in a forced romance. She didn't want to watch her friends play out false happiness in front of her, knowing full well that she was broken and he was an egotistical bastard. She felt like, if David wasn't with her now, she could break down and burst into tears. The good thing about David was that he never knew how she was feeling. The bad thing about being with David was that he never knew how she was feeling.

'Martha, will you and Willy move in with me now? If Mae and Peter have another one coming, another baby I mean, then it's probably time to move out.'

He continued to stroke her body, any piece of skin which he could touch. Martha was staring at the ceiling feeling more empty and cold than she had done in a very long time.

'Yes, I think it's time we did.'

She rolled over and kissed him. He, in a delighted euphoria, kissed her heavily and began to remove her nightgown. She allowed him and let him believe she was interested but her mind couldn't have been further away.

CHAPTER SIXTEEN

Martha hadn't slept well that night, and thus, she was the first one up in the house. She got washed and dressed quietly and went downstairs. She was quite glad to be on her own now that she thought about it. She sat out on the backdoor step. It was a crisp, typically May spring day. The skies were clear and all was still. Martha was just sitting there, looking around and taking deep, meaningful breaths. She wasn't thinking of anything. Her mind was completely clear. She wished her mind was this quiet more often, but it seemed so rare. She was so deep in this moment of newly found clarity that she hadn't heard Peter come downstairs and into the kitchen.

'I've made you a coffee.'

He handed it to her, looked up the garden, and inhaled deeply. The small garden had a low brick wall edging around it, separating the small patch of grass from a concrete area immediately by the back door. There was a concrete path to the right of the lawn running all the way to the top of the garden. It wasn't a particularly pretty garden but it wasn't too much work either. Peter sat on the wall so that he was facing Martha as she sat in the doorway. Peter never made Martha coffee. In fact, he didn't share his precious coffee supply with anyone, as it had been so difficult to get hold of any during these times of rations.

'And to what do I owe this surprise act of generosity?' Martha accepted the mug of warm coffee and cradled it in her hands to warm them.

'I just thought you might like one. No one else is up, so I didn't have to spare much of it.' They both chuckled at his confession.

'Why are you up so early? Have you been awake long?'

'I couldn't sleep. I just decided to get up in the end. I've been down here for about half an hour.'

'A lot on your mind, eh? I know that feeling.' The conversation wasn't flowing. The two of them were awkward.

They both went to speak at the same time.

'Martha, allow me, please. I don't know what to say about what has been happening. I just...I mean...'

'You don't need to explain Peter. You didn't act alone. I'm moving out this week anyway, so let's just put the whole thing behind us and hope that it never comes out.'

'Moving out? Where? Why?'

'I'm moving in with David. It's for the best. You and Mae need space to be together as a family, and let's face it, it really *is* a good idea. We've been fools.'

Peter lit up a cigarette and slowly walked around the garden. Neither of them said another word. They did glance at each other a few times. If Martha caught David's stare, she would look away, but he seemed to want her to look right into her eyes.

The sound of life was coming from upstairs. The rest of the house was stirring. Peter threw his cigarette to the ground and stamped it out with conviction before heading back into the house. He was trying to deliver a message to Martha. He wasn't happy. It annoyed her when he became like this. She didn't know what is was that he wanted or expected. Peter turned on the wireless and began preparing breakfast for everyone. He didn't normally do that, but he obviously wanted to keep busy this morning. Mae came down beaming from ear to ear and wished everyone a good morning. Martha reciprocated the greeting whilst Peter pecked his wife on the cheek. Mae moved around the room as if she was gliding almost. Pregnancy suited her. She turned off the wireless and Peter snapped.

'Turn that back on at once, I was listening to it. We are expecting an announcement from Winston Churchill shortly.'

Mae seemed genuinely upset about being snapped at by Peter. Martha thought it was probably the hormones, although she knew it was more than that.

'I'm sorry, darling, I didn't realise.'

Mae looked as though she could cry. Peter instantly went to his wife and comforted her. He hadn't done that much since Martha had been with them.

'I'm sorry. I didn't mean to snap. It's just today is a big day. It's looking more and more like the end of this ghastly war, and we are expecting an announcement that the Germans have surrendered and left Italy today. I just really want to hear it.'

He pulled out of the embrace and took her

head in his hands. He stared into her eyes and kissed her on the nose and then the cheeks and then the mouth. At this point, the two young boys came bounding down the stairs and David followed behind them.

'Anyway, my love, I have started preparing breakfast, so you don't need to do much.'

He sat down at the table and took his place as man of the house. Mae and Martha picked up where Peter had left off. David joined Peter at the table.

'It's nice seeing you two so romantic. I hope me and my Martha will be like that in as many years.'

Peter ignored David and pretended to be watching the boys play out of the window. Martha had been watching the men, and David looked around at her. She gave him a smile and decided not to say anything, as he would only be embarrassed, but they both knew Peter had heard him loud and clear.

The breakfast was interrupted by a knock at the door. Officer Pembrooke had called around to follow up on the meeting at the village hall the night before. Martha analysed him as he explained what the latest was to everyone sitting around the table. She thought how hard his job must be. There was so much expectation placed on his person, and that's all he was, a person. He couldn't create results out of thin air. It had to be fact. *People are so quick to speak badly of the police and judge them,* she thought, *but how good would they be at it? Finding clues? Working tirelessly. Giving something, anything to the public just to reassure them.* It was not an easy job, and Martha had the utmost respect for the police.

Peter, not so much. If Peter was to be reincarnated, he would be a peacock. Full of himself and not as attractive as he thought. He seemed to get a kick out of belittling people. He wouldn't be where he is now if it wasn't for his family background. Martha began to wonder what it was she ever saw in him. In front of her now she has Peter, who is being deceitful to his wife and taking Martha just because he believes he can, with no interest in either of them whatsoever. Maybe there is interest, but there is no thought for how either woman feels because, if there was, he wouldn't be doing it. There is no intention for one or the other. There is only intention to satisfy his own desire. It is all about accomplishment for him. It's for his ego and nothing else. Then, there is David. A self-made man. A man of virtue who would never do anything to hurt Martha. He would give her himself completely and was utterly dependable. Both men had their appeal, she thought. If only she could amalgamate Peter's confidence and arrogance with David's love, passion and sincerity.

She was suddenly drawn back into the conversation around the table. She had heard the name 'Evelyn' mentioned a few times.

'Sorry, who is Evelyn? I drifted off, sorry.' Office Pembrooke appreciated the rare apology he had received and blushed as Martha made him feel important and respected, not something he was used to.

'No bother, mam, I was just explaining the latest developments. Peter was quite unhappy at last night's meeting, so I thought I would visit him and some others and bring them up to speed like, you know.'

He was definitely blushing. She found that very sweet and humbling. He must have seen so much across his career. He had to be in his fifties, she thought, and it had been a rough ride, judging by his drinker's nose. And crikey, if he blushed because *she* gave *him* the time of day, he must get it rough. She admired him but didn't want to patronise him by telling him that.

'Evelyn is Simon's mother. She lives not far from here. She is not from here. She sold up when her husband died and bought a place closer to where Simon was being kept as the travelling got too much. She is a dear old woman. The mind...well the mind boggles. She knows he's a bad man but she is his mother. I suppose she still loves him. How can you not love someone you created?'

The table all sat silently and pondered Officer Pembrooke's question. You could see them each thinking about it, deep thoughts on each face at the table: Peter's, Mae's, Martha's and David's. They were all wondering how they would feel if they had a child that had grown into an adult like that. Peter, unsurprisingly, broke the silence.

'Well, no child of mine would be capable of such vulgar crimes. It *has* to be the parents. Perhaps the old witch neglected him and this is his revenge.'

Peter got a glass out for the policeman and topped everyone up. Officer Pembrooke accepted the offer of a drink gratefully. Martha could see he did not agree with Peter's opinion, and she thought he was the better man for saying nothing of it. He must have met all the worst people, the biggest, the baddest, and the saddest. He knew what made people tick, and he knew the inexplicable. Of course, some people don't have the best of upbringings, but there had to be those who gave their children everything for them still to turn out in a way they would never have expected. It was the whole nature versus nurture debate. What we are born with and what we learn.

'I am sure I know an Evelyn, but I just can't place her.' Martha racked her brain.

'Leave this to the men, Martha.' Peter, once again, putting someone in their place, she thought. He needed that to feel good about himself, she thought. She didn't need anyone to make her feel good, so she let him have it.

'And what of this Evelyn character, Pembrooke? So, she's the mother of the lunatic. I take it she is in custody now for aiding and abetting? Has she told you where he is? Where can we find him? Or have you got him as well?'

Martha thought Peter was a fool. She didn't find it attractive for a man to tell another man how to do his job when he had no relative experience of how that job works. He wouldn't last five minutes as a policeman, she thought. He hasn't got the patience or an open mind, and with that, she tutted out loud. Peter turned to look at her, and he had venom in his eyes.

'Did you just tut at me, woman. I am trying to get answers.'

He was on full peacock parade now, she thought. She did tut at him but she hadn't meant for it to come out loud.

'No, I did not tut at you, Peter, for heaven's sake. I am just tutting at the sheer travesty of the situation. Of course, I was not tutting at you.'

She wished she could tell him that, of course, she *was* tutting at him. That she thought he was a fool and not nearly as intelligent or as articulate as he thought. That he lacked tact and compassion, but, no, she had been raised better than that. She was an opinionated girl deep down, it's just that no one knew it. She may come across as quiet but she had a loud mind. She used her father as a tool of approval. In her mind, she would say whatever her father wouldn't mind her saying out loud. Anything and everything else, she kept to herself.

Officer Pembrooke continued to tell everyone around the table what he knew, which wasn't much more. He told them that Evelyn was cooperating now and that they believed Simon would revisit the house and that they would be keeping a 'constant eye on it.' Martha tuned out again. She sipped the brandy that Peter had given her. Another evening and another petal off the flower that she thought she was. As each day, each occurrence, each situation passed, that is how she visualised it. As if she were once a tulip, but slowly and gradually, with each challenging moment, a petal was being stripped from her already wilting stalk. Except, now, she didn't care so much. You could say she had given up the fight, but then again, you could say that she stopped fighting and started letting the petals of the past fall rather than being stripped of what she thought was hers.

CHAPTER SEVENTEEN
8TH MAY 1945 – VE DAY

There was so much joy and happiness in the house that it seemed that even the walls were smiling and celebrating. The fear had gone and the excitement buzzing around the place was like a constant source of electricity giving power to thin air. When the news had delivered confirmation of victory in Europe, Peter punched the air. Martha and Mae embraced tightly and let out tears of joy. It had been a long and nasty six years. The two women hadn't seen much of the chaos, but Peter had been to the city a few times, and he would regale the women with the horrors he had seen and stories that his fellow officers and soldiers had told him. Stories of holes in the ground larger than numerous double decker buses lined up together. Stories of policemen walking around with buckets collecting body parts. Stories of heartache as mothers had to send their children off to live in the countryside. Both Martha and Mae were certainly glad to already be living in the countryside. Neither could bear the idea of sending their children away at any time, let alone this time, a time of fear that they had all been living in.

When it became official that the war was over in Europe, Martha let Willy sleep in her bed with her that night and she held him all night. She stroked his hair as he drifted off to sleep. She ran her fingers lightly down his cheek and could feel warm air coming from his little nostrils; she felt overwhelmed with relief and love. They had been some of the lucky ones. She cried quietly as she thought of those who hadn't been lucky, and that evening she did a prayer to God to send love and healing to those who needed it. When she woke up on the morning of VE Day, the two of them hadn't moved, and she realised it was the best night's sleep she had had for quite some time, and it seemed to be that way for her little boy, her own little soldier, William, too.

The 8th May was a beautiful day. It was glorious sunshine, an absolute scorcher. It almost seemed like the whole country had been covered with a blackout blind and now it had finally been lifted and the sunshine was making up for being away for six years. It was a stunning day. A perfect day for a street party.

The whole village was alive like it had never been before. People were bumbling about, saying hello to everyone they saw. You could hear people humming tunes to themselves or whistling as they walked along with a skip in their step. Everyone was milling about getting ready for the biggest street party anyone had ever known. Tables were being laid out in the middle of the road, the whole length of the street. Everyone was getting involved and contributing in whatever way they could. Some people gifted flowers for table decorations and every household had been baking and preparing food since the night before. This was to be a momentous occasion. Children were skipping around and giggling. There was laughter all around. Happy laughter and lots of it. Everyone was elated.

Martha and Mae got the two boys dressed in their smart clothes. They both wore shorts, a shirt, a tie, and a tank top. Their hair was combed smartly to the side and their shoes polished by Peter. He gave them both a lesson on how to polish their shoes and the importance of it.

'Smart, respectable men have polished shoes. People notice things like shoes. If you want to be treated like a real man you must have clean shoes. You want to be treated like real men, don't you?'

Both of the boys nodded in unison and with admiration at Peter. By the time he had finished with the shoes, you could see your face in them. Peter dressed up too. He was always well turned out but he had made extra effort today. Taking slightly longer to shave. Perfecting his hair just a little bit more. That extra slap of cologne on his cheeks. Even the sting from that seemed to last a little longer but it was more satisfying than normal. Everyone wanted to try that little bit more today. The two women were no exception. They were dressed up to the nines. Once again, they stained their legs with tea leaves, the classic red lipstick was on and some for blusher, too. They looked super glamorous and captivatingly gorgeous. They wore tight blouses and flowing skirts, showing off their female prowess, and it had not been lost on Peter. His eyes lit up like he had taken something hallucinogenic when they appeared together downstairs.

'Oh my. Can this day get any better? I think not. With you two beauties by my side and a day of celebrations ahead. What a time to be alive!'

They all moved around the kitchen as if they were dancing that morning. It was as if they glided past each other. The atmosphere was of pure joy and sheer delight. The boys played happily together. Romance was in abundance. The birds could be heard chirping and tweeting louder than normal. Flowers were in full bloom. The melancholy and trepidation that had once consumed the house and soaked the walls was no more. It was as if the house had been decorated. It was as if the village outside was brand new. The jubilation that filled the street was like something that could only be compared to a film set. Never before had everyone all been so happy at once, but today was a day where everyone could rejoice in triumph.

Today the front door would be open all day. The whole street was an open house. The long table was gradually being covered with all the bakes that had been made. Jugs of juice were spread the length of it. All the food that had been saved for a long time, saved for this day, was being laid out. It was going to be a day of indulgence, which was a feeling no one had experienced in recent times.

Martha was more excited than anyone as her sisters were visiting for the day. She hadn't seen either of them for so long, and the three of them hadn't all been together in years. Susannah was on leave from work and had been staying with Jane as Jane had the space to offer. Martha couldn't wait to be able to do the same one day. She hadn't discussed it with David but she knew he would do anything to keep her happy, so she knew it wouldn't be an issue. She could invite the whole village if she wanted, not that she would; she just knew he would do anything for her. Whilst his parents were still alive it would be difficult to have anyone to stay, and she wouldn't want them to feel like she was taking over their home in any way, but it didn't seem likely that they would be around for too much longer, two to three years at most. She would probably invite Susannah to come and stay when she and David had a child. He was very much a family man, and although she was scared, she realised that she would have to give him his own child soon. He would probably want one before his parents passed, she thought. She wouldn't invite Jane to stay. Jane wouldn't want to. Jane would visit, give an expensive and thoughtless gift for the child, stay for what she thought was a reasonable length of time, and then leave again, showing no real interest in the new baby. No, she wouldn't invite Jane to stay. Susannah, however, would always be welcome, be happy to come, and Martha would be glad to have her. She would be great with the baby and she would be a great help to Martha. She could come and stay for a week and get to know the new addition. It occurred to Martha that if anyone could hear her thoughts, they would think she had it all figured out. She would tell them not really and that, if anything, she just loved to fantasise about marital bliss.

'How is my gorgeous girl doing? Can I help with anything?'

David had crept up on Martha and put his arms around her middle and began to kiss her neck whilst she was preparing food in the kitchen. Martha felt genuinely happy. She smiled at his touch and stopped what she was doing and turned to kiss him. She kissed him intensely to his surprise and he reciprocated. The two held each other, and for Martha, this was the first time she had felt that she wanted

David emotionally. She had got her head around things and had come to terms with her life now. She needed to move out of Peter and Mae's house and start building a life with David and Willy. She realised that she barely thought of Peter when he wasn't there. His fascination in her caused confusion, but now that she had realised she didn't want him, she felt empowered and in control. Now that she felt in control, she found a new confidence. With her newfound confidence, she found clarity, and with clarity she found happiness.

'I know we were going to wait until the end of the week, but I think Willy and I should just move in with you now. First thing tomorrow morning we could start taking our things to yours.'

She looked right into his eyes and her heart fluttered as she saw his smile grow across his face.

'Why wait until then. Let's do it today.'

David was like an excited little boy. He picked her up, twirled her around, and showered her face and neck with lots of loving little pecks.

'Oh, look out. Love's young dream are at it again.' Peter came in the room and broke up the romance. 'Don't stop on my account. It's nice. It's nice that everyone is happy. What a great day.'

He smiled at them and raised his mug as if to congratulate them, and it seemed sincere. He left the room and David and Martha gave each other a look of bewilderment and then giggled like teenagers before kissing again.

'I can't move today. It's the party of the century, and my sisters are coming. They should be here soon. But, tomorrow. Let's do it tomorrow. I can't wait to begin my life with you.'

David pulled her close and held her head against his chest. He had never been happier than he was right now.

Mae's pregnancy was in full swing, and she was suffering from terrible morning sickness. She had come into the kitchen and seemed fine, but within minutes she was throwing up in the sink. She apologised to David and Martha.

'Please excuse me, I am so sorry but I can't help it. It comes on so quickly.'

Martha began to pour Mae a glass of tap water.

'Don't be so ridiculous. If you need to be sick, be sick. Is there anything I can do to help? Do you want me to get you anything?'

Martha pulled out a chair for Mae and beckoned her to sit down and handed her the water.

'I think I'm having a girl this time. I wasn't

anywhere near this sick when I was carrying Charlie. Anyway, I'll be fine. There is a street party to be had, and this little madam will not keep me away,' she said, stroking her tiny but growing bump.

The three of them went about taking all the food they were contributing outside and laying it all out on the tables.

As they went outside, Martha saw her two sisters walking towards her. Jane's driver had dropped them off around the corner as the road was in use for the street party. Jane would normally be dropped right outside wherever she needed to be, and Martha felt the need to apologise that this couldn't happen today. She ran to both of her sisters with open arms and called out their names.

'Susannah. Jane. You made it. I am so happy to see you both.'

She gave them each a tight cuddle and a peck on each cheek. Willy had noticed the commotion and was looking with confusion as to who his mother's new friends were.

'Come over here, darling. It's Aunty Jane and Aunty Susannah. Come on.'

Willy slowly walked over to the three women and headed directly for just behind his mother. He leaned against the back of her legs, just looking out slightly so that his aunties could only see half of his face. He hid the other half in her skirt and behaved all coy. Straight away Susannah bent down so that she was the same height of him and started making a fuss. She told him how handsome he was and how he looked just like his Daddy. She told him she couldn't believe how big and strong he was now and that she didn't believe for a second that he was 'really that shy.'

Jane, however, seemed even colder and more distant than she normally was, which saddened Martha. She appeared stiff and continued to hold her bag in front of her with both hands. She did acknowledge Willy, but she seemed despondent somehow and not present. Martha hoped she might find out during the day what was happening in her life, but she knew that was unlikely. Jane was very secretive and didn't believe in sharing thoughts or feelings and went about her life with the stiff upper lip attitude. Martha led them towards Peter and Mae's house, and they talked about how the journey was and complimented each other on how well they all looked.

Peter came out of the front door and went to light up a cigarette. When he saw the three women approaching, he put his cigarette back in its box. His jaw almost dropped when he saw Jane. It hadn't occurred to Martha, knowing of his wandering eye, that he would be interested in her sister. Of course, he would be. When she saw his face, the penny dropped. Jane was extremely glamorous, immaculately dressed, and gave off an air of wealth. Martha wasn't jealous of this realisation. If anything, it had just occurred to her what she already knew. Peter was an insecure man who constantly craved and sought approval from women to make himself feel better. Perhaps it was because his wife Mae was beautiful and his friends would tell him so, regularly. It was as if he needed to know that other women saw him as an attractive man, not just his wife. Either way, Martha thought, Mae deserved better. Yes, Mae could be hard work and seem ungrateful at times; yes, Peter had provided her with a lovely lifestyle but she was the mother of his child, or at least he assumed he was, and now she was carrying their second child and all he could do was ogle other women. Martha left Peter to pander over the new female specimens that had arrived that day whilst she went to find David.

'Mae, have you seen David?'

Mae was getting the rest of the fancies ready

to take outside and trying to do far too much at once in the kitchen.

'He's in the back garden doing something.'

Martha tiptoed out of the back door and found David cleaning up two old paint tins.

'What are you up to now?' she lovingly quizzed her beau.

'Well, I am making the boys a time capsule each.'

Martha felt her heart expand and flutter with pride for this man she had met. He was such a wonderful man and so good with children.

'You see, today is going to go down in history. It's Victory Day. They will be learning about this for the rest of time in schools across the country and across the globe. So, I was going to get the boys to write a note each, I'll help them, like, and maybe put a toy into each tin and then we will bury them. One day someone will find them, and it will be like a glance back in time.'

David was genuinely excited with his idea, and Martha loved him even more for it.

'I think it's a wonderful idea. Do the boys know?' She put her arm around him.

'No, not yet, it only came to me a minute ago. I'm going to take these tins out to them once I've scrubbed them up. I'm trying to get them so that they are the same. I don't want them fighting over who has got the shiniest tin.'

Martha thought in that moment that she wanted to make a baby with David tonight. Of course, she would wait until they were married, but there was nothing to stop them from practising.

'Well, I think it's a wonderful idea and I think you are a sweetheart. My sisters have arrived now. Why don't you come out and meet them and tell the boys your idea?'

David jumped to his feet and was smiling enthusiastically, as he did with anything that involved Martha. They shared a kiss, and then Martha took his hand and led him through the house.

They went outside and Martha conducted the introductions. To her surprise, Peter was in deep conversation with Susannah and not Jane. He seemed genuinely interested in her career in nursing and didn't seem to be lecherous either. She expected to find him emulating Jane's status and showing off in general. As Martha introduced her sister, she could feel Peter's eyes on her yet again. She chose to ignore it and put her arm around David and showed her sisters a display of affection for her recently discovered new love.

The afternoon slipped by, and everybody went about enjoying the day. They ate, the children played, they talked. It was a lovely day and the sun stayed out for all of it. Mae enjoyed seeing the three Henderson girls back together again and they reminisced about old times. Peter and David talked more than normal, but that was only because Peter wanted to seem like the good guy in front of his audience. As the day drew to a close, Jane said that they must be leaving. They had a two-hour drive back, and she wanted to get back before it was too late. They all kissed and hugged goodbye, and Martha walked them to her car where her driver was patiently and dutifully waiting for her. They said goodbye once again, and Susannah got in. Jane closed the door behind Susannah but stayed outside the car.

'Martha, what is going on with you and Peter?'

Martha was somewhat taken aback.

'What do you mean?' she scowled at her sister.

'Oh, come on. You two are not fooling anyone. He's mad about you. Everyone can see it, and I mean everyone. The only one who is blind to it is poor David. Tread very carefully, Martha. Very carefully.'

With that she pecked her sister on the cheek

and got into the car saying, 'Yes, lovely to see you too,', which was for Susannah's benefit.

Martha waved awkwardly and watched them drive off. Once again, her happiness and contentment with David that day was now short-lived.

CHAPTER EIGHTEEN

The very next day Martha was moving in with David. The day was surreal to her. It seemed as if it happened in slow motion. The rumpus commotion from Victory Day seemed to have passed so quickly now that moving day was here. As she had waved her sisters off the night before, she had told David it would be wise for him to go home that evening and spend it with his family and prepare them for her and Willy's arrival the next day. What she didn't tell him was that she had been completely flummoxed by her sisters' acumen with the Peter situation.

What David didn't know was that Martha didn't sleep a wink that night. What David didn't know was that Martha went through every possible emotion that the human body is capable of that evening. Firstly, she experienced surprise. She was completely shell shocked that Jane had come to the conclusion she had. Martha thought that she hadn't given anything away. She was sure of it. If anyone did, it was Peter, but even then, she had until that moment believed it was between the two of them.

If Jane, Jane whom she rarely saw, if she could detect it, then how many others could? Could Mae? The thought petrified her. She never meant to hurt Mae. That was never the plan. There was no plan. Martha couldn't bear the thought of Mae thinking she had wanted all of this. Jane said that everyone knew, apart from David. She wished she had questioned her, but at the time she was speechless. Now that Jane had gone, she had a million questions. She had spent the early hours of that evening after her sisters had left, ruminating over who knew what.

She busied herself with helping out with the cleaning up process. She made small talk with the neighbours. They rejoiced the whole time in what a stupendous event the day had been. She insisted on Mae taking some rest 'in her condition,' but it was about 'Martha's panicked condition' if anything. She played with the boys, Willy and Charlie. She got them to talk about the day. She wanted them to remember this day for the rest of their lives. They were only five years of age now, but she wanted them to remember the heinousness of the time that they had lived in. She knew that in years to come people would ask them what it had been like, and she felt it her duty to not make them permeate within the experience of which they were in, but not currently aware of, but to take something positive from it and convey the message of hope.

They were just small boys but, with no doubt, people would seek more interest in them in years to come. No one would question her or Mae or Peter or any of their peers because, if they were friendly enough with them, or old enough to ask questions, then, surely, they would have lived through it themselves or have family that did. No, she knew that they would not be asked. Willy and Charlie would be asked time and time again, 'What was it like living through the war?' At least that is what she had hoped. She lived in the hope that no other wars would happen, this would be the one that was asked about, and she wanted to make sure her boy, and as much as suitably possible for her to influence

Charlie, she wanted them to talk about it positively.

Gosh, there would be enough families on this street who would go down the melodramatic route. She wanted her boy to tell everyone a story of success. She had learned that misery and negativity was rife but did no good. People fed off it. The weaker were influenced by it. The strong used it as a tool of power. What she had learned from the war was more than death and the devastation it caused. She saw the power in fear and weakness. She didn't have much to offer Willy but she could teach him courage. She could teach him not to be afraid. The hypocrisy behind it all was everywhere, but she could feed him strength. She could empower him with vision and morals, but the reality was, she was more knotted than a fisherman's net.

Once she had tucked the boys into bed, her emotions had turned from surprise into sadness. There was nothing to distract her anymore. She had busied herself all afternoon and now she had run out of all those routes. She was left with only her thoughts for company, and right now, they weren't helpful. Once she had tucked the boys in and kissed their warm sun-blushed cheeks goodnight, she took herself downstairs. Peter and Mae had gone to bed. They had wanted an 'early night,' and of course, Martha was happy to oblige. At the time, she was more than happy to agree. She was looking forward to being on her own, but now that her alone time was here, she regretted it deeply. She sat herself down at the kitchen table.

She ran her fingers over the mahogany top. She ran her fingers over every scratch. Slowly, wondering how each mark and how every engraved scratch had happened. She imagined that Charlie's toy cars or trucks had caused much damage to a once beautiful table. She wondered if Peter had put something on the table he shouldn't have or whether Mae had. She imagined the row that might have erupted because of such an incident. After pondering whether it could have been Peter, Mae, or Charlie that had damaged the table or all of them, she realised that her brain had become so tired that she had forgotten what had led her to here. She stopped feeling the scars of the table and took a moment to feel her own. Twelve hours earlier she had been so happy, but Jane's statement had spiralled her right back to everything she thought she had left.

She stood up from the table and walked to the larder. She took hold of Peter's brandy and picked up one of his Waterford Crystal glasses and poured herself a drink. They had never used these glasses whilst she had been there, and she got the feeling they hadn't been used for a long time, if ever. She didn't care tonight. He wouldn't know. Even if he did find out what would he say? He could question her about touching his precious possessions, but all he would get from her would be a nonchalant attitude back. She didn't care anymore. She would be gone in the morning anyway.

'Damn, Jane,' she said as she knocked back the large brandy she had poured. She rarely drank. She had never drunk on her own before, and she had never drunk more than what she had had under this roof in her life. As she sat there and felt the warmth of the brandy flow through her body, she felt sadder now than she had for such a long time. She had moved here with such hope. She knew that she couldn't stay here with Willy forever, but she never ever believed it would go the way it had.

She had only had a couple of brandies before taking herself to bed. She was glad of this because she was wondering what path she was on, having sat there drinking on her own. Luckily, she felt queer after the two she had and decided, despite her best efforts, she was not going to create a problem such as alcoholism in her life. She realised she had enough to deal with. As she got in to bed and sank her head on her pillow, her anguish moved to happiness. She let go. She realised that whatever mess she was in, whatever Peter wanted from her, whatever Jane thought she saw, she realised that none of it needed to happen. She could control it. She could be in complete control. She *was* in control. And she *would* be in control. She would show them.

Once she had gotten out of this godforsaken house and started her new life with David, all of this would subside. It would all blow away like tumbleweed. No one knew and nobody had to know. Jane was wrong. Jane knew, but that didn't mean that everyone knew. Of course, Jane knew. She was related. Of course, she could sense something from her sister's behaviour. That didn't mean that everyone else knew. Martha reasoned with herself and that gave her a great amount of satisfaction. What did Jane know? If anything, Martha wondered if she had said that to her to give them something to talk about. She had noticed how distracted she was earlier that day; she must have been looking for a problem to talk about. Martha closed her eyes, suitably satisfied that the problem was with Jane and not with her.

But what if Jane was right? Martha tossed and turned, and it became clear she was not going to be asleep anytime soon. She began to panic. What if David was a mistake? What if she moved in and realised her feelings were not strong enough to keep them together? What if he could detect that something was up? How would that affect his behaviour towards her? Maybe he would become aggressive? In the comfort of his own home, maybe he would become a tyrant and this would be the biggest mistake of her life? Martha realised that her inability to get to sleep was causing her to become irrational. She sat up and rubbed her face. Her heart was racing. What was she so afraid of? She didn't want Peter. She wanted a man like David. Her mind was racing. David was everything she needed and Peter was the last thing she needed. She was tired of being tired and now she was winding herself up. *No more,* she thought. This just had to be cold feet. Everything would be fine in the morning. She lay down once again and tried to get some rest.

Morning broke through the blind in Martha's window. A bright gleaming ray of sun seeped through the tiny gap in the net curtains, and it was glowing right onto her face. It was almost as if this ray of sun was especially for her. It was a sign. A symbol of hope and positivity for moving day. She rubbed her eyes and sat upright. The warm shard of sun made her smile. It told her everything she needed to know, and now she felt no fear, no anguish, no confusion. She was happy. She finally felt sure that she knew what she was doing. With that, she almost leapt out of bed. She stood up and stretched her arms above her body. She felt good.

Martha went downstairs and joined Peter and Mae in the kitchen for one last breakfast together. Mae had already seen to the two boys who were now playing with a train set in the front room. Martha had popped her head in on them on her way through to the kitchen and wished them a good morning. The three adults were all in the kitchen for breakfast for the last time. It occurred to Martha that breakfasts wouldn't be like this again. When she moved in with David, Willy would be on his own with a house full of adults.

'Charlie must come to stay from time to time. Willy would love to have some company in the new house, for sure. I hope he copes with the change. I do worry about him.'

Martha picked up her cup of tea and blew on it. The steam was still rising off it, so she thought better of it and put it back down.

'Oh, he'll be fine. Children are tougher than

us and pretty resilient,' Peter assured Martha. 'Anyway, you are not going to be strangers, are you? You are going to keep popping in. I need you to keep an eye on this one for me. She'll need more help soon as the pregnancy develops.'

He stood behind his wife and rubbed her shoulders. Martha liked Peter when he was like this. When he was being a good man and tending to his wife. It gave her a warm feeling inside, and it made her think that they could all have a happy future together. Peter and Mae, Martha and David.

'Of course, I will still be popping round. Try and keep me away. As soon as it is ok, you know, I don't want to tread on anyone's toes, I will have you all over for dinner. We can have a big dinner party. You should see the size of the kitchen they have there. It must be at least three times the size of this one. It is in desperate need of a good clean and a de-clutter, but I will sort that, once I am in there.'

Just as they were talking about all the changes, David came in through the front door with a knock and a call. He didn't need to be asked in anymore; he was going to be part of all their lives. Peter was very welcoming to him and even gave him a pat on the back as he pulled out a seat from the table for him.

'We're having a big breakfast this morning, David. Something hearty to send you all on your way. You'll have a bit of everything, won't you?'

David's eyes were sparkling like never before, and his face exuded his sheer delight that this day was finally here.

'Yes, thank you, that would be grand.'

He took Martha's hand and brought it to his lips. He kissed it gently whilst looking into her eyes, and once again she felt safe. She knew this man adored her and would do anything for her.

'Right, then, Mae, it looks like everyone is having a bit of everything. I've put all the goods out on the side.'

Peter sat down at the table feeling very good about himself having sourced some real treats for their breakfast. No one asked where he had got them from, which he was probably hoping they would. He had managed to get bacon, eggs, bread, tinned tomatoes. They would be having the works this morning.

Breakfast that morning was the perfect send-off. The women chatted without a care in the world. They talked like two best friends who hadn't seen each other for a while. The men talked about business and what Britain would look like over the next few years. They were predicting what impact the war would have and how long Britain would take to rebuild itself. The boys played happily, and you could hear them laughing at times. The scene was picture perfect.

Mae was positively blooming with her pregnancy, now in full swing. Martha was a lady very much in love and seemed at ease. She was quite different to the woman that arrived at that house almost a year ago. She wasn't the anxious, mousey character she had once been. She would never be as gregarious as Mae, but she was quietly confident now. She walked with a new air about her. Her back was straighter and her shoulders further back. She glided rather than tiptoed. Willy was not as clingy either. His confidence had grown. He was a boy now, not a baby, and his mother could see that. He was still very much a mummy's boy, but it was a different kind of love. He wanted to show off and impress her now, rather than curling up in her lap or pulling on her sleeve whilst hiding behind her. He would greet guests at the house without being asked. He would ask questions. He was growing up to be quite the charmer, and he was intelligent and inquisitive. Despite the troubles and tribulations of Martha and despite the emotional turmoil she had been suffering from, this house had done them both the world of good. If they had stayed in the last house much longer, they were at risk of living the same life forever.

Moving in with Peter and Mae had pushed them both out of their comfort zones, and although it had been tricky at times, she was so glad they had done it. Now she could move on to her next chapter with David as a better-improved version of Martha. She was beginning to find herself. She was beginning to feel sexy again. She was beginning to want happiness which, in itself, was a strange concept. She hadn't realised the cloud she had been living under. Even when she thought it had passed, she hadn't realised it was very much still over her, it just wasn't raining. But, now with the war over, things seemed different. Mae was bringing new life into the family which was always exciting for everyone involved. Everything just seemed so sunny now.

Martha went upstairs to take one last look at the room that had opened doors for her. She stood by the door and just pushed it open gently. As the door widened, the room became flooded with sunlight. She leaned against the doorframe and crossed her arms. She could see the dust particles floating in the sun's rays across the room. Martha thought it was like some sort of magical dust. It was happy dust. You could only see it when the sun shone this bright, so who couldn't be happy to see the dust floating around everywhere?

She crept in the room slowly and with grace. She sat on the edge of the bed and smoothed down it's already smooth covers. She looked around and took a deep breath. The duvet and wallpaper were almost matching. Creams and pale greens. The furniture was ornate and made of dark mahogany wood with little brass handles. She stood up and walked around the room slowly, tracing her fingertips over the surfaces of the furniture. She picked up a trinket box on the dressing table and opened it. She knew it was empty inside; she just wanted to have a look. She put the lid back on it and placed it back down carefully. She sat down on the stool and held up a hand mirror to look at herself. She picked up a brush and gently stroked her hair with the soft bristles a couple of times. She got up and went to the sash window. With her long, dainty fingers she opened it just a tiny bit. It was stuck and required a bit of strength to push it up, but she managed. After a deep inhale, she thought the room would benefit from an airing. She went back to the door and turned on her heels. She took in one last look and smiled. Martha closed the door and went downstairs. David had loaded the car already, and everyone was waiting to say their goodbyes, not forever, but goodbye to living together and on to pastures new. New beginnings all round.

CHAPTER NINETEEN

A few months had passed, and already a lot had changed. The country was picking up the pieces from the war ending, but more locally, no more had been heard about the murderer on the loose. He hadn't been caught, but there had been no reporting's of any further crimes by him either, so it had been assumed he had gone into hiding somewhere or had moved on to another town. Apparently, the police were in contact with his mother, Evelyn, paying her regular visits to keep an eye on things, and to offer her their support should she need it.

Mae had her baby. A girl this time, and they called her Anna.

Both of David's parents had passed. His

mother passed within two weeks of Martha moving in and then his father passed a month later. Both of them had died in their sleep. Everyone said that David's father had died of a broken heart. The couple had been together since they were teenagers. Some people said the relief of the end of the war had made them go, and some said that David's mother was hanging on for someone like Martha. Now that Martha was here and David was happy, she felt like she could go, knowing that he would be looked after. Once she was gone, his father had nothing to live for, according to many, and so, his heart gave up for the love of his wife. Although it was extremely sad and a lot more stress than David or Martha felt they could cope with so soon, Martha found the romanticism behind those ideas comforting and, in an odd way, hoped that when she died, it would be of an old and broken heart, rather than that of tragedy or disease.

Martha hadn't wanted to take over the running of the house so soon, but after the death of both of his parents, David needed someone to take hold of the reins. He hadn't said as much and probably wouldn't have asked, but Martha meant more to him now than ever, and he allowed her to guide him through the next chapter of his life. His brother, Michael, was also very accepting. She wasn't sure how he would react to her, but he had been nothing but kind and sweet. She wasn't sure if he saw her as the sister they didn't have or as a mother figure, but she was very glad for how welcome he made her feel; in return for his warmth, she was growing quite protective of him. Both David and Michael were excellent with Willy, and she felt that they were better role models for him than Peter was.

They were good men with big hearts. They both had lots of skills they could teach Willy such as mechanics, carpentry, and household maintenance skills. All of this she thought would be of great benefit to Willy growing up. She wanted her son to be a good man. Not a pretentious, chauvinistic, and self-centred man like Peter. What could Peter have taught Willy, really? He hadn't been awful, but in the grand scheme of things, he could only share knowledge on cigarettes, alcohol, and one-upmanship.

David and Martha had had Peter and Mae over for dinner one evening just before Anna was born. It was a nice night, if not a little awkward. Martha had been looking forward to hosting them for an evening after everything they had done for her, but it became clear that neither of them were relaxed when out of the comfort of their own home. At least that is what she had hoped it was. She wondered if David's house was not good enough for them. She wondered if Peter didn't like not being the man of the hour, as he so usually was.

After allowing her mind to run away with her, she decided that Mae was probably exhausted with her pregnancy, now that it was almost done, and Peter was exhausted with having to support her. He wasn't very good at doing things for others when required. He was happier being helpful when he didn't need to be. The evening ended with Martha feeling deflated and wishing they hadn't had them over, but David seemed oblivious to what Martha had sensed, and he talked about what a great success the whole night had been whilst helping her clear up and put the dishes away. She was glad that he was oblivious to her feelings at least in times like these. It helped give her a clear head and not allow her to dwell on things. She decided to move on from it but felt that she was in no rush to have them over again.

Shortly after Anna had been born, David drove Martha and Willy over to visit them all. Mae seemed genuinely happy to have them there, and she was a wonderful mother. She had already been a great mother with Charlie, but from what Martha could observe, having a girl had softened Mae. She didn't seem so brash in her opinions nor her mannerisms. Martha thought that Mae seemed like a new woman, and she liked the new version of her. She was soft, she was tender, and she seemed delicate now. Martha wondered if some women needed to bear a daughter to make them see the world differently. She wondered if some women put on a hard exterior so as not to be seen as a pushover, to be seen as 'one of the boys,' and to not allow anyone to think they could be easily hurt. Martha wondered if having a girl made some women give up the pretence, if that's what it was, and not care about any of that anymore. Then Martha thought that perhaps she thought too much at times and to just let things be. It had been a calm and lovely afternoon and early evening. Even Peter behaved in a more civilised way towards David. He didn't seem to be so patronising. She decided his behaviour must have been due to the lack of sleep that a new a baby brings. She was fairly certain that he had not turned over a new leaf.

During the visit, Mae invited David and Martha to Peter's award presentation. She told them he was being presented with a 'War Medal' for serving 28 days at sea during the war. Martha had realised that her Johnny would have at least been receiving that or something similar if he had survived. He had spent most of his time away. She didn't know what he would have got; he was in a lower rank than Peter, and he hadn't been at sea, but if Peter was getting an award for spending a small amount of time away on a boat she thought, then Johnny would have been up for several awards. She realised that she was allowing her grief to take over and cause her to have negative and bitter thoughts. She told herself that thoughts like that weren't pretty. If Peter was up for an award, then he was entitled to it, and so they should all be there to show their support.

David took a real shine to baby Anna that afternoon. Not because she was a girl but because he was so desperate to be a dad himself. Martha watched him hold her as if it came so naturally to him. He stroked her cheek and rocked her gently from side to side. He ran his index finger down her tiny forehead and to the tip of her nose. He did this repeatedly, and she dozed in and out of sleep in a completely fulfilled and delirious state. Martha realised that he deserved to have his own child. He had done so much for her and Willy. She should give him the one thing that he couldn't make on his own.

She knew it would make him the happiest

version of himself there had ever been. Perhaps not tonight, she thought to herself, but very soon, she would see if they could make it happen. There had been so much change in that house already, a new baby would be too much. She knew David wouldn't hesitate right now, but whether he realised it or not, she felt that he needed to get used to his parents not being there before throwing the responsibility of parenthood into his lap. You can't fix change with more change, she believed. You had to come to terms with change first so that when the next change came, the right version of you was there and ready to deal with it. Present change with an emotionally unstable person, and the results could be very different than what the outcome could've been. They don't say time is a great healer for nothing.

When David and Martha arrived home that night, she got Willy ready for bed, but David insisted on reading him his bedtime story. So, with that, the three of them curled up on Willy's bed and they all sat together whilst David read. He was very good at it. He pulled silly faces and he put on different voices for each of the characters. Willy gasped and giggled in all the right places, and Martha felt so glad that she had all of this. She never thought she would find another Johnny. He was so rare, and although David was not replacing him, she thanked her lucky stars that she had found someone who was so kind, not only to her but to her son too. David treated Willy as if he was his own. He had more patience than anyone she had ever known, and that trait alone was a big part of the attraction for her. After they had tucked Willy into bed and both kissed him goodnight, they got up and left the room, leaving the door slightly ajar as a defence system to keep monsters at bay. The light melted monsters, according to Willy.

Out on the landing, David walked ahead of Martha and took her hand to guide her down the stairs behind him, but she held back. He stopped on the step and looked behind him, and she stood there staring right back at him. She bit her bottom lip, and he was instantly aroused. All the blood began to flow to inside his trousers immediately. That simple signal told him everything he needed to know, and he was not about to say no. She was the most beautiful woman he had ever seen. She could be dressed in rags with her hair in a mess, and he would still want to make love to her over and over again. Even if she did only have rags for clothes, there was no chance her hair would be a mess. One of the things he liked about her so much was how much effort she consistently made, not only with her personal appearance but with everything she did. She continuously gave so much without ever asking for anything back. David walked back up the two steps he had managed to get down and put his hands on Martha's hips. She loved his big hands. His physique was different to Johnny's, and although she hadn't planned her next love to be that way, she was glad he was. It made it easier for her to be with him, knowing that his shape was so different. His hands were like shovels and his fingers were big and thick. He had the hands of a workman. Small cuts and scars everywhere told a story of his hard graft since childhood. His whole build was stocky, and he was built mainly of muscle due to his labour-intensive lifestyle.

With both of his hands on her hips, he was almost able to hold her whole waist. He kissed her hard and she kissed back. There wasn't a lot to David. He wasn't a deep soul but he was kind, and whilst Martha considered that thought, she found herself becoming extremely aroused and had this overwhelming desire to be with him. She kissed him back heavily and almost allowed herself to sink into his hands. He must've felt it because, in that moment, he picked her up and carried her into their room, kissing her the whole time. He placed her on the bed as if she was a delicate patient who needed gentle care. Martha allowed him to take the lead.

She completely surrendered herself to him, and her burning desire to make love to him. As she lay on the bed, David slowly traced his fingers over her face. He traced the outline of her lips and then down to her chest. He traced the line of her collarbone and then began to kiss her neck. She began to breathe heavier as goosepimples rose all over her body. He slowly began to unbutton her blouse. With each button he undid, he would kiss his way down her body. Once he was at her navel, she sat up and took his head in her hands. They both sat together on the bed staring into each other's eyes. Martha leaned in and began to kiss David passionately. She kissed him as though she hadn't seen him for five years, or as if this was the last time she was going to kiss him. They began to undress each other quickly, David holding Martha's head in his hands and kissing her with force and meaning. Once naked, David pushed Martha up the bed; she held on to his arms and, again, she appreciated how strong he was as she wrapped her fingers around his biceps. David pulled away from kissing her so that he was hovering just slightly above her mouth. They could feel the breath of each other on their faces. He held her stare and entered her. He moaned with pleasure and she gasped with passion. He slowly began to make love to her, and she rocked her body in time with his. She had one hand on the bottom of his back holding him close to her and one hand on the back of his head. It wasn't the most furious lovemaking the two had shared, but it was loving, sensual, and extremely intense for them both. With gentle motion, they both came together and they stayed in their embrace for quite some time after, saying nothing, just lying there, in pure ecstasy together.

CHAPTER TWENTY

The days flew by into weeks which quickly passed as months, and Martha was settling in well with David and his brother. Peter and Mae would visit regularly, and likewise, they would visit them. Willy remained good friends with Charlie, and the two of them became more like brothers than friends. Little baby Anna was a few months old now and was already growing into a strong woman just like her mother. She had both her parents and her big brother wrapped around her little finger.

Peter seemed more distant as the time went on, and Martha believed that he was jealous of the baby. He loved her without a doubt, she was the apple of his eye and would definitely be his little princess that would never go without, but Martha could see that he resented the lack of interest Mae had for him and the abundance of interest she had for her new baby. Whenever they all met for dinner or lunch, he wouldn't even put on his usual alpha male display for David. David misinterpreted this as Peter accepting him and liking him, but Martha didn't think that was the case. She wouldn't tell David as he was too sensitive to handle that kind of revelation, plus Martha thought one of the greatest things about David was his innocent mind.

Christmas was fast approaching, and it had been decided that they would all celebrate together at Peter and Mae's. David was slightly put out by this, as his house was bigger, but Martha reassured him that they were offering to host as they were more comfortable financially and wanted to be able to share what they could put on the table.

'We are not a charity, Martha. I can provide for us just as much as Peter can. In fact, I could probably put on a better spread than them. I know this year is still tight for food, but I could get us a pretty good murkey. I heard someone talking about them the other day. It's like a turkey but it's made of something else. Sausage meat, I think. It's got breadcrumbs and stuff on it. I don't know. Ask one of the local lasses, they'll be able to tell you, and then next Christmas we'll have a real turkey.'

She loved his enthusiasm, but her mind was made up. She wanted to get out of the house. It was a nice break for her in a way. She liked being there but she often felt alone, despite David being there most of the time. She thought it would be good to have different company. He was aggrieved that she wouldn't let him look after her. He wanted to be the alpha male from time to time, despite his apparent soft demeanour.

'I know, darling, but look at it this way, it will be their house, their mess, their chaos. All we will have to do is help lay it all out and help clear up. We are getting off lightly if you think about it. The boys can play together and then we can have a family boxing day here, together.'

She gave him a cuddle, and he responded limply. It was their first Christmas together, and he couldn't understand why she wouldn't want to spend it on their own with Michael and Willy, a proper little family unit. Instead, they would be there, and he would have to listen to Mae patronise Martha all afternoon, and he'd have to pretend to be on Peter's level. He didn't care for either of them much, but he daren't tell Martha that. He just thought she was a much better person than the pair of them put together and that she deserved more respect than they ever showed her, but she liked them, and he didn't want to upset the apple cart.

David had long been confused about the relationship between the three of them. He thought that it seemed complicated and unpredictable. He couldn't understand how they all did it. He was a calm man with little or no complications in his life. He was a quiet man, but he knew more than he said. He was very observant and he analysed most situations. He noticed that one minute, Peter acted like Martha was his little sister. He would defend her and protect her with his life. The next minute he would be cold and rude and treat her like a passer-by in a shop that had knocked his cut loaf out of his arm. She never seemed to object to his hot and cold behaviour. Then there was Mae. One minute she would act like she idolised Martha. She would act like she was her hero, and as if she wanted to be her. The next minute she would seem jealous of Martha and put her down in front of people. It was odd to David. Something else he had noticed was that the two of them were out of sync. If Peter was being cold with Martha, then Mae would be nicer. If Mae was being a bitch to Martha, then Peter would be in his protective mode. David just couldn't quite put his finger on it, but he wished that Martha would take off her rose-tinted spectacles and see them for who they *really* were. She deserved the moon in his opinion when all they gave her was the dark night sky.

CHAPTER TWENTY-ONE

It was December 21st, 1945, and Martha and David were preparing for Christmas. Willy was sitting up at the kitchen table making home-made paper chain decorations. Earlier that day, he and Martha had painted some old paper, as new paper was still hard to come by. She thought that making their own decorations was nicer and said that they should do it every year despite rations and availability. David had sourced one of those 'murkeys' that were all the rage this year. He said it would do for Boxing Day, but secretly he was hoping that Martha would change her mind, and they would all spend their first Christmas together alone as the family unit that he had craved for so long. He looked at Martha and Willy making their paper chains, and he was glad that he had them.

He might not get the Christmas he wanted this year, he thought, but he had more this year than he did last year. Despite the loss of his parents, which upset him greatly, he had the love of a good woman, and he really did love Willy as if he were his own. Maybe next Christmas there would be an additional family member. He would love that, but Martha hadn't expressed much of an interest yet, and he didn't want to push her. One step at a time he told himself. All will come good in the end.

'I'm going to head out to the barn and get some kindling for the fire. I wonder how long your paper chain will be by the time I get back.' David nodded at Willy as if to suggest he was against the clock and might win a prize for his efforts. Willy's eyes boggled, and he got back to business frantically, desperate to please his new father figure.

David and Martha had made the house look as best as they could with what they had. Rationing was still in force and everyone was trying to muster up whatever Christmas they could manage. Homemade decorations, 'murkey' instead of turkey, homemade presents or hand me downs. Resources were low but spirits were high. Martha sat with Willy by candlelight in the kitchen. She enjoyed special moments like these, and she loved to light a Christmas advent candle. She always found that most children didn't need to have fancy toys. She felt that they needed stimulation and interaction. She loved teaching Willy new things and seeing how thrilled he was when he accomplished something. The two of them were giggling away when the front door burst open, and David was standing there, out of breath, barely able to hold himself up and ashen-looking, as if he had seen a ghost. Martha panicked.

'Willy, darling, stay here. Mummy will just be a moment.' She got up from the table and left the kitchen, closing the door behind her. 'David, what's wrong? You're scaring me.'

David could hardly speak. He was pale and shivering and couldn't compose himself. He turned and pointed to the barn.

'In there. Oh, God, Martha. In there.' She went to leave the house, and he stopped her by pushing her against the wall. 'No. You can't go in there. Please. Do as I say. I just, I just need a minute to get my breath. Find Michael and tell him I need his help without disturbing Willy.'

He was beginning to get himself together. He stood up and rubbed his face with his hands.

'Ok, darling, I will, but I need to know what is happening? What are we dealing with?'

David looked up to meet her eyes.

'There's a body. A woman. In our barn. It happened not long ago. We need to get the police out here.'

Martha gasped and brought her hand to her mouth. She looked scared and then confused.

'A body? What? Who? How?'

David became flustered.

'Martha, for God's sake, will you just get Michael. We don't have time for this now. The killer could still be nearby.'

The colour from Martha's face drained. She rushed upstairs to get Michael. David heard her gentle tap of his bedroom door, and seconds later his brother came bounding down the stairs.

'What...' Michael began to speak loudly.

'Shhhh,' demanded David. 'Willy is sitting in there. He can't know about this. Michael, I am going to have to drive into the village and get the police out here. Martha, you need to get Willy to his bedroom, and do not tell him about this. Michael, I need you to guard the house and protect all three of you. Whatever happened out there... this madman... this psychopath... it looks like it was within the last hour.'

Martha gasped again.

'I will be as quick as I can.' He grabbed Martha and kissed her hard on the lips. Then he took Michael by his upper arms. 'You can manage, can't you? I will be straight back. No more than twenty minutes. Lock the door, close all the curtains, turn the lights out if you think that's best. I won't be long. Do not go out there and do not look in that barn.'

He looked at them with fear in his eyes and made his way out to the car. Martha and Michael were left speechless in the hallway. Michael turned to Martha and offered her a cuddle. He wasn't normally an affectionate man and would wince at having to touch anyone, but he knew he had to step up to the plate for his brother tonight. Deep down he was petrified. He was a quiet boy. David was the man of the house, but Michael wasn't going to let his brother down. Martha was speechless and was looking at Michael for answers.

'Ok, well, like David said, I think you need to get Willy up to bed, and I will keep a lookout down here. Do you think you can manage that? Will you be ok?'

Martha nodded, and he could see she was shaking. He wanted to reassure her, but firstly, he didn't know exactly what he was reassuring her about, and secondly, that would be pushing him out of his comfort zone. He felt pathetic as he watched her walk into the kitchen whilst he stood there gormlessly. He wished human behaviour came to him as easily as it did for his brother. Michael struggled socially. He never knew the right words to say, his head was always scrambled when it came to knowing what the right thing to say was, but give him a puzzle, and he could fix it.

Martha walked into the kitchen and saw Willy at the table innocently playing with his paper chains. He looked up at his mum and beamed with pride, whilst showcasing his mountain of work. She smiled back at him. She glanced over at the window and froze. She wanted to close the curtains but was terrified that the killer might still be out there. If it was a murder, and if it was the same killer from earlier in the year, he had only gone for women. She was the only woman in the property. She was feeling sick but trying not to show it. She was scared for Willy, and for David and Michael. She heard Michael clear his throat and she realised she had been standing there frozen to the spot. She nervously went to the window and unhooked the curtains and drew them quickly, closing out any ghastly scene that might be out there.

'Willy, let's clear this up and get ready for bed. We can do some more in your pyjamas upstairs if you like. I will do some with you.'

Willy was happy with this deal and hadn't seemed to notice that anything was going on, which she was relieved about. She wished that a deal about making paper chains was enough to make her happy right now, but she had a feeling they were all in for a long night.

Everything that followed passed in a blur. David arrived back with Officer Pembrooke, along with a handful of other policemen. They had arrived quietly, as David had explained that there was a child in the house, and they didn't want to alert him. The police had been good and said that they understood, and so they were discreet when they arrived. They also said they didn't want to cause too much of a commotion in case the killer was nearby, that's if they were looking for a killer. This was indeed confirmed as soon as they saw the body. The young woman had been murdered; there was no doubt about it. She could only have been in her early twenties. David had gone back into the barn with the police and had managed to observe the scene for longer this time around. The victim was almost naked. Her ripped, blood-stained clothes were strewn across the hay bales that she was resting on. She had marks around her wrists as if she had been tied up and various wounds to her body, the most severe being that her throat had been slit. David realised she was a local girl from a farm not far from his, a few miles down the road at most. He knew her parents. He let out a sigh and then he began to sob. Officer Pembrooke patted him on the shoulder.

'David, let's get you out of here. There is nothing you can do. This is where we take over. Let's get you inside. I expect that new lady of yours will need you for a while following this. Be strong for her and that little lad.'

Officer Pembrooke put his arm around David's shoulders and walked him to the house. They went into the kitchen where Martha was pacing up and down, and Michael was sitting at the table biting his nails. Martha threw her arms around David and hugged him tightly. He nestled his head into her shoulder and was more vulnerable than she had ever seen him before. She sat him down at the table opposite Michael and said she would put on some tea for all of them.

'No, you won't, I'll do that. It's the least I can do.'

Officer Pembrooke started opening cupboard doors trying to find a teapot. Martha sat next to

David and held his hands in hers. They all sat in silence, in a state of bewilderment. Officer Pembrooke cut the edgy atmosphere.

'I will need to ask you all some questions, but I think that can wait for the morning. Let's get the body removed and off the premises. Is there somewhere else you can stay tonight? The press will be all over this place by the morning, if not before.'

David rubbed his head in his hands.

'I can't believe this is happening to us. What has happened is terrible, and that sick bastard needs stringing up. He's tainted my perfect home. Everything was going so well. My girl has moved in, and we are getting ready for Christmas, and now this has happened. How will I ever look at her parents again? How will I ever be able to go out and get kindling again? Or go in the barn again? This is a horrible, horrible mess. People will now know us as the family that had the murdered girl in the barn. No. No. No. This isn't fair.'

David became very emotional, and Martha's attempts at comforting him were of no help. Officer Pembrooke put a pot of tea on the table and put out some cups. He pulled up a chair at the head of the table.

'David, what you saw tonight no man should

ever have to see, but for now, you need to be strong. You need to be the man of the house. You need to protect your good lady here and protect that little lad upstairs. Michael will help you. I think it's best that you stay somewhere else, just for tonight. Martha, your friends? Peter and Mae? Will they take you all in for the night? We can transport you over there?'

Martha nodded but looked miles away.

'Martha, I really don't want you and Willy to go and stay there. You haven't long been here; please don't go and stay with them.'

David pleaded with Martha. He was aware that he looked desperate and he couldn't believe he was being that way, but something inside him just didn't want them going back to that house. Martha looked panicked. There was no way she wanted to stay on the farm tonight. She wouldn't sleep a wink. It was unlikely she would sleep at Mae's, but she would feel more comfortable there. Officer Pembrooke could detect the frustrations all around and stepped in again.

'David, I think you should all leave tonight. None of you should stay here. We need to do our investigations anyway, so you would be helping us, but more importantly, you've got a family to take care of now, and that includes your brother, Michael.'

Officer Pembrooke's words were the formula to get David on the right track. The words, 'you have a family' rung in David's ears and filled his heart with pride, and he knew this was his time to step up. This was his time to be the real man of the house, to be the leaning tower of support for all of them. This wasn't a time to be scared. With that he stood up and began to slowly pace the kitchen.

'Officer, you are right, I was being so selfish.'

Officer Pembrooke started to fan his hands as if to say, 'Think nothing of it.' He was a modest man, but he was good at his job.

'David, you were not being selfish. You have experienced a horrendous ordeal this evening, but like I say, for now, you need to take care of your family and deal with your trauma later.'

David continued to pace the kitchen, chest puffed out with his new responsibility. 'Ok, Martha, let's get ready and get out of here. I suppose you had better get Willy out of bed. We don't need to tell him, do we? Just make something up? A surprise sleepover or something?'

Martha had already gone upstairs and was packing her bag before David had even finished his train of thought.

CHAPTER TWENTY-TWO

David, Martha, and Willy arrived at Peter and Mae's and gave them the rundown of what had happened. The two women took the boys and baby Anna up to bed whilst David gave Peter the detailed version of the evening.

'Stay with us as long as you need to,' Mae said.

Martha knew she wouldn't have had it any other way. If it wasn't for the circumstances which had got them to being there that evening, Martha was quite glad to be under their roof again. She liked it there. It was odd, she never had felt quite at home whilst she was there, but now that she was at David's, Mae's house seemed like home.

'That's very kind of you, Mae, thank you. I would love to stay longer, truth be told, but David will be keen to get back. You know what he's like. He's not ungrateful, it's just that he is quite a private man.'

Mae knew exactly what Martha was saying, and they both hoped that the visit would last a little longer than one night. Mae would be happy if they stayed all Christmas. It's not as if they didn't have the space. Once the children were in bed, the two women headed back downstairs where Peter had already got the brandy out, and he poured them one each as they came into the room. He topped up David's, although it looked like David hadn't touched his first one.

'Get that down you, David. It'll help you sleep.'

Peter pushed David's glass closer to him. David picked it up hesitantly and sniffed it. He grimaced at the smell but knew it would help to knock him out, so he drank it down in one go. He flinched his whole body and screwed his face up as if he had just eaten a lemon. He never was much of a drinker. Peter passed his cigarettes around and they all took one each. Martha thought this was just like old times, apart from David being there.

'How are you holding up, Martha darling?'

Peter looked at her intently and seemed genuinely concerned. He was good at this kind of stuff, always had been. She reminded herself of that and told herself not to get sucked in.

'I'm ok, thanks, Peter. I'm shocked, but I am ok. I didn't see it. I mean, when I say 'it,' I mean the girl.'

Martha looked down and scoured the table for some relief. She felt guilty for saying 'it' when she had meant the poor girl.

'We know what you meant, Martha, don't worry. The 'it' refers to the scene. You didn't see the scene that David stumbled across. Don't beat yourself up. You've all been through the mill tonight. It's not nice for anyone involved, and it means that awful, horrible, sick bastard is on the prowl again. Look, I am sure Mae has already said it, but you are all welcome to stay here for as long as you like, ok?'

With that, he reached his hand out across the table and placed his hand on top of Martha's and rubbed it with his thumb. He looked her in the eyes, and once again her stomach fluttered. David didn't like what he was seeing. He wished he had Peter's confidence, Peter's charm. He always seemed to know what to say to women. Martha could feel herself blushing and pulled her hand away.

'Thank you, Peter, that means a lot. Mae did say the same. You are both very kind, and we are lucky to have you as friends, aren't we?'

She put her hand over to David and gestured for him to give her his.

'Yes. Very lucky.' David smiled awkwardly, almost through gritted teeth. 'But I was hoping to have us all at home over Christmas, apart from having Christmas Day here of course, and hopefully, that can still happen. We will just have to wait and see what the police say, I suppose.'

He picked up his glass and realised it was empty, but Peter was on hand immediately to pour him some more.

Over a couple of hours, the four adults smoked and drank until David and Martha were numb enough to go to bed. David was the first one to suggest it. The brandy had gone to his head, and he needed to lie down. Although he might regret it in the morning, Martha was glad that he would at least be able to sleep tonight. She knew she would probably struggle to get to sleep, and she didn't need David awake as well. She wanted to be left alone with her insomnia that today's events would inevitably bring. They all said their goodnights. Martha offered to help clear up, but Mae and

Peter insisted that they go and get their heads down.

'There will be plenty of opportunity to help clear up in a couple of days when the old fat boy has delivered all his gifts.'

They all managed a slight chuckle, and David and Martha headed upstairs. As expected, David went out like a light. Martha lay there with her small bedside lamp on, softly lighting up the room. She looked around the room, again and again, remembering what it was like being there before. It wasn't that long since she had left, but so much had happened that it seemed like a long time ago. Everything was slightly hazy. She had had quite a bit to drink. One more drink and the room would be spinning. She closed her eyes but opened them immediately. As soon as she closed them her mind started creating images of the girl in the barn.

She knew the details now of what had happened to the girl, but she hadn't seen it, and nor did she want to. She tried to close her eyes again, but all she could see was a lifeless naked body slumped across some hay bales with blood everywhere. She sat up in bed. David was out for the count. It was no good; she wasn't going to be able to drift off yet. She turned and let her legs out of the bed and sat on the edge. She tried to take some deep breaths and get some clarity. That didn't work. Her drunken, foggy, and chaotic mind would not rest. She decided to get up and go and get a glass of tap water. As quietly as she could, she crept down the stairs trying not to disturb Peter and Mae and the children. She tiptoed from the bottom of the stairs into the kitchen and flicked the light switch.

'Can't sleep?'

Martha jumped, not expecting Peter to still be up.

'No, I can't. Sorry, I didn't realise you were still up. I was just going to get a glass of water.'

She poured herself a glass of water and stared straight ahead into the dark night outside through the window. Peter was watching her, and she could feel it. His eyes were like hot pokers digging into her back. She didn't move. Peter was staring. He was looking her up and down and admiring every inch of her body. She had fascinated him since the day she moved in. He hadn't noticed her prior to that, but now he couldn't help but be fixated by her whenever she was around. He had drunk quite a bit of brandy tonight.

He was tempted to go for it. Would she let him, he wondered? Would she scream and wake the house up? Or does she want him just as much as his curiosity wanted her? He thought he hadn't had enough alcohol to eliminate the risk, but he had just enough in him to make his move. He gulped down the last of his drink in his glass and put it down on the table, pushing it across so that it stopped in the middle. He sat there for a moment and continued to stare at her. His heart began to beat harder. He noticed she wasn't drinking her water anymore. She had finished it and was just standing there as if she was waiting for him, he thought. He stood and began to slowly walk over to her.

They didn't know it, but both of their hearts were racing in unison. She knew he was coming for her. She knew what was about to happen, and yet she didn't do anything. She didn't know if she wanted it or not. All she knew is that she was just going to see what was going to happen. He stood right behind her and pulled her hair away from her neck. He began softly kissing her neck. Her knees went weak as he got hard. He kissed her more and put his hands on her breasts. She wasn't stopping him yet, and he was eager to see how far this could go.

He turned her around to face him, and they began to kiss frantically. He pulled her nightgown up and put his hands on her naked breasts. Her nipples became erect as soon as he touched her. Inside his trousers, he was throbbing. In his mind, he begged her to let him have her. He put his hand between her legs, and still, she didn't stop him. She moved her legs apart to allow him in. He knew this time that he was going to take her. He was going to make love to her so hard, he could almost climax now as the desire was so strong. He pulled his braces off his shoulders and begun undoing his trousers as quickly as he could. They kissed messily, lips and tongues everywhere. He dropped his trousers and revealed his very large, erect penis, and her stomach flipped. The pair of them were locked in a trance of lust that neither of them could deny in that moment. They weren't thinking straight, and they weren't thinking of anyone else or anything else. All they knew was what they were doing right now.

Peter picked Martha up and entered her. He was huge. She hadn't experienced a man like that before. The rush of euphoria flooded both of their bodies; it was running through their veins like a hit of sex injected with a needle. He carried her to the wall, her legs wrapped around his waist and he still inside her. Once against the wall, he began thrusting. She felt totally different to Mae. She was less confident, and she was shy, and that turned him on even more. The pair were silent, and the passion was raw. She had pulled her nightgown off, and he had his mouth all over her breasts. He thrust in and out with pace, and she clenched her hands on his shoulders, biting her lip, not daring to let out a sound. Both Peter and Martha became sweaty at the same time, their breathing patterns matching, and his thrusts becoming closer together.

She was captivated by how strong he was. She never thought he would be like this, but she wanted more of him, as much as she could take. She could feel her thighs tighten around his waist, the grip of her hands became stronger, her stomach became taut, and her body began to shake. He began thrusting harder and harder; he was so big she almost asked him to stop, but just before she did, she climaxed, and then so did he. The pair embraced and clenched with ferociousness. He slowed down his thrusts and let out a little sigh with each one until eventually coming to a complete stop. He continued to hold her, and she noticed how tightly he did so. He carried her away from the wall and lay her down on the floor where he lay with her. The pair stayed there for the next ten minutes or so in silence. A silence that had never been louder.

CHAPTER TWENTY-THREE

Martha woke up with a jolt. She had an arm wrapped around her and a body that was spooning hers. She carefully opened one eye to take in her surroundings without making it known she was awake. She was in bed. She was in her bed in her room in Peter and Mae's house. Suddenly the fear-like guilt ripped through her as if she had just stepped out in front of a bus. The panic rushed through her like cold blood in her veins. She felt sick. She felt dirty. She wanted to cry. What on earth had she done? Why couldn't she resist Peter after a few drinks?

It was the alcohol. She wouldn't have done it otherwise. She tormented herself repeatedly, going over the events of last night, again and again, wishing she could turn the clock back. David's arm pulled her closer to him, and she wanted to cry, her eyes filling up and bottom lip quivering. He was still half-asleep. How would she ever be able to look at him again? She felt his erection push against her. He didn't ask; he never had since they began dating. He was a gentleman and always waited for a sign that she wanted him. To her surprise, she wanted David right now. She didn't want Peter to be the last man that had touched her. She desperately wanted to make passionate love with David and eradicate any wrongdoing from last night. She couldn't engage in sex with him now; she hadn't cleaned herself since last night. There was no way she could let David near her when she was still carrying Peter within her. Every time she thought of him, or his name, she felt sick to her stomach. She knew she would just have to ride this out. No one could know. She would take this secret to her grave. It was done now. David and Mae wouldn't find out.

Mae. Poor, poor Mae. She began tormenting herself again. Would she ever be the same again? Could she put this behind her, or had she just ruined her and Willy's best chance for a decent future? She decided to go ahead with her idea of sleeping with David, which she herself found bizarre. Just the notion that she wanted to left her perplexed, but she saw it as the next step. It is not the reaction she thought she would have had to this kind of situation, but it was what she thought she needed to happen next. Once she had felt David's touch and received him, then he would be the last man to have had her, and she felt this was the first step in her recovery from what she had done. She gently peeled back the bed covers trying not to disturb her innocent, doting lover.

David did stir, however, and he tried to pull her back into bed. He put his arm around her and brought her face down to face his and gave her a kiss. She gave him a quick peck and pulled away abruptly.

'Give me two seconds, I just want to freshen up. Don't move, I'm coming back in.' She smiled at him, trying to convince them both that everything was fine and perfectly normal.

'You are a silly girl. You don't need to freshen up. You always look beautiful.'

'It just makes me feel better. I won't be long.' She crept out of the room, straight into the bathroom, locked the door, and sank to the floor with her head in her hands.

Once freshened up, Martha crept back into bed. She realised that she wasn't at all in the mood to be intimate with David after all, but she had started it now. He was expecting her. What could have happened for her to change her mind so quickly? Perhaps she just needed to get out of the bed quickly, and now that she was back in it, she realised that this didn't seem normal, but she had offered it to David now, and so she would have to go through with it. She felt sick again, she felt more ashamed by the minute, but she knew what she had to do.

Eventually, all four of the adults and baby Anna were downstairs and around the table again. The boys were playing and had been told to be good. Otherwise, Santa Claus wouldn't visit them. They were behaving impeccably as a result of said threat. Mae had once again excelled herself with a more than generous spread for everyone's breakfast. There were no signs of poverty in this house.

'Tuck in, you two, you probably need a good breakfast in you.'

'Martha and I can't thank you enough for your hospitality. You're good people. After breakfast, I will head over to the police station and see if we can return to the farm today. We don't want to put you out.'

Peter and Martha didn't say a word.

'Well, as I have said to Martha already, and

to you, there is no rush. We can manage for a few days if you need it, but we understand you want to get back to your own bed, don't we, Peter?' Mae began to chuckle.

'What's funny?' Martha asked gingerly.

'Peter must have had more brandy than his usual amount last night because he fell asleep down here. I was laughing as I said David must want his own bed and Peter is in his own home and isn't even using his. He hasn't done that for years.' She continued to chuckle, and Martha offered a small, false and nervous chortle.

'Sorry, doll, I must've drifted off. I don't know what got into me.' Peter's eyes met Martha's, and they both looked away.

The four of them tucked into their breakfast with Mae giving Anna little scraps of hers. Martha wasn't sure if anyone had noticed, but they ate in silence for the duration.

As soon as breakfast was over, David made his excuses and headed for the police station. He was keen to go home regardless of how unsettling it could be for everyone, but little did he know Martha was very keen to return there as quickly as possible. Martha offered to clear up whilst Mae got baby Anna ready for the day. Well, get her ready for the second time of the day after the mess she had made with her breakfast. Peter loitered in the kitchen waiting for the coast to be completely clear.

'What the hell do you think you are playing at?'

Peter startled Martha at the sink. She looked genuinely scared of him; he was very much in her personal space.

'What? What do you mean?' She spoke in a hushed tone.

'Do you think I don't know why you two were late coming down this morning? How could you after last night?' Peter looked over his shoulder, checking once again that the coast was clear. 'How could you? Did last night mean nothing to you? I'm gobsmacked. I risked my marriage and you risked your, whatever it is you have going on with David, and a friendship with Mae, and now you are back in bed with him? I didn't have you down as that kind of girl, Martha. If I had known that was how it was going to be, I wouldn't have risked it. Not for a slut.'

He wandered out to the back door and went and smoked in the garden. Martha was shaking. Tears began to fill her eyes, and a tidal wave of emotion was sitting in the middle of her throat ready to pour out at any minute. She had to control it. She was trapped, frozen to the spot.

She couldn't let Mae see her like this, and she did not want to give Peter any gratification for his insults towards her.

She ran her hands under cold water. This seemed to help her get her emotions under control. Her despair quickly became anger, as she watched him through the window. *This man drives me crazy,* she thought. She looked over at the wall where they had been less than twelve hours ago. She looked at the floor where they lay after. She looked back out of the window and observed him standing there, puffing away on his cigarette nonchalantly. She slapped down the tea towel on the side and decided that enough was enough. *How dare he treat me like this.* she thought. He had no idea what he was doing to her, but she was about to tell him. She marched out to the back garden and stood straight in front of him. She snatched his cigarette from him and took three deep inhalations. With her hand on her hip and the other hand holding the cigarette away from her, she told Peter exactly what she thought.

'How *dare* you speak to me in that way. You listen to me, Peter, and you listen good. You started all of this. You picked on me when I was vulnerable and lonely. You chose every moment. You made sure that I had just enough alcohol in my body to consider you and me together. Yes, I could have said no, and that's what I bloody well should have done. I wish I had never laid eyes on you. You make me sick. You disgust me. I don't steal people's husbands. That is not me. That has *never* been me. But you saw how weak I was and you pounced. Mae is my best friend, and because of you, I have committed the worst crime any friend can do to another. But do you know what? I disgust myself more. I am disgusted that I was too weak. Disgusted that I inflated your already oversized ego. But worse than all of that, I am disgusted that I actually enjoyed it. Disgusted that I couldn't get enough of you and that I want more of you. I hate myself for loving what you can do with your fingers, your tongue, and your penis. I've never known anything like it, but for the record, what is the point in good sex if the personality is dire? You've got nothing upstairs; it's all in your trousers. That's your problem, you're inadequate compared to most men, so doing that, doing this, makes you feel better. What's the matter, Peter, did Mummy never tell you she loved you? If I want to sleep with my partner the morning after we made a terrible mistake, then that is *my* choice. I've only been with three men. Johnny, David, and you. I dread to think how many pathetic women like me you have lured into the bedroom. You don't deserve Mae, and you don't deserve me. One more thing, if I am a slut as you said, what the hell does that make you?'

She took one long, animated suck on the cigarette whilst staring at him, and then threw it to the ground and stamped it out whilst maintaining eye contact the whole time. As she walked off and made her way back into the house, she didn't see Peter smile.

Martha stomped her way up the stairs in a state of exhilaration, frustration, triumph, nausea, and adrenalin. She decided to pack up the things that her and David had brought with them the night before and get ready to go back to the farm. Whatever nightmares were waiting for her there were better than living in one here, she thought. She began picking up their clothes and was caught stuffing them hastily into a holdall by Mae.

'Martha, darling, what are you doing? Surely you can't be thinking of going back there? You won't get any sleep. Stay with us for Christmas.'

Martha looked around over her shoulder to see Mae had her puppy dog eyes on. She knew that Mae loved having her around. Peter didn't offer her anything emotionally, but that's what she got from her friend Martha. If only she knew that Martha was now ten times worse than Peter. Martha became morose and began to sob.

'Oh, hang on, let me put Anna down in her cot. Don't cry.'

Mae quickly put Anna in her cot in their bedroom and went in to Martha's rescue. She knelt next to her and rubbed her shoulders. 'You can't go back there tonight. Look at you. You're scared stiff. Do you want me to speak to David for you?'

Martha shook her head.

'There is no point putting it off; we have to go back sometime. We might as well go today. You know, rip the plaster off.'

She lifted her blouse and used it to dry her eyes and then tucked the wet bit back into her skirt. Mae exhaled loudly.

'Look, just think about it. I've said my piece, but I think it's too soon. Come on, let's go and have tea. Tea solves everything, isn't that what they say? Doubt it solves a murder, but still, it will make us feel better. I think Peter is down there. I'll tell the useless sod to make it for us.'

Mae pecked Martha on the head and left the room.

'Don't stay up here too long, I want to see you downstairs in two minutes.'

She closed the door, and as she walked away;

she didn't see Martha get up on to the bed and scream and sob into the pillows.

When Mae went downstairs, David had just arrived back from the police station. Peter had begun making the teas. He hated it when Mae bossed him around in front of other people, but he'd had enough conflict with women already this morning, so decided to do as he was told, aware that at least one of the two women would be happy with him.

'Where's my girl?' David asked.

'She's upstairs packing... and crying.'

Peter's ears pricked up, but he pretended not to listen.

'What? Why? I'll go and see her.'

'I'd leave it, David. I am not supposed to say anything. She's packing because she thinks you should all go back sooner rather than later, and I think she's crying because she's terrified. Just give her a minute. I told her to take a minute and come down for tea.'

David sat down at the table and took his cap off. He rubbed his face, put his elbows on the table, and held his head in his hands.

'Well, the police don't want us to go back anyway. They have asked if we can stay away for a couple of days whilst they keep an eye on the place and collect clues. I don't know; I am keen to get back. I feel like I have been pushed out of my home by another man. I feel like I have failed Martha and Willy. I feel helpless. Useless. Worthless.'

Mae gave David a sympathetic look whilst Peter patted David on the shoulders and said,

'You're not any of those. You've done the right thing. You took your family somewhere safe. You are protecting them. The right thing would be to stay here, as the police said. You were going to be here for Christmas Day anyway, so what harm does staying a couple of days extra do? You will have peace of mind, and you have us for company. If you go back to that farm now, all you will have to talk to each other about is what happened the other night. Why not go back with stories of the Christmas you had here, with us.'

David nodded and sighed.

'You're right. Plus, I suppose I am only thinking of myself. She loves spending time with you, so that will make her happy if we are all together. As long as you are sure.'

'Wouldn't have it any other way,' Peter said, feeling pleased with himself.

David went upstairs to go and check on his Martha and try and soothe her worried mind.

Meanwhile, Mae was full of admiration for her husband.

'You really do surprise me sometimes, do you know that, Peter Wilkins?' Mae looked like a giddy teenager at her husband.

'Really? How so?' He walked around behind his wife and draped his arms over her shoulders, as she sat at the table.

'I know how you like your space. I know you don't *really* like David, and here you are offering your home to them for the next couple of nights. I think that's really nice of you, and it makes me love you even more.'

She held his hands and placed them on her heart.

'We have to support them. They don't have anywhere else to go. I don't mind them being here. In fact, I wouldn't have it any other way. I can handle, David and as for his brother, well, it's like he's not even here. Has he emerged from his room?'

'He came down for a drink earlier. I told him to make himself at home. I think he is very shy. We will have to get David to coax him out, even if it is just to sit and have dinner with us.'

Peter continued to stand behind his wife, swaying gently as she held his arms around her, believing her husband was a true gentleman.

CHAPTER TWENTY-FOUR

The house was filled with an abundance of festivity and jubilance. The children's laughter was a cacophony of noise that ricocheted off the walls. The smell of turkey and potatoes wafted through the house like a comforting blanket of happy memories. It rained down memories of Christmases past, before the war. There was to be no 'murkey' in Peter's house. He had money, and he had connections, so today they would be eating like royalty. Not a scrap of hardship in sight. Not a crumb of poverty to be seen. Not in this house. The wireless was on louder than normal, and everyone bopped around each other whilst getting the house prepared for a feast to be remembered. A day that would go down in history. The first Christmas after the war. Bing Crosby, Billie Holiday, and songs by Ella Fitzgerald played and brought animation to what were normal tasks. The music brought life to the laying of the table, the chopping of the veg. The music that was reverberating through the house was bringing the morning to life. Frank Sinatra's 'The House I Live In' came on, and Peter stopped what he was doing and took his wife for a dance around the table. They laughed and, to everyone else, seemed in love.

Martha had begged David the previous afternoon to take them all back to the farm. He hadn't seen it as pleading. He thought she was saying it for his benefit, and he thought she was being selfless yet again. He loved her for that. He thanked her for it at the time and he pulled her close. 'No, no the farm can wait. I know you like being with your friends, so we will stay here. I can manage, but thank you for trying to please me.'

Martha had nothing to say. She sobbed into his arms, and he believed she was distraught about the murder. He stroked her head, and he promised to take care of her. He promised that he would never let any harm come to her. He told her he knew how lucky he was and that she deserved more than he had to offer, but that he would give her everything he had. Martha sobbed harder and harder but said no more. She decided this was her punishment. She believed that her God wanted to torment her, to make sure she was never as stupid or as weak again.

———

David's brother, Michael, had become a godsend. He was better with the boys than anyone else. No one wanted to exploit him, but he was a welcome break. It worked well for all of them, as he was painfully shy. He got to come out of his room without being intimidated by Peter and without feeling sheepish around the women. He loved children; they were innocent and non-judgemental. He was comfortable in their company and rarely relaxed in adult company. Willy and Charlie were happy, and Michael was happy. Peter was happy, and Mae was happy. David surprised himself by enjoying the day more than he thought he would. It dawned on him that being the guest on Christmas Day was a treat compared to being the host, just as Martha had told him. They wouldn't let him lift a finger. The women did most of the work whilst Peter began to drink early and got out his cigars for special occasions. Most of all, David was happy because his girl was happy. She was comfortable here, and he felt that he had given her the greatest gift of all, and by doing so felt that he had received the greatest gift of all.

Martha was in a silent hell. She had gotten up that morning and decided to carry out the day with conviction. She decided to wear her best fake smile and be the most gregarious soul in the house. This was the pact that she made with God, in exchange for a solemn vow that she would never be deceitful or weak again. She had been brought up in a religious family but had let this side of her life drop as she got older. She didn't know what she believed. She believed in something. Even if it wasn't God as such, she believed there were forces working for the greater good, but they watched everything you did, and your luck depended on your behaviour. That's what fate was all about, she reckoned. Sometimes, she would do something that she considered frowned upon, but Martha's 'frowned upon' was mildly mediocre compared to the everyday bad man. Martha considered not opening a door for someone, or being too busy, or not paying a compliment when she had thought it, as a bad act.

She would churn it over in her head, kicking herself that she had an opportunity to do a good deed or carry out an act of kindness and she didn't do it. When she was aware of these kind of teachings, she would feel that God, or whoever it was that was looking over her, would sweep down almost immediately to remind her she should have been kinder. It would be a small reminder like breaking a teacup or spilling something down a freshly worn outfit. A small penance for a missed opportunity of good. On Christmas Eve, she silently prayed to God for forgiveness for her adultery with Peter. David had lain asleep next to her as she held her hands in a praying position to her face and silently prayed, begged, pleaded for forgiveness. She explained that she felt lost and that she didn't know who she was anymore, but that it was clearer to her now more than ever before where she wanted to be, and that if God could protect her, she would never let him down again. In her mind, she believed she had his forgiveness that night, as long as she turned it around the following day and became the partner that David desired and the friend that Mae deserved.

Christmas Day 1945 went by without a glitch. There was food aplenty. The children played with a multitude of gifts. Some were hand-me-downs from Peter, David, and Michael who had all taken the time to find old possessions that they no longer needed, that they felt the boys would feel privileged to have, but David and Michael had been the stars of the day having handcrafted toys for the children. Michael was particularly good at woodwork and had made a dolls house for baby Anna. She was far too young to enjoy it now, but ever since he knew they would be spending Christmas Day there, he had gone straight to work, having always wanted a little sister. The house was a piece of perfection and a work of art. Everyone was taken by surprise when he unveiled it. They had all thought he had been hiding up in his room all this time, when what he had been doing was making a handcrafted masterpiece that would undoubtedly become a family heirloom for a child he didn't really know. He and his brother had hearts of gold. David thought he was going to win everyone over with his handmade plough and tractor he had made for the boys. He looked extremely pleased with himself, and so he should, as they were also very good and very thoughtful, but Michael's *pièce de résistance* was the gift that stole the show.

Martha had decided that after today she would make no effort to return to this house again. She decided that she would invite Mae over; it would make sense for the boys to play together. She would avoid all opportunities to be near Peter again. If she was invited, she would make an excuse that she either had something to do or that she was needed back at the farm. She knew she couldn't avoid the house completely, but she wanted to make sure that she would not be left alone with Peter anytime soon. What surprised her was that she managed to handle the day better than she expected. She had gotten off to a wobbly and nervous start, but once she realised that no one could detect her awkward behaviour or maybe, more to the point, no one had noticed, she began to relax. How relaxed she became disappointed her. She was knee-deep in a path of self-discovery that she had been thrown on involuntarily and was racing along it at the speed of lightning. She was scared but thrilled. She was spooked but exhilarated.

The day passed with high jinks and merriment. They ate more than they needed. They laughed more than expected. They drank more than required. The day was nothing short of a huge success. By the end, Michael surprised everyone yet again by coming out of his shell after a few drinks and whisking Mae off her feet for a jive dance. Everyone cheered him on, but they wouldn't realise what a wonderful sight it was until the morning due to the excess alcohol and camaraderie. That's if they remembered it.

The boys went out like a light having revelled in the splendour of the day. They were blessed with the love and gifts that had been given to them, and surprisingly, they seemed to know it.

The adults stayed up and continued to nibble on leftovers but the music was turned down and the thronging atmosphere drew to a close as a post-Christmas Day lull crept in. Eventually, they all began to clear up and made their way up to bed. It wasn't as late a night as normal, but every single one of them had overeaten, over-drank and over-enjoyed themselves and were more than ready for rest.

Martha and David got into bed, and he languidly tried to pull her in with his arm that was like a dead weight. He was a few short breaths away from the land of sweet, sweet slumber. A place that seemed dreamier than an actual dream to her right now. She gave him a peck and turned rigidly. He wanted to spoon her, and she felt like she was rolling around in a bed of stinging nettles, but she reluctantly allowed him to latch his body on to hers. Now that all the commotion was over and the house was silent, Martha became inhibited. Being alone with her thoughts was not where she wanted to be, and Martha was many things, most of all, self-aware.

She lay there telling herself that each night that passed would become easier, and especially once they were home, she could get things back to normal. She loved David, but she had realised over the last couple of days that she was not *in* love with David. She loved him very much, and she knew how good he was for her. She knew how safe she was with him and she knew that it didn't matter whether she was in love with him or not, she loved him enough just to be with him. He didn't give her the burning, passionate desire that resided within her, but what he did give her was worth so much more. What she had come to realise was that if something is burning, it will eventually go out. That wasn't what she wanted or needed. She wanted longevity. She wanted understanding, and right now she wanted an all-forgiving love. Or at least she wanted forgiveness but she knew that would be asking a lot of anyone let alone God or David.

She began to ponder whether she should tell David what she had done and beg for his forgiveness. The thought only lasted a second. David was many things, but he would not forgive

341

betrayal. His moral fibre was strong. After a day of overindulgence, she was parched and hadn't taken any water up to bed. She listened out for noise of life coming from the other rooms. She had been in such deep thought she hadn't actually heard the snoring sound resonating through the walls from Peter and Mae's room and hadn't noticed David's breathing, which by now resembled a deep-sea diver. With the house in a food and drink coma, she thought she would be safe to tiptoe downstairs and get a glass of water before quickly returning to bed.

As she drank her water by the sink, she heard life upstairs. She should have known he couldn't resist. Did she know, and is that why she went? She didn't know the answers to her own questions. There was no way she was going to dart and have an awkward passing on the stairs. She would wait for him to come in and then she would tell him clearly that she wasn't interested. At last, she felt like she had a good idea. *This would be perfect*, she thought. Tell him once and for all that enough is enough and leave the room before he can speak. Tomorrow life will go back to normal; we will return to the farm and get away from this madness. She assured herself that she was now in control. The footsteps came in the room, and she finished her water.

Without turning, she said, 'I should've known you would come. Why can't you just leave me alone and keep your grubby little mitts to yourself.' She turned hastily and could just about see a figure in white in the darkness of the room. She went upstairs as quickly but as quietly as she could. As she got to the top of the stairs, Peter was standing in his doorway. Martha froze with fear for a moment and looked at Peter. She pushed past him and went into her room to immediately see David lying in bed, still sound asleep. It wasn't Peter in the kitchen, it had been Mae.

CHAPTER TWENTY-FIVE

'Sir. Sir, I am glad I have caught you. Are you heading out?'

Officer Pembrooke was normally a busy man, but crime had, thankfully, been quiet for him recently, and he was on his way to interview someone who had reported vandalism in their garden.

'Well, I was just on my way out, PC Jones, but I can spare you a few minutes. Always happy to help you youngsters.' Just because he wasn't that busy, he didn't think the kid needed to know that.

'I've had a gentleman come in who lives on Everest Road. He didn't say the number.'

'Right...'

'Well, he claims to have seen a tall, dark figure inside number 28.'

'And...'

'Well, I thought you might want to know that. I thought she lived there on her own?'

'Who? What are you talking about, Jones, you've lost me.'

He hung his thumbs into his jacket belt hoops and leaned back as if extending out his slightly rotund belly. PC Jones looked at his senior, slightly baffled, and then looked around to see if anyone was in earshot. The coast was clear, so he leaned in and whispered;

'That nutter that's on the loose. His mum's house. His mum lives at number 28, doesn't she?'

The penny had dropped with a thud and a clink in Pembrooke's head as the realisation dawned on him.

'Very good. Of course, I knew what you were referring to; I was teaching you the benefits of not... beating around the bush as it were. I was heading over there now, actually.'

PC Jones didn't entirely believe Officer Pembrooke but wasn't too bothered. He could understand his sense of pride.

'Can I come with you?'

Jones was looking at Pembrooke like a dog that had rolled, begged, offered his paw, and was now sitting obediently waiting for his reward.

Officer Pembrooke let out a deep sigh as if to indicate that he was unsure that this was a good idea, and then he agreed, reluctantly. What PC Jones didn't know was that Officer Pembrooke was glad he was coming, as he wasn't sure now what he was going to walk into today. The vandalised garden was to be put on the back burner whilst he investigated real crime.

The two policemen arrived at Everest Road and decided to walk up and down the street first before making any contact with Evelyn. PC Jones, who told Officer Pembrooke on the way that he could call him James, filled Pembrooke in on what he knew so far and what he suspected could be happening. It turned out that, although James hadn't been working on the case, he had taken a particular interest in it, as most people in their village had been affected by it either directly or not far off. It was a small village and most of the residents knew each other. All the men in the village wanted the killer to be gone whether it was the result of an arrest or a vigilante. Most would prefer the latter, probably.

When the neighbour of Evelyn had arrived at the police station to say that he thought something suspicious was going on, he wanted to remain anonymous, but James was more than happy to collect the details with the hope of being allowed to help on the case. Pembrooke listened intently, mainly because he was surprised by how much this James lad seemed to know. He told James that he had done his homework and that none of what he was telling him was news to him, and of course, he was up to date with it all. He had learned a few minor details from James, and he had gained some insight into potential theories, but he did not reciprocate on the offer of first name terms.

As they slowly walked the pavements of Everest Road, James noticed the neighbour that had come forward anonymously peering out from behind a net curtain, directly opposite Evelyn's house. It occurred to James that this man was much more than a concerned neighbour, he was an extremely reliable witness and probably knew more than he had said. He had come across as a bit of an oddball when he came in, but James had already learned early on in his short career that the slightly odd, nervous, stay-at-home-and-peer-out-of-the-window-types were one of the police force's most valuable assets. As soon as they made eye contact, the man quickly disappeared behind the heavily smoked-stained, yellow, net curtain. James kept quiet about having seen him. He knew he could use that card later, plus he already suspected that Pembrooke knew less than he said he did. He didn't want to dent the man's pride any further than he already had. After all, he didn't say that he could call him by his first name. *Slowly, slowly, catchy monkey*, he thought to himself. He wanted to work his way up the ladder, and upsetting his senior was not the way to go about that.

After walking the length of the street, Pembrooke announced that they would now go and call on Evelyn and see what they could find out. James had said it had been a useful walk, as he had spotted three alleyways between the terraced houses and had noticed that most of the gardens were open and that he suspected a lot of the back gardens were shared. Pembrooke looked at him, baffled by his interest in such minuscule things. James could see that his comments had gone over his head.

'I was looking to see how easy it is to get in and out of this street. You know, if this Simon character is being put up by his old dear, how easy is it for him to come and go incognito, like? From what I can see, he can easily hop across gardens and take back alleys, so he wouldn't need to be seen out on the main street. If he is coming and going in the night, it is likely no one even knows he is living on this street.'

Officer Pembrooke felt all the blood rush to his cheeks and his head went light as if he had stood up too quickly. He hadn't even given any of that any thought. The more time he spent with his new protégé, it dawned on him how rusty and out of practice he was. Nothing serious had ever happened in their village; he had never had to put much of his training into practice. Now, here he was up against a fresh, young whippersnapper who was revelling in the severity of the situation, getting to put good use to all the training he had received. Pembrooke felt a pang of envy but also a pang of pride. He needed to encourage this lad, he thought. All it can take is one negative influence or experience to have your dream crushed. Pembrooke wanted this lad to go on and be the best version of himself he could be, and so he decided from this day on he would take him under his wing and give him the support and encouragement he needed.

As they approached Evelyn's door, James went to go around the back of the house through the communal alleyway.

'What are you doing now, kid?' Pembrooke looked bemused at his new student.

'I'm going around the back. You knock the front door; I'll scale the back in case he tries to escape,' James was whispering.

Officer Pembrooke was embarrassed, and proud yet again. He expected that James may be taking it all a bit too seriously but laughed on the inside at his gusto.

Officer Pembrooke peered through the living room window. It was hard to see anything through the net curtains, but he thought he could make out Evelyn sitting in her chair with her back to the window. He walked to the door and knocked three times.

What he hadn't seen was Simon kneeling in front of Evelyn, with one hand around her throat and the other covering her mouth. She had a black eye and a cut on her cheek. Officer Pembrooke knocked three more times. Simon stayed still and silent. He could feel the hot breath of Evelyn on his hand, but he didn't look at her. He was looking at the door the whole time.

Pembrooke was sure he had seen her in her chair. Perhaps she was asleep, he thought. He went back to the window, which he tapped lightly. There was no movement from the chair.

She must be asleep, he thought, hopefully not dead. He decided to come back and check on her later or tomorrow. He reassured himself that she must be asleep, but it wasn't sitting right with him. He felt odd and didn't know why. In the end, he told himself it was just worry. He didn't like to think of the elderly being alone and especially in the winter. That's when a lot of them seemed to pass. He hoped she wasn't dead. James hadn't come back around, so Pembrooke made his way to the back of the house to tell him they would come back later. As he reached the back of the house James was nowhere to be seen, then he saw that the back door was ajar. Officer Pembrooke cautiously entered the house; he felt very unsettled but decided that if his junior was in there, he had to go in as well. He prayed that they wouldn't discover Evelyn's body rooted to her chair with deep-set rigor mortis.

Once Pembrooke was in the kitchen; he realised he could hear a deep voice. He tried to listen, but the pounding of his heart in his ears was making it hard for him to hear.

'You are supposed to protect me, you old witch. You're my mother.'

The sound of heavy footsteps pacing followed.

Thump, thump... thump, thump.

Officer Pembrooke wondered if he was going to have a heart attack. He was frozen with fear mixed with panic and a tiny dose of adrenalin. He needed to find James, and he needed to find him quickly.

'They'll be back, you know. They'll be back, and then they'll find out you've been keeping me here, and you will go to prison. Oh, they won't be kind to you.'

He laughed which sent a shiver down Pembrooke's spine. Pembrooke shifted slowly through the kitchen and picked up a long knife on the way. He just hoped that he didn't have to use it. He felt trapped in a horrendous nightmare that he wasn't prepared for. He had only ever dealt with petty crime. He was completely out of sorts. As he got out of the kitchen and into the hallway, he saw James with his back against the wall, who then gestured to him to be quiet. James saw that Pembrooke had the knife and gave him the thumbs up. He motioned towards his truncheon and mouthed 'after three' with a nod. Pembrooke waved his hands in a surrender way. He was not ready for this.

He knew that they needed to take swift action, but he had never been so terrified in all his life. He looked at James, and he knew it was happening. He had to follow James' lead and pray that this would go smoothly.

James tiptoed to the living room door and

slowly poked his head around. He saw Evelyn in her chair. She looked horrendous. Her hands were bound with bailing twine, her face was black and blue, and she was so thin. She looked very frail, like she was going to die. Her hair was a mess, and she had what looked like soup all over her top. Soup that was days old. James felt sick but empowered. He raised his truncheon above his head, and Evelyn looked at him and raised her eyebrows.

Simon knew instantly someone was there. James hit him with every bit of strength he could muster. As the truncheon cracked across Simon's head, his eyebrow split and a bead of blood appeared which then began to trickle. Simon launched into James. He picked him up by the scruff of his neck with what seemed like supernatural strength and slammed him against the wall, and then headbutted him, knocking him out. He then threw him to the floor with an almighty force. Officer Pembrooke was right behind him and was crushed mentally when he saw what had happened to Evelyn. If it wasn't for the same house, he wouldn't have known it was her. He drew the knife and hesitantly thrust it forward at Simon. Simon completely dodged the move and immediately took the knife right out of his hand in one easy swipe. Officer

Pembrooke stood there, ashen-looking and completely petrified. He begged Simon, who was cowering over him.

'Please. Please, don't do this. I have a wife and children, please.'

He cried as he pleaded with and for his life.

Simon leaned forward and penetrated the blade deep into Officer Pembrooke's neck. Pembrooke gasped and stared at Simon with broken eyes. He lost his posture, and his body slid into a slumped position against the wall. James was still unconscious. Evelyn was crying. Simon showed no feeling. He looked around the room and laughed. He threw the knife across the room and pounded his chest like Tarzan whilst laughing loudly. Evelyn was breaking down, and Simon was not interested. He went about removing the officers' uniforms and making an outfit for himself with a combination of the two. Once he was dressed, he calmly walked out of his mother's house without so much as looking back, leaving her there, sobbing, black and blue, and tied up with bailing twine.

CHAPTER TWENTY-SIX

It had been two weeks since Officer Pembrooke's death. The whole community was shocked and saddened. The aftermath of the attacks on the girls had been awful, but the death of a long-standing, friendly, and people-passionate policeman took its toll on the villagers. Everyone liked Officer Pembrooke, and a lot of people saw him as a father figure; he was a loving family man.

His junior, who had been with him on that fateful day, spoke of his admiration for his colleague when he got out of hospital. He said he showed true bravery and that he hoped he could be as good as Pembrooke in his career. Then he vowed to find the killer and get justice for all his victims. The villagers believed him as he delivered his speech with tears rolling down his cheeks. He confirmed that the police station would be holding a commemorative celebration for Officer Pembrooke's life and service to the force, but not before the commemoration party planned to mark the end of the war that had been planned by local councillors. They had discussed whether they could make Pembrooke's passing a part of it, but it had been voted against as they felt that the village would benefit from a celebration. They also felt that Pembrooke deserved a dignified event that was exclusive to him.

It was the morning of the 'end of the war' party, and Martha was trying to get Willy ready. Willy was not making this easy for her, and she felt she had little patience for him today. She had noticed she had little patience for anything recently and had found that her moods were up and down more than usual. She hadn't been to Mae's house since Christmas. On the morning of Boxing Day, Mae had enjoyed telling everyone how she had caught Martha sleepwalking and how she was lucky she had been there, in case she had injured herself.

They all laughed it off, apart from Peter. Since then, which was only a couple of months ago, she had refused all invites. She had told Mae that she hadn't been feeling great, which wasn't actually a lie. She had felt rubbish in recent weeks. The ramifications of her actions were still manifesting within her and her everyday life, and she couldn't shake them off. She felt tired, she felt sick, she felt restless, she was off her food. She realised it would take time for her to get over her actions. David had noticed a couple of things but didn't seem too worried. If anything, he was sweeter than usual. Good old, reliable David. Where would she be without him? She secured Willy's tie and then combed his hair to the side. She had managed to control his unruly cowlick thanks to the use of Uncle Michael's 'Jeris' antiseptic hair tonic. Normally she wouldn't allow him to put any of these horrible products on his beautiful blonde locks, but she needed perfection for today.

The party was to celebrate the end of the war. It wasn't an official party, as such. It had been organised by local councillors as a 'lift me up' for the local, tight-knit community. It was to be a day of celebration, and they were going to give out awards for outstanding members of the community. They knew Peter was getting one. She wished they hadn't known so that they could not go, but Martha realised that not going for no reason would appear odd. The whole village was going, and everyone was looking forward to it. Everyone apart from Martha. Once Willy was dressed and Martha was happy with her work, she told him he could go downstairs and do some drawing whilst she got ready.

'I want to stay here with you, Mummy.'

He said it angelically, and he looked angelic like a little cherub. Sometimes she was afraid of how much he was growing up and how he was slowly pulling away from her in his ever-developing independence, but little throwaway comments like that would remind her he was a very small boy, and he needed her just as much as she needed him. She took him by the hand.

'Very well, young man, perhaps you can help me choose which dress to wear.'

They smiled at each other and went into her room.

They laughed and played as she tried on various dresses to sounds of vomiting if Willy didn't like it or clapping if he did. Between the two of them, they had whittled down the choices to three. They had picked out a short-sleeved, paisley-patterned dress. She held it up to her again, and they decided it was too summery. The next one was a long-sleeved, sleek dress with a floral pattern. She decided it was too 'Mumsy' despite Willy saying he 'really liked it.' The last dress was by far the most glamorous. The top half was cut like a long-sleeve shirt. The sleeves would roll up and button at the elbow. The bottom half puffed out like a meringue. It was olive in colour, but the fabric changed colour depending on the light. It went shades of terracotta and brown and gold. She slipped into it with elegance. She had already applied her makeup and styled her hair earlier that morning before anyone was awake. She couldn't sleep, and it seemed like a good use of time. Her victory rolls had set at the front of her head perfectly, and her makeup, for once, looked flawless. Her red lipstick screamed 'icon.' She couldn't see it, of course. She buttoned up her dress and then secured the belt around her waist. As she patted down the skirt, she looked up and saw that Willy's jaw was on the floor, as was David's, who had been standing in the doorway watching her get dressed. She looked at them both and came over all coy.

'Baby, you look a million dollars. What on God's green earth did I do to deserve a girl like you?'

David was grinning from ear to ear, holding his mug in his hand. He was covered in engine grease and knew now was not the time to go in for a cuddle and a kiss.

'I will do my best to scrub up for you, m'lady, but you will be the belle of the ball, that's for sure.'

He gave her a mock curtsy and walked off shaking his head in disbelief.

Martha had been racking her brain about how today would go, seeing Peter. She had seen Mae since Christmas, but she had not seen him. Mae had been to the house once, and then they had met in the village one morning. Both meetings had seemed to go ok, but Martha hadn't instigated either of them. She was aware that she was being a bad friend to Mae, but she felt that if she was the one pushing to meet up, then that would make her even worse. She obliged with the meetings Mae had requested, but Mae hadn't suggested another meet up since. Martha didn't know when she would be able to suggest it, if ever.

They all piled into David's truck to head into the village. He had cleaned it especially for his girl and his step-son. They both looked so smart, and he couldn't have been prouder. He felt that they were a different calibre to him; but they were there, they were by his side, and he would do his damn best by them. He hadn't scrubbed up too badly anyhow. Martha had made some small changes to his outfit choice. She told him that his shirt didn't go with the trousers so one of them had to change, and he let her choose. She did and then she changed his shoes too and then she felt that he looked dapper and handsome. She felt an outpour of love for him. She could see how much he wanted her, and she wished she could feel the same back.

They pulled up outside the village hall and there was already a stream of cars and a crowd of villagers gathering by the entrance. David told Martha to get out with Willy and that he would find somewhere to park the car. She did and was immediately greeted by an extremely glamorous Mae with her children.

'Martha, darling. There you are. I'm so glad to see you. Peter is off discussing when he has to go up and collect his award, or whatever it is they are doing. Of course, there are loads of people here we know, but I wanted to see you. You know, someone more normal.'

Martha knew what Mae meant and didn't take offence. She would be glad of Mae's continuous, babble-like chatter today. Mae beckoned them inside, and Martha told her she needed to wait for David.

'Oh, very well then, I will take Willy in. He

can sit with Charlie. Come and find us, we are inside on the left, third row from the back.'

The village was very lucky to have a grand hall. It wasn't any old hall. It doubled up as a theatre, although it hadn't been used as that since before the Second World War began, but it also had changing rooms and backed on to local playing fields. This was the first major event they were holding since the end of the war was announced the previous spring. It was to be the party of the year; that's what had been promised. People were advised to expect a second Victory Day-style celebration. From what Martha had seen so far, everyone had certainly dressed up for the event. She was glad she had gone for the dress she had. She hadn't felt confident in it earlier, but some of the women that were arriving were making her look positively plain. At least, that's how she saw herself, but she was one of the most stunning women there. Her elegance and candour would make her one of the most beautiful women there.

Everyone piled into the hall and took their seats. There were lots of faces Martha had grown to recognise. David seemed to know almost everyone that came through the door. Well, most of the normal people. Peter wasn't friendly with those types, but the ones David didn't know were exactly the type of friends that were exclusive to people like Peter. When David saw someone he knew, there seemed to be a mutual head nod or a wink of an eye which seemed sufficient, thought Martha. If one of Peter's silver spoon-fed friends came in, there seemed to be a waft of arrogance that would flow through the building. The thing is, thought Martha, these 'upper class' were outnumbered by the normal folks. They could walk in here with their airs and graces, but they weren't impressing anyone apart from their small clique. She was happy to be on the side of the larger group, the 'normal' people.

The doors closed and the town's head councillor began with an opening speech. He began by welcoming everyone to what was going to be the biggest party of 1946. Standing behind him in an orderly fashion were those who were to receive awards from him shortly. There was a mixture of folk as this was a community event. There were war heroes, which is the category Peter fell into. Martha didn't think he deserved it. He hadn't been out there fighting like Johnny had. He hadn't gotten his hands dirty or even shed any blood. She didn't know exactly what he did, but she imagined him seated on an oversized leather chair in an office filled with books that he hadn't read.

In her daydream, she imagined him being told he had a visitor, and he told his secretary to give it five minutes and then let them in. He was signing something. Something important? Who knew, it was just a daydream. She thought that was about as much as he could manage. He was probably responsible for signing things off that he had little or no understanding of the consequences. As she came out of her daydream, she realised she had been staring at him the whole time. He had been scouring the whole room, probably assuming everyone was there for him. He was scouring the audience, and then their eyes met.

He looked at her, and she looked at him. It was back. The racing heartbeat. The beads of sweat appearing on her upper lip. Her hands were becoming clammy again. This was ridiculous, she told herself. She looked down and then she looked up. He was still staring right at her and then, promptly before her, he became Johnny. The face looking back at her was Johnny. She desperately wanted to be as far away from this hall as possible. Her mouth began to fill with warm saliva, and she knew she was going to be sick. She grabbed the gift bag that she had been given on entry; it contained a balloon and a leaflet detailing the order of the day, and she promptly threw up in it just as Peter's name was called for him to collect his award. David began to pander to her, and she said she just needed a minute, got up, and went looking for the facilities to freshen up.

She found her way into the men's changing rooms. She could have ended up anywhere. Once she had got up and left her seat, she had darted around aimlessly, looking for somewhere to continue being sick. The first glimpse of a toilet, and she was in there. She had been violently sick and then found she needed a minute to relax, to get over the heaving. Once she had calmed down, she went to the sink and rinsed her mouth with water.

Luckily, she had some mints with her, and she knew this morning that she hadn't felt too good. The nerves had gotten the better of her. No sooner had she thought about seeing Peter did he appear in the room right before her. She took a step back and placed both of her hands on the sink behind her. Peter smiled at her softly. He smiled in a way she hadn't seen before. It seemed genuine, it seemed caring. He began to walk towards her.

'Martha, I don't want to not see you again. I

know what we did was wrong, but I want you to know I do not think badly of you. This has all been me. I know that.'

All she could see was Johnny. She wanted to cry. She inched towards him. Closer and closer until they were nose-to-nose.

'Johnny? Is that you?'

Peter said nothing, but before he knew it, Martha was kissing him and pulling at his shirt. His perfectly waxed hair fell out of place, and their hands were everywhere. Martha was saying, 'Johnny, Johnny,' over and over again. Peter didn't stop her.

He pushed her up against the sink and entered her. She wrapped her legs around his waist, and they both embraced each other passionately as she allowed him to have his way with her.

Directly behind them was a frosted window that was ajar. Simon was the other side of it. He was watching every detail of what they were both doing and was aroused by it. He could see Peter's naked rear going back and forth. He loved the slapping of the skin. He wanted in on the action. It had been a while.

'Mummy I need a wee.'

Charlie was pulling on his mother's dress whilst she chatted with some of the wives.

'Okay, darling, well you know where the loos are. You can go but come straight back. I think your dad is out there somewhere, so see if you can find him.'

Charlie ran off clutching his crotch as most children his age did. There was no, 'I need to wee soon.' It was always, 'I need to wee *now.*'

Charlie did know where the facilities were, as his father had taken him here many times before for various events. As he got closer to the door, he could hear some strange noises. He prized the door open with his little fingers. Through a gap of about an inch wide, all he could see was his dad with Aunty Martha. She was sitting on the sink with her dress around her waist and his father's trousers were around his ankles. His father was connected to his Mummy's friend. He wasn't sure exactly what was happening, but he knew that it wasn't normal. He let the door close, and he wet himself.

Martha and Peter only had a moment to enjoy the post-coital embrace. They both knew they were 'missing,' and that they must be seen by all that knew them soon. They kissed passionately unlike last time. It was different this time. It was if they had started something. It was as if they realised this desire was out of their control. Peter got dressed hastily.

'We can't go down together. It will look suspicious. I'll go down first, and you come down after five minutes.' Peter dressed hastily.

Martha agreed, and they kissed once more before he left. She hopped down off the sink and enjoyed the sexual hot flush that she was feeling. She looked down and began doing up her buttons. She couldn't see that Simon was now standing only a few feet away from her wielding a knife.

Peter got back to find Mae sternly quizzing their son. He could see that she was trying to tell him off but trying to control herself as they were out in public.

'What's going on? Leave the poor boy alone.'

Peter tried to pull the three of them away so as not to drag any attention to themselves.

'Peter, the boy has wet himself. He is almost five, and he has wet himself. I thought he had been here before. I thought he knew where the toilets were.'

Peter and Mae began a small tit-for-tat argument about whose fault it was that their son, who was now crying, had wet himself. Around them, the party had begun. Everybody was dancing to Glenn Miller's 'In the Mood.' David interrupted Peter and Mae's squabble.

'Has anyone seen Martha? I heard she was sick, but I can't find her.'

In that moment, the music was switched off, and a screeching could be heard from the changing rooms. The crowd began moving in every direction, and various screams could be heard. David ran towards the screams; somehow, he knew he had to. When he got to the changing room, he had to wade through the partygoers that had assembled around the door. He had to push through to see exactly what he didn't want to. His Martha embroiled in a scene that could only resemble something from a horror. Blood everywhere. All over her, all over the floor, on the sink, on the tiles, on the mirror. He scooped up her lifeless body. The crowd around them gasped. Peter had made his way in, insisting that Mae stay with the children. When he saw what David was seeing, he leant down the other side of her and helped David hold her, the two of them, believing with the amount of blood lost that she was dead.

Martha was alive when they got her to the hospital. Just. She was rushed to theatre immediately, and David, Peter, and Mae had the agonising wait for news. David barely spoke; he just paced the corridor for what seemed like hours. Peter would demand answers any time a member of staff walked past. Mae would cry, and then stop, and then cry, and then stop. Michael was back at Peter and Mae's house with all the children.

In the early hours of the following morning, a doctor appeared. He told them that she was in a critical condition but that he had good news.

'It's been a tough twenty-four hours for you, David, but I have good news. I am fairly confident that she will make it, and so will the baby.'

David leapt to his feet. He kissed the doctor. Peter and Mae stood up and hugged each other. David kissed the both of them, they all hugged, and they all let out tears of joy.

Having received the good news, Peter and Mae knew they were ok to leave David on his own now. They agreed to take Willy and David's brother, Michael, home to the farm if he didn't want to stay at theirs that night. They told David again that their house was an open house and that they would do anything he needed, anything at all.

Once home, Mae tucked Charlie into bed. She kissed him on the head, and as she turned off his lamp, she told him how much she loved him and how she would always protect him. She was about to leave his room when he said;

'Mummy...?'

'Yes, darling?'

She went back to his bedside and knelt beside him once more.

'What is it, angel?'

'Mummy, you know yesterday, when I wet my trousers?'

'Oh, darling, it was one of those things. Don't worry about that. These things happen.'

'Mummy, there is a reason I couldn't get into the toilet. I did know where the toilets were, but when I got there, I saw Daddy. He was with Aunty Martha, and they had their clothes off. They were kissing. I didn't want to go in there.'

Charlie began to cry, worried that he had said something he shouldn't have. Worried that his dad might beat him.

His mother pulled him in and stroked his head.

'Shhh. Thank you, dear boy. Thank you for telling me. Don't worry. Daddy was just helping Aunty Martha. She wasn't feeling well.'

Mae stroked her boy's head and let the tears roll down her cheeks.